The Last Aliyah

What They're Saying about Mark Alan Leslie

[The Last Aliyah] could turn out to be a definitive book, from the shame of replacement theology to the Christian involvement in the rescue of the Jews.

—**Frank Eiklor,** president, Shalom International

[The Last Aliyah] is a compelling, fast-moving, and timely story, and unfortunately, begins with a very scary, but very plausible scenario. I enjoyed the book and kept wondering how [Leslie] was going to get out of the corner he had painted Omri into. Very clever using the sci-fi version of 2 Kings 6:18."

—**Neil Lash**, co-founder of Jewish Jewels

The Last Aliyah is one of the most intriguing stories written about the plight of the Jewish people in the End Times. What makes it memorable is the author's resurrection of the use of the Underground Railroad that originally brought the slaves freedom to Canada, and now used to bring Jewish people home to Israel. A must read for Christians who stand with Israel.

—**Mitch Forman**, vice president of Chosen People Ministries

Other books by Mark Alan Leslie:

With a genuine flair for compelling, entertaining, and deftly-crafted storytelling, *The Crossing* is very highly recommended ...
—**Midwest Book Review's Small Press Bookwatch**

A gripping story told with the maturity of a seasoned wordsmith. I'll put Chasing the Music in the class with John Grisham or other secular novelists touted for producing today's best fiction … Readers can't go wrong with the intricately woven plot, intriguing characters, and crisp writing style.
—**Randall Murphree**, editor, American Family Association's *AFA Journal*

One word to describe *Chasing the Music?* ADVENTURE! ... This was Indiana Jones wrapped up in Romancing the Stone overlaid with National Treasure—all my favorite action movies between the covers of one book … It definitely reads like the best action adventure movie I've ever seen ... I definitely recommend that adrenaline junkies read this book.
—**Pam Graber**, *BookFun* reviewer

I was blown away at the many scientific connections and historical ones in *Chasing the Music*. The extensive depth of information was exceptional. Well done!
—**Lynda MacDonald**, Heart to Heart Ministry, Nova Scotia, Canada

Fast action and high suspense … The read [*Chasing the Music*] was exciting, following clues and moving from place to place. I loved it."

—**Randy Tramp**, freelance writer and author of *Night to Knight*

Compelling… It [*True North: Tice's Story*] is a fast read that will stay with the reader far past the last sentences.

—**David Shaub**, Union Historical Society

It [*True North: Tice's Story*] is educational and relevant … Living in Nova Scotia in an area that served as one of the terminuses of the Underground Railroad—a Black Cultural Center housing historical archives relating to it being nearby—and knowing descendants of some of those slaves, I found it educational and relevant.

—**MaryAnn Gilbert**, Ship Harbor, Nova Scotia

Midnight Rider [*for the Morning Star*] is engaging, entertaining, informative and convicting.

—**Jamie Lash**, Jewish Jewels, Fort Lauderdale, Fla.

Midnight Rider [*for the Morning Star*] is an exciting, exhilarating story that challenges the reader in an intense way.

—**Dr. Dennis E. Kinlaw**, founder, The Francis Asbury Society and past president Asbury College

[Midnight Rider for the Morning Star] is a stimulating and imagination-provoking book.

—**Patch Blakey**, executive director, Association of Classical and Christian Schools

An exhilarating historical novel, helping readers experience the heart and mind of this 'saint.'

—**Chris Bounds**, assistant professor, Indiana Wesleyan University

This [*Midnight Rider* [*for the Morning Star*] is a fast-paced ride and read through the new Republic with America's most influential religious leader.

—**Darius Salter**, church historian and pastor, Richardson (Texas) Church of the Nazarene

The Last Aliyah

By Mark Alan Leslie

Elk Lake
PUBLISHING, INC.
PLYMOUTH, MASSACHUSETTS

Cover Design: Jeff Gifford
Interior Design: Cheryl L. Childers
Editors: René Holt, Deb Haggerty
Published in Association with the Steve Laube Literary Agency

---

Library Cataloging Data
Names: Leslie, Mark Alan (Mark Alan Leslie)
The Last Aliyah / Mark Alan Leslie
398 p. 23cm × 15cm (9in × 6 in.)
Description: The United Nations' resolution that changed Omri Zohn's life ricocheted across America and around the world. They must activate the escape route for the last aliyah, the final return of God's chosen people to their homeland—if they can flee.
Identifiers: ISBN-13: 978-1-946638-88-5 (trade) | 978-1-946638-89-2 (POD) | 978-1-946638-90-8 (e-book.)
Key Words: Israel, Jews, UN Resolutions, Emigration, Travel Bans, Underground Railroad, Persecution.
LCCN: 2018939248 Fiction

Dedication

This book is dedicated to the many Christian organizations who minister and reach out to God's chosen people, the Jews, and the land of Israel.

"This is what the Sovereign LORD says: 'See, I will beckon to the nations, I will lift up my banner to the peoples; they will bring your sons in their arms and carry your daughters on their hips.'"

—Isaiah 49:22 (NIV)

"'Behold, I am going to send for many fishermen,' declares the LORD, 'and they will fish for them; and afterwards I will send for many hunters, and they will hunt them from every mountain and every hill and from the clefts of the rocks.'"

—Jeremiah 16:16 (NKJV)

ACKNOWLEDGMENTS

When you bounce a book idea off most people, they nod or shrug, maybe ask a question or two, suggest they'd like-love-consider reading the final version. When I present a plot to my wife, Loy, she's like a super-taut trampoline. She sends ideas soaring to another stratosphere while keeping them within the bounds of believability, that is, without landing hard on unforgiving ground. So she gets my number-one acknowledgment as encourager-in-chief trampoline mate. I also want to thank my sons, Rit and Dax, for their support, especially Dax because he is also a talented author who can tell me when I, or my hero, should not actually jump off the cliff unless I/we first strap on a parachute.

Also, my gratitude goes out to my agent-retired, Les Stobbe, whose middle name, I think, is Persistence, and to my editors with the gentle touch, René Holt and Deb Haggerty.

Bless you all.

CHAPTER ONE

The call that changed Nobel laureate Omri Zohn's life came at the hour when the most distasteful acts are perpetrated in Washington, DC—when Congressmen board flights home before the news hits the airwaves.

Omri forced one eye open and squinted to see the phone's caller ID. 202 area code. His friend, US Senator Joseph Frank. His heart fluttering—maybe even skipping a beat—he tried to calm his shaking hand as he reached for the phone.

"Omri! It's Joseph." The voice boiled with tension, urgency. Zohn sat up in his bed and struggled to open the other eye. He looked at his clock: 2:58 a.m.

"They've done it, Omri!" Joseph Frank's hoarse utterance quaked between a rasp and a gasp. "The Senate just approved enforcing the United Nations Resolution."

A crushing weight settled on his chest. "Oh, my Lord."—more a moan than a statement.

"We Jews are now essentially prisoners in our own countries," Frank said. "Not allowed to go to Israel or any country that defies the UN Resolution outlawing emigration to the Holy Land. Get your escape plan in motion, now, as I will mine."

"You said *we*, Joseph. Even *you* can't leave?"

The three-term senator from Florida grunted. "Even I. Beware of men in black suits at your door. They'll hold you here."

Omri shook his head in the dark, then said, "My brother, Ariel, just called me yesterday. He's got stage-four cancer."

Joseph groaned.

"Are there no exceptions, Joseph? Any chance at all I can get permission to visit him?"

"'Fraid not."

Aargh! Omri gritted his teeth. "Joseph! You know my son and his wife and child moved to Israel a year ago. Are you saying I can't see them again?"

"Not a chance, unless Benjamin and his family come back to America. But if they did, then, of course, they wouldn't be allowed back out of the country. Not unless they've obtained their Israeli citizenship already."

"Not yet."

Omri flicked on the light of his nightstand and swung his legs off the bed. If the sky was falling, he had to move, get his plans in motion.

"Homeland Security had representatives in the chambers, sitting on the edge of their seats, waiting to give the go signal to headquarters," Frank continued. "Making it more repulsive, today is August second, the last day before the six-week summer recess. My colleagues—the brave sort they are—are about to vanish into the countryside and avoid any nasty questions."

Omri chuckled ruefully. "No surprise there."

A pause, then Frank added, "You realize this begins the curse on America."

Omri knew the Scripture: "I will bless those who bless my people, but those who curse them I shall curse."

"Godspeed, my friend!" Joseph said. "Hopefully, we'll meet again in Israel. Shalom."

The line clicked off.

Omri set the landline phone in the cradle gently, as if a grenade. He peered at his bedside clock: 3:01 a.m. Appropriate, he thought, recalling the words of Psalm 3:1: "O, Lord, how many are my foes! How many rise up against me!"

He spoke softly the seventh and eighth verses: "Arise, O Lord! Deliver me, O my God! Strike all my enemies on the jaw; break the teeth of the wicked. From the Lord comes deliverance. May Your blessing be on Your people."

He took a moment to reassure himself the plan he had in place was truly what he wanted. His wife and daughter were buried in Israel, killed by a terrorist bomb at a bar mitzvah celebration for their nephew a dozen years ago. His boyhood home was there. Besides Benjamin and his new family, Ariel and his family, many cousins and friends lived there. This ban would prevent him from ever seeing them again, ever paying respects to Adina and Devorah, ever setting his feet in the Old City, ever praying at the Western Wall. Besides all this, Israel was the only country in which the Jews could defend themselves.

Omri stiffened his back, placing his feet on the small sheepskin rug on the wooden floor. *The time has come. This will be the last aliyah, the final return of Your people to their homeland, Lord … if we can get there.*

—~—

Vice President Daniel Fireside walked to his office, a Secret Service man at each shoulder. The hall filled with the hum of phone calls and the tapping of fingers typing tweets. Senators hurried to get out of Washington even though daybreak was still three hours away.

The chills of triumph gave him a buzz, but Fireside fought to contain his elation. He'd proven he could indeed push measures through a stubborn Congress—and this particular legislation was the most contentious in his twenty-two years in this combative Congress in this quarrelsome town, the hub of what was more and more a belligerent country. While he had needed to merely cajole many colleagues into his and the president's way of thinking, he had to bludgeon others with substantial threats before they succumbed. The eighty congressmen who had flipped their votes on Obama trade overnight years ago paled in comparison to this victory.

The atmosphere outside the Senate chambers crackled with electricity. Obviously, Fireside wasn't the only one grinding his teeth. Senator Halsey was leaning on one leg, then another, agitated. Senator Franceour was maybe one decibel down from shouting at an aide.

Standing in a wide hallway with gleaming floors and walls soaked with two centuries of rich history, Fireside thought of the consequences. The Party had surely alienated the Jewish vote, but the Muslims' high birth rate had already overtaken the Jews in numbers—just like they would in Israel with this ban—so they had a net win at the polls.

Chuck Claiborne, Fireside's chief of staff, was doing his job, refereeing a scramble of senators pushing each other aside to get the vice president's ear. The atmosphere was just one step removed from a Macy's bargain basement free-for-all.

"Fireside, you'll pay dearly for this. Your career's over!" yelled Senator Bill Bloom.

Fireside winked, smiled and—the trifecta—shot him a thumbs-up. *Billy-boy, dream on. I just jumped aboard a rocketship, pal.*

Fireside tapped one of his Secret Service protectors on the shoulder. "Wait here by the door. Nobody comes in."

The agent nodded, and the two men took up their posts as Fireside escaped to his office. He closed the door, leaving the hubbub behind him. He had to place a most important phone call.

Taking a seat behind the historic double-pedestal, mahogany, Wilson desk, he wondered how many of his predecessors could have pulled off this coup.

None, except perhaps LBJ, who, like Fireside, had used this office as an elegant and convenient setting for informal party caucuses, press briefings, ceremonial functions, and—ahem, this was the bend-your-arm-'til-it-breaks part—private meetings. LBJ might have been considered the master, but Fireside had just one-upped the big Texan. *Check and mate.*

Placing his hands on the desktop, he took a deep breath, picked up the red telephone, and punched in a number he knew well.

—~~—

When the phone rang, President Harold Smith switched on a low-wattage bedside lamp. Unable to sleep, he had fidgeted under the sheets for hours, awaiting this call. He'd spent his last drop of political capital on this UN Resolution, declaring failure was not an option. Though no one but his wife knew it, his future beyond the presidency hung on its success.

His neck hairs prickled in anticipation. Was it good news, bad news, or some dire gray-area result? Smith despised gray areas.

Picking up the phone, he murmured, "Yes?"

"It's done, Mister President. We're a go!" Smith could almost see Fireside glowing on the other end like a schoolboy after his first successful prank.

Smith's eyes shot wide open, and he released a breath. "Fallout?"

"Some outrage, plenty of grumble. Good thing Lieberman and Shumer retired. A few almost stalked out of the chambers. Well, Frank and Weiss did—as we predicted. Frank's leaving was okay because I thought I'd shoot him, he was so distraught, so righteous, so—Jewish. Broke an arm here, a leg there, but we avoided insurrection and got the law passed without a real bullet being fired, although I'm glad Armstrong and Bloom weren't armed.

"Great work, Dan! Glad you're at my side. Nice to have a majority in both the House and Senate, eh?"

Hanging up, the president turned to his wife.

"The vault door's slammed shut on the Jews," he said with cold certainty.

In the faint shadows of the room, Theresa Smith smiled back and whispered hoarsely, "Well done, my love.

Smith nodded, then asked, "Like a drink in celebration?"

"In the middle of the night?" Theresa reached for her robe, hanging on a nearby chair. "Good idea."

Smith swung his feet over the side of the bed. "You know when I first saw this could happen?"

"When?" The First Lady was now slipping her feet into slippers.

"Back in 2017 when UNESCO finally voted the Jews had no connection to Jerusalem."

"M-hm. Shows how much the UN hates the Jews."

"They're not alone," Smith said. "Gin and tonic?"

His wife nodded. "You know me so well, Mr. President."

Why am I so agitated, so nervous? Whatever's bothering my spirit, I hate it! Bunyan "Jacko" Jackson forced himself from his bed and through the sliding doors to the patio. He stood—all six-foot-four inches and two hundred thirty-four pounds of him—and pressed his hands against the waist-high railing, peering out onto the dark Atlantic Ocean beyond his expansive lawn.

He tightened the sash of his flimsy cotton robe over his pajamas. The summer night on the outskirts of Portland, Maine, was warm. The nightglow of the city to the north turned the sky a pale fluorescent green. A faint scent of salt drifted in the air. *Tide's out.*

The first couple bars of Louis Armstrong's "What a Wonderful World" on his cell phone wafted through an open window in his bedroom. He hustled back to his room. Who was in the hospital, or who died? What would cause a call at this hour?

He answered, "Jackson."

"My friend, it's me." The distinctive Israeli accent of Omri Zohn made Jackson stand straight in anticipation. "Aliyah is on. Plan B."

Click.

Jackson's mouth went wide. He scowled at the phone as if the instrument were a Yankee pitcher or an implement able to answer the stark questions: How could we? How could the United States do this to its own people?

Dismayed, he murmured, "Well, Satchmo, today it's not such a wonderful world."

He laid the phone down on the bedside table and sat on the king-sized bed. He inhaled deeply and peered at a shelf below the tabletop. Reaching down, he pulled out a leather-bound copy of *The Pilgrim's Progress*, handed down by his great-great-great-great-grandfather Tice, who had escaped slavery in 1860.

Jackson thought of the book's story, then recalled the passage in the ninth chapter of the Book of Amos: "I will bring back My exiled people Israel."

This was it: the last aliyah. And here he was—retired Major League baseball player, Hall of Famer, and descendant of a slave—positioned to pay forward what so many good-minded people had done for Tice. Jackson brought the little book to his lips for a light kiss. "We'll get them to Jerusalem, Grampa Tice. I promise."

He set the book down, picked up a thick, well-worn manuscript in a homemade binder—Tice's hand-written account of his own escape from the South. With a deep love for an ancestor he'd never met, Bunyan frowned at the thought the world had come to this. He stood and walked to a two-shelf, glassed-in bookcase and pulled out a world atlas. Opening up the book, an encrypted mobile phone was revealed, hidden in a hollow. He grabbed the phone and texted an encrypted message. When deciphered, the note read: "Aliyah is on. Plan B."

Giant red eyes hovered above and behind Ethan Rosenbaum. He hunched his shoulders in the moonless night. Adrenaline pumped energy through his veins, but he felt like he was running through deep sand. He could feel sweat behind his ears, an aching right calf—and raw terror.

He crested a hill, heaved himself forward, and landed on the ground. A hissing sound, a snarl slashed the silence. Heavy breathing crowded his ears. Breathing and the death threat.

Ethan pushed himself off the ground and raced down the back side of the hill. He turned to look. Giant eyes rose up over the peak only twenty feet or so behind and ten feet high. His remaining moments in this world were numbered unless … unless a miracle.

A sudden high-pitched jangle shattered the night sky—and the dream.

Ethan shuddered, half relieved he was dreaming and half afraid the dream was a portent.

Jerking awake, he pushed himself to a sitting position, opened an eye to look at his oversized clock, and groaned. Trying not to awaken his wife, Naomi, he reluctantly picked up the phone.

"Aliyah is on," said the Israeli-tinted voice. "Plan B, ASAP."

Click. At those words, heaviness cloaked Ethan, as if the darkness in the room had become a physical cloak. The giant red eyes of oppression.

Suddenly he was wide awake, but he sat motionless as if his body had been shot with Novocain, trying to absorb the impact of the news.

Since the United Nations had voted for the extraordinary resolution stopping all Jewish immigration to Israel, he had entertained thoughts of what would happen if, God forbid, Congress were to vote in agreement.

Few had actually believed America and other countries around the world would acquiesce when it came to enforce ent of this type of resolution.

And now, in the wake of the vote, the Jewish and Christian outrage obviously paled to the "hoorahs" of the anti-Semites and anti-Zionists and failed to dissuade Congress.

How could America, "home of the free because of the brave," abide by such a decision? Surely there would be rebellion in the streets. Right?

Nevertheless, though he and Naomi lived in Charleston, South Carolina, and Omri lived outside Boston, they had devised various plans for aliyah—just in case. *That's what we scientists do: devise tests, plans, and contingencies for various scenarios. Another thing we do: harden ourselves to trust provable facts, no matter the substance or depth of beliefs indicating the contrary.*

The men had a Plan A for Monday through Thursday, and a Plan B for midnight Thursday through Sunday.

At his side, Naomi stirred awake. "Who called, Ethan?"

"Congress." His voice cracked. "Lost their collective mind."

She shot up out of the sheets. "No!"

"That was Omri," he said. "They did the deed. Congress sold us out."

"So, we're going ahead with our decision and leaving friends, synagogue, jobs." A statement, not a question.

Ethan locked his eyes on hers. "I'll take the visiting fellowship Doctor Ibram offered at Technion—Israel Institute of Technology."

"The MIT of Israel," Naomi nodded with a half-smile. "My brilliant husband."

Ethan laid his hand on her neck and pulled her softly to his embrace. They stayed like that for a minute or so, absorbing how earth-shattering was the moment.

"I'm so sorry, Naomi," he said. "I know you love your job too. Something awaits you there."

She pulled away just enough to look up in his eyes. "Leaving our friends and neighbors is worse, darling." She sighed. "But I know the Lord will help and console me in this. Leaving is going to be emotional, but He'll strengthen me—us."

Ethan couldn't muster a response. Naomi had the faith for both of them. She believed; he hoped.

"When do we leave?" she asked.

"Omri said ASAP. Normally the plan would mean this moment, but today's Friday, so Plan B's different. After Congress's vote, if I don't show up for work this morning, someone will figure out we're on the move and finger us to Homeland Security. No, we've got to pretend everything's copacetic. You'll go to work; I'll go to work. We'll come home—and then scuttle out of here on the first train."

Ethan again glanced at the illuminated clock: 3:16 a.m.

"I'll get the coffee brewing," Naomi said, "then start packing, but only as much as we can carry in duffel bags. No curling iron, no hair dryer."

"And no board games."

"Spoilsport."

Somewhere in the distance, a fog horn croaked hoarsely, and as if in response, a boat's stack bellowed. One fog, Ethan thought, was causing nautical confusion just as another kind of fog had clouded the thinking of Congress.

Chapter Two

8 a.m. Friday

President Smith stalked back and forth in the Oval Office, now and then glancing out the windows to the Rose Garden while holding a telephone tight to his ear. This was the call on which his future would rely once he left the presidency. The next minute or two would portend whether his next challenge would be on the world stage.

A majority of the nations on the globe have deferred many forms of power to the United Nations. As the world's high court, or military or treaty mediator, the UN now holds real power—an authority with an armed force behind it. To rule the UN? Well—

"Thank you," Smith said in response to congratulations offered by Prince Hamza Al Fahad of Saudi Arabia, chief of the League of Arab States.

"You'll find I'm a man of my promises." Al Fahad spoke in perfect English. After all, the Saudi was educated at Harvard and Columbia universities.

"I hope so, Prince Hamza, because I've put everything on the line. I've got just a few months left in office, but, starting today, my name will be a curse word for many people—"

Al Fahad interrupted him. "On the very first day, in the very first hour, of the next session of the United Nations, the entire Arab League will propose a change in the rule preventing a citizen of any of the five permanent members of the Security Council from being the UN Secretary-General. The door will open and, with the League's support, you are—as they say—'a shoe-in.'"

"And?" Smith said.

"You'll find one hundred million dollars already in your Zurich bank account."

"And?"

"And after you are sworn in as secretary-general—*if* you continue on this glorious road you've chosen, to support the Arab peoples and our goals, you will see fifty million dollars a year added to that bank account. You'll be a welcome guest, with all the privileges that entails, at all of the houses of our leadership all the days of your life. Besides, Allah will smile upon you."

"Very good," Smith said. He took a seat behind his desk and exhaled deeply. He looked down. His right hand was trembling.

A minute later, the call ended. *Not a bad promotion from "Leader of the Free World" to "Leader of the Entire World."* He grinned, and a tear of joy wet the corner of his eye. *Strange, I haven't shed a tear since Mom died.*

He kicked back, put his hands behind his head and closed his eyes.

My, what grand successes await those who are patient, lay out a finely tuned strategy, and march on undeterred by difficult circumstances. The Administration had spent the last seven years skillfully turning the minds of half of Americans against the Jews, against Israel. The country had flipped—from a majority supporting Israel to a minority.

Smith chuckled at his own genius at having used the media to make Jews the scapegoats for a faltering economy.

And now, as he neared the end of his presidency, just hours ago his forethought had culminated in this masterpiece of international legislation.

He only wished he had taken up Sandra Molitor's bet the Senate would not comply with the UN resolution. *Ha, you say! I'll double-down, Sandy. Just watch.*

He swung his chair about and again looked out to the Rose Garden. The grass shimmered as he edged close enough to crack open a window and breathe in the aroma of newly cut grass.

Ah, Secretary-General Harold Smith. The world is your plaything. His thoughts moved to the international community. As usual, Marshall Islands, Micronesia, Nauru, and Palau had followed the US lead and abstained in the UN vote. But he wondered about Prime Minister Daniel Donaldson of Canada, Prime Minister Lukas Arnesen of Norway, Prime Minister Warren Joyce of Australia, President Václav Gauc of the Czech Republic, and President Pratibha Tagor of India. They represented the major countries voting against the ban on Jewish immigration.

Who could be turned? He had used all the personal persuasion he could muster and was as yet unsuccessful with these leaders.

So, if America's Jews wanted to get to Israel, they did have one way—into Canada—to sneak off the continent and fly out. Smith and his leadership had conferenced *ad nauseum* about how to persuade Canadians to rethink their position and support the travel ban, but not one good, let alone tantalizing, idea had materialized. There was no way to strong-arm them. And they had enough of the currency ruling the world—oil.

Smith rocked back and forth, picturing himself at the helm of the United Nations in about one year. He stood at the secretary-general's lectern, representatives of the nations of the world below and before him in the stadium seating, all eyes attentive, all ears on alert. The leader of the world was about to speak! The United States had used considerable might to save the faltering UN from life support in the 1990s, then empowered the organization at every opportunity, so now the organization wielded real authority and clout.

Smith grinned, then a motion outside the window twisted his revery into apprehension. A White House Office of Communications crew was beginning to set up for a Rose Garden press conference. He might have to face some unsettling questions. But, of course, he knew which reporters to point to in the question-and-answer portion of the conference. Teleprompters? He didn't need any Obama-type help. He could think on his feet. He was Harold Smith, the next secretary-general of the United Nations!

Secretary of the Treasury Hank Blasted slammed his fist on the conference table and swore. He scowled, his chubby red face contorted with anger. The meeting had started the previous day, a Thursday, and lasted deep into the night, only to begin again early this morning. Four high-ranking officials—Inspector General Stanley Brown; Victor O'Malley, head of the Office of Domestic Finance; Sam Johnson, head of the Office of Terrorism and Financial Intelligence; and Miriam Mazar of FinCEN, the

Financial Crimes Enforcement Network—had walked out, submitting their resignations en masse. Blasted was physically exhausted, mentally fatigued, angry enough to strangle a child, and ready to go home.

This morning's news from the Senate did little to assuage his frustration. Those people were concerned with keeping down the Jewish population in Israel so the Arabs could out-populate them and take control at the voting booths. Blasted didn't care a bit about such an outcome. Israel be overrun or not. The same with Christianity, Islam, Buddhism, Hinduism, Taoism, Confusionism and all the other "isms," except maybe skepticism. He didn't give a giraffe's neck about any of them. Money was what drove his world.

"I don't care if you don't agree. What I care about is plugging the breach in the dam, stopping the money from pouring out of America into other countries, especially Israel. The Jews!" He cursed again, aware Brown, O'Malley, Johnson, and Mazar were no longer seated around the table. "They care more for Israel than their own country! Here they are, finding ways to get around American law and get their fortunes into Israel. Every red cent leaving here to bolster their economy hurts ours."

His head was spinning with fury.

Two dozen officials, from the Office of Tax Policy to the Office of Legislative Affairs to his deputy secretary of the treasury, Charvi Gupta, sat silent around the table. John Casey, sitting across from Blasted, began to stutter a response, but Blasted cut him off. "This is a done deal, John. Congress passed the law years ago. Years! Obama signed the thing. But we've never implemented the rule fully. When Congress doubled down last week, they were serious. I don't get a vote. You don't get a vote. But your job is to uphold that vote. So prepare to enforce the law, or you can go home to Indiana without your job. Simple. And that goes for all of you!"

He swept his arm in an arc around the table. Casey was emotionally tossed back into his chair by his public dressing down. Casey wasn't the only one in the room who was uncomfortable with the law, Blasted was certain. Brown, O'Malley, Johnson and Mazar—they could and would all be replaced. Some might at this moment be calculating their chances of promotion, and this could work to Blasted's benefit. Nevertheless, a mantle of tension weighed heavily in the room, and Blasted hoped browbeating one person would prevent the need of going head-to-head around the table.

He needed to squelch this unrest and now, not tomorrow, not next week. This was the rule of the land, much as years before in Brazil when, in the midst of extraordinary inflation, the government in Rio de Janeiro outlawed money leaving the country.

And Blasted carried the burden of authority in financial matters. His job was to oversee enforcement, and he was darn well going to do so.

He leaned forward, placing his palms on the edge of the table and, in a measured voice, said, "If I have to send a field worker to knock down every door of every Jewish home in America in order to investigate their finances, I will, people."

The face of Joseph Stein, who had fired Blasted from his first job, flashed across his mind and he scowled and tightened his jaw. *Jews! The scourge of the earth!*

Blasted looked to his immediate left at Gupta. She returned a look of encouragement, like a churchgoer in the front row, giving an "amen" to the preacher.

Blasted lifted his intimidating six-foot-three, three-hundred-pound frame from seat."Are we ready to move on, people?"

He scanned the room, looking for a weak link, especially Casey and Sandra Waltham, the Florida bureau chief, who was averting her eyes from her seat near the other end of the long table.

Mumbles of agreement were his answer. "Remember, results. Quantifiable results. Weekly reports and calculable results."

Around the room, twenty-four men and women pulled together their stacks of papers, spelling out how to conduct direct operations to keep Jewish money—actually, anyone's fortune—in America.

Blasted slapped his attaché case shut, locked it, , and strode from the room. Snapping open his video phone, he punched in the number for the Oval Office.

—∾—

8:22 a.m.

Dressed in his familiar brown tweed sport coat, black slacks, and light-blue button-up dress shirt, Omri Zohn stepped off the Red Line on Boston's "T" at Kendall Station. The crowd of commuters and students bustled and jostled around him. A middle-aged black man strummed an acoustic guitar hooked to a tiny amplifier, softly singing "Sunshine in the Morning." Omri flipped a dollar bill into the man's open guitar case and gave him a thumbs-up.

The man stopped singing long enough to say, "Thanks, professor."

Omri scurried up the subway stairs and at the top, dropped a plastic bag containing the shredded pages of his personal address book into a trash container. Next to the container, the headline of the *Boston Herald* in a vendor's box screamed, "Murderer!"A large photo showed a man who bore a disturbing likeness to a forty-year-old Charles Manson. The Congressional vote had come too late for the day's papers. *Under the cover of darkness. Smart move. Scurrilous.*

Omri stopped in his steps. What was this urge? This dreadful conflict? The left side of his brain was wrestling with the right side—a match started after Jacob Frank's call. He looked down the subway steps. He could retrace his steps, take the "T" to North Station, and catch an Amtrak Downeaster. The train would leave for Portland, Maine, at nine o'clock and arrive shortly before noon.

"Morning, Dr. Zohn!" The voice of his student Bobby Scott, his long curly hair making him look like a teenaged Art Garfunkel, brought Omri back to the moment.

He forced a smile and nodded. "Good day, Mr. Scott."

As Bobby hurried off, Omri again considered the option. Even if he got to Portland by noon, he and Bunyan would have to wait an entire day and a half. If the Rosenbaums were to fly to Portland, they would put themselves directly in the crosshairs of Homeland Security, so the train was the better choice.

So, multiply the variable (the Rosenbaums) by the coefficient (thirty hours), add the constant (the two-and-a-half-hour train ride they would all need to take from Boston to Portland), and you get the solution (wait and don't let anyone quantify your intentions). Display tranquility, not anxiety. Give no hint you're fleeing the country. Be happy, even jolly.

Teach the classes at ten o'clock and one-thirty. Spend the normal few hours in research with one or both of your graduate assistants from mid-afternoon into the evening. *Stick to the plan.*

Omri shrugged, turned back, and strode to the Massachusetts Institute of Technology campus, nodding and smiling hellos on the way. The campus seemed diametrically opposite that of neighboring Harvard University, whose brick buildings were covered with ivy. The school's Lincoln Lab—a monument to modernism with walls of glass—was representative of the university's buildings, posing the oddest array in the universe of peculiar architecture.

Omri recalled his first visit when he'd shuddered at the campus's cold expansiveness and off-putting structures. He had nearly done an about face and left Boston without an interview. But, here he was, more than two decades later, and the place was like home to him.

As much "home" to him as Israel? Well, no. He'd grown up rambling through the hills of the Golan, streaking down the beaches around Haifa, camping at Dag Al Ha'dan, swimming in the pools at Ganey Huga Park.

Once he'd spent the morning of Pesach in the Old City, the afternoon floating in the Dead Sea, the evening eating St. Peter's fish outdoors at a Galileean seaside restaurant in Tiberias, and the night sleeping under the stars at Yarden Kineret off the Israel National Trail.

What a dissimilar "home" Boston was. Within minutes, he'd settled into his cozy little office in the School of Engineering, like sitting down in his den at home.

—⁓—

Bunyan Jackson was again on his patio looking out to sea. His gaze settled on two large boats—one a trawler, one a cruise liner steaming toward Casco Bay and Portland Harbor. A mug of hot coffee warmed the palms of his big hands. "Mitts," one reporter for ESPN had called them. Whatever. He peered down at them. *You used to swing a baseball bat in a boys' game for twenty million dollars a year. Now you're about to risk everything for nothing. But this is the Lord's work—priceless.*

He turned and looked at his home. He loved this place. A local architect had designed the traditional Maine coastal home—grey shingles and white trim; a grey wraparound deck with white railings on three sides, and patio at the back—for Bunyan and his wife, CeCe. Inside, a winding staircase with startling hand-carved pine railings, led to three second-floor bedroom suites, each with triple windows, looking out on the landscape or ocean; native oak and pine floors throughout; and a widow's walk atop. He lowered his head. *Or a widower's walk in my case.*

After Omri's phone call, a peculiar combination of excitement and trepidation had made any sleep fitful. He had been visualizing the next couple of days, helping three Jews escape America, carrying out a plan they had hoped and prayed they would never need.

The door to the patio from the dining area slid open, interrupting Bunyan's thoughts.

"Would you like me to bring your breakfast out here or to the dining room?" A slim, tiny Latino woman with a matronly air cocked her head, awaiting his reply.

"I'll take breakfast out here. And please, Lana, bring a plate for yourself and join me, will you?"

She hesitated.

"Please."

"Of course, sir."

Bunyan sat at one of four round patio tables. In this early morning light, the shade from the table's umbrella was cast halfway toward the house.

A minute later, Lana delivered a tray filled with homemade biscuits, Canadian bacon, scrambled eggs, two bowls of hot oatmeal sprinkled with brown sugar, a carafe of coffee, two tall glasses of orange juice, one pitcher of milk, butter, and a small jar of Maine-made blueberry jam.

She set the tray down in front of him, then removed a bowl of cereal and glass of juice for herself.

"Looks wonderful!" Bunyan said.

"Thank you."

"Lana," he said, "you've been with me for seven years now. I trust you implicitly."

"Why, thank you, sir!" Her brown eyes lit up.

"Well, your trust is crucial, because I need to rely on you."

Her brow wrinkled and she leaned forward, prepared to listen. She was a pleasant lady, probably beautiful in her youth, with long black hair pulled behind her ears and dark Costa Rican skin. A gray dress and white blouse covered her thin, athletic body.

"Tomorrow, if you're here, you could be put in jeopardy."

"Jeopardy?"

"Danger. If things go wrong, if you're found complicit—"

"Complicit?"

"That means you're involved in something illegal."

Bunyan put a hand on hers and leaned in.

"What I'm going to do will be considered against the law, and if you help me, the law might say you're involved."

He proceeded to tell her about Omri and the Rosenbaums and asked if she was prepared to do something with which the government would not be happy. At first she frowned. Then her face lit up. "Why are you doing this, sir?" she asked.

"Bunyan," he corrected.

"Bunyan." She smiled.

"I'm paying forward a debt, Lana, kind of like a balance due for my ancestor Tice."

He proceeded to tell her Tice's story from his fateful moment in Ripley, Ohio, on the north short of the Ohio River, when the very first person to help the dripping-wet slave in his escape was a Jewish lady.

"So, your Grampa Tice loved the Lord," Lana said.

Bunyan nodded in agreement. "Love of God was the most valuable thing he handed down to his descendants. The most valuable thing in my life."

"Anyone who comes into this home knows that's true," Lana said, "with your plaques and Bibles and devotions. My favorite is by the front door: 'As for me and my house, we will serve the Lord.'"

Bunyan smiled. "If not for Him and my close friends, I don't know how I would have survived CeCe's death."

Lana's eyes filled with sadness.

"Don't be gloomy, Lana. She's in a glorious place now—a heaven where there's no sin, sickness, or death."

"You're so right." Lana paused, wiping away a tear. "So, your Grampa Tice came this way, up through Massachusetts and Maine to Canada?"

He nodded his head. "A hundred and fifty years later, my family is still close to a couple of the families who helped Grampa Tice all those years ago. One family in particular up in the mid-coast."

"The Callahans," Lana said.

Bunyan smiled an affirmative, thinking of Frank and Margaret, to whom he had sent the encrypted message five hours earlier. Margaret was the great-great-great-great granddaughter of Caleb Chadwick who, with his parents, had helped Tice on the last leg of his escape. Their families had remained close ever since.

"I'll do whatever you need," Lana said, "and thank you for trusting me and giving me the chance."

Chapter Three

President Smith set the telephone in its cradle, resisting the urge to slam the receiver down. His rage tightened the muscles of his face into a taut mask. The Prime Minister of Australia, Warren-bleeping-Joyce, had just called him "a spineless wallaby and unworthy of being used as crocodile bait."

Minutes before, he had called the Czech Republic's president, Václav Gauch, whose response pushed Smith to forever file him under Personal Enemy Number Six—higher than the number he reserved for his last presidential opponent, whom he detested.

Smith was toying with the idea of lowering himself to call the president of the Marshall Islands, just to resurrect the joy of victory, of power, when his secretary buzzed his desk.

"The vice president is here to see you, Mr. President."

The recollection of his last root canal occurred to Smith. He swallowed hard, then said, "Send him in, Martha."

The door opened and the tall, wiry figure of Daniel Fireside stepped through the threshold. Smith waved him into the room and came around his desk to shake his hand.

"Fine job, Dan. An amazing achievement. What can I say? You've helped accomplish the impossible. You've already received my endorsement, but I'm now pledging to work every day from here to November for your campaign. I'll do whatever I can whenever I can to get you elected president. Fund-raisers, personal appearances—"

"Thank you, Hal. I appreciate your offer very much."

"So, tell me, what favors do we owe and who do we owe them to?"

"We're talking a long list."

"But do-able?"

"Sure. Quite an array—from Nick's demand to replace Harry as Ways and Means chairman all the way down to Trent demanding the IRS take down his brother-in-law's firm."

"His brother-in-law?" Smith's mouth fell open. "Hateful."

"Sure is. I don't believe what drives some of these people, how their constituents could re-elect them and their personalities time after time." Fireside shuffled the papers in his hands. "That said, some requests on this list will be painful."

Omri walked through the paces of his day with a smile on his face. He was not naturally devious, so he hoped the grin looked genuine.

He taught his ten o'clock class about the possibilities of molecular memory to twenty-eight mushy-minded undergraduates. Then, strolling along the corridor toward the faculty lounge, he pretended not to hear a conversation between two students in which one asked the other, "What would you do if you were Doctor Zohn and were told you couldn't go home?"

"Well, Israel's not his home now. He's lived here for ages." The reply was sharp, as if the girl was offended, angry.

"But still—" said the first. "What if he wanted to visit family there?"

Reaching the faculty lounge, Omri opened the door, half frosted glass, half wood, and scanned the fifteen-by-twenty-foot room. Several men and women were eating lunch; others were chatting in the conversation area.

A radio, sitting on an end table beside one couch, blared what Omri recognized as a Boston talk show. "The Jews run this country—from Wall Street to Hollywood," a man's angry voice railed. "Time for them to pay up and stay put."

The host responded, "That sounds pretty bigoted, Henry from Cape Cod. And I thought you people on the Cape were all about freedom—sexual and otherwise."

"There's a reason they're called 'wandering Jews,'" the caller responded. "They always outstay their welcome."

"So you want them to stay here, held hostage," the host countered. "If you don't like them, why not cheer as they leave?"

The caller began to stammer a response. Omri shook his head and took a seat at a nearby table.

When leaving, he even engaged Doctor Jurewicz, one of his least favorite colleagues, in a discussion of Jurewicz's simulation and visualization software at the Plasma Science and Fusion Center.

Later, he taught an afternoon seminar to seventeen postgraduate students on Condensed Matter, in particular the hidden electronic order in uranium-based material.

Fully aware of the phrase "Keeping your wits about you," Omri strolled to his lab, even whistling "America the Beautiful" on his way.

Both of his graduate assistants, Mark Poulter and Dennis Wade, looked up when they heard the door open. The look on both faces appeared to be relief, though perhaps surprise on Mark's. Had they also been discussing his fate? Was he a topic of dialogue outside the walls of MIT? Outside his circle of academia? His thoughts flew to the offices of the US Department of Energy and the Department of Defense.

"Good afternoon, Doctor," Mark said.

Wade simply waved hello.

"Gentlemen," he replied.

Omri studied the lab table before Mark, who was researching whether invisible particles could enhance thermoelectric devices. The table looked like a miniature convergence of a Kentucky still and a NASA wind tunnel.

Wade, his usual unkempt self with uncombed hair, shirt-tail hanging out over his trousers—*probably wearing mismatched socks,* Omri chuckled—stood at a very large whiteboard working out an equation in regard to Omri's research into nuclear fusion.

As Omri stepped into the room, his telephone rang. He hastened to pick up.

"Dr. Zohn?" The voice on the other end had the distinctive Southern accent of Henry Webster of the Science and Innovation arm of the US Department of Energy. "Just checking to see how things are going with our favorite nuclear scientist."

Webster was more politician than scientist, a man polished in the art of servile deference, Omri thought. *He should go far.*

"Well, I just stepped into the lab and found Dennis and Mark hard at work."

"Any closer?"

"I should be able to demonstrate Sunny in a week or so. I know the secretary wants the president to be present with a handful of others and for it to be behind closed doors. Let me give you a call Monday or Tuesday—Wednesday at the latest—to firm up a date."

"We're on the cusp of greatness!" said Webster, whom Omri had discovered was ever willing to include himself when "we" were a success but to distance himself when "they" failed.

Omri looked down at his desktop calendar. Every day was full next week. By mid-morning on Monday, people would start to wonder about his whereabouts—perhaps even send out an all-points bulletin. He wondered if they might entertain the thought that he had been kidnapped by some "bad guys" from the Middle East, or even "bad guys" from the energy-producing companies that would be devastated by such a cheap source of power.

Only mildly attentive to Webster, mouthing on about arranging a private flight from Boston to Washington, Omri began to calculate all the hours he had devoted to developing sonufusion, using sound waves to produce nuclear-fusion reactions., leading to developing an inexpensive tabletop device carrying a fraction of the cost of the historically large multibillion-dollar nuclear-fusion reactors.

Yes, Omri's Sunny, which created tiny bubbles that implode with tremendous force, was something Webster, the secretary, the president and many others would enthuse over, using the inclusive word we.

Omri ended the conversation, saying, "Let's finalize our plans when I call you next week."

Hanging up, Omri wondered if Webster's call was legitimate, or if he was checking to see if he was even there, or perhaps escaping the country. He'd given Webster no reason to think his mind was already in his beloved Galilee.

He looked up at the whiteboard. Dennis was stuck, ruminating on a mathematical obstacle, apparently aborting his efforts.

Omri's eyes widened, and he rose to join his prize student. "Mr. Wade," he said, "you're on the verge. Here, let me show you." He picked up a length of blue chalk and immersed himself in the mesmerizing world of numbers, equations, algorithms—the graspable things of this earth so very unlike human nature, overfilled with foibles and feelings and nuances no one can fathom, let alone firmly grasp.

Two hours later, at four-thirty, Omri said, "Mr. Poulter, Mr. Wade, why don't you begin your weekend? Have a barbecue tonight. Go to the beach tomorrow. Take in a movie. You've earned the rest."

Once they'd left, Omri stayed for a few minutes, pretending to be busy.

At exactly 4:37, he was out the door. Leaving the building, he felt fingers gripping his shoulder. Turning, he couldn't stop a smile crossing his face. The fingers belonged to Anton Francoeur, a visiting fellow from the Sorbonne's Université Pierre et Marie Curie.

"My friend," Francoeur said, "I weep for your people. I truly do. This day is a day of mourning for our Creator, a dark day of infamy for America, a day when the world has truly turned against God's people and against his land."

Omri looked over the man who had been at MIT only since January and yet had become a valued friend. He stood only five-foot-four but possessed the heart of a giant.

"Yet a day foreseen by the prophets," Omri replied, allowing a sad smile.

"In my own France, the National Assembly and Senate are voting on the United Nations ban at this very hour. I hear they have debated through the day and midnight is approaching over there. I dare not guess how the vote will turn out."

"Badly, I suppose," Omri said, "especially with the enormous influx of Muslims in recent years."

"Can your dual citizenship get you to Israel?"

"I'm told my research is my captor. I cannot legally leave because of Sunny's importance to national security and my contract with the government."

"Told by whom?"

"A friend in the Senate."

"But your son, your grandson, your brother! Their being in Israel means nothing? You cannot visit them?"

Omri shrugged.

Francoeur shook his head, looking dismayed. "You must feel betrayed, no?"

"Yes, very." Omri hesitated, then said, "but life must go on, Anton."

"Let life go on with us tonight, Omri. Come to my apartment. Élise will cook up a chicken chasseur with croissants and a crème brûlée. I have your favorite coffee, Café Shachor, to top off the feast.

"You found Café Shachor for me?" Omri couldn't hide his enthusiasm.

Francoeur's eyes brightened as he nodded assent.

Omri shook his head in wonder. Here he was, in a hurry to escape, and yet to do so, he had to leave friends such as Anton. He was a scientist and as such, spent that "scientific" part of his life necessarily dispensing with sentiment, avoiding emotional conflict with facts, proving or disproving theories with dispassionate formality. He fought back a tear that struggled to escape the corner of his right eye.

Anton's wife, Élise, had told them both, "You scientists need to delve into another world. Poetry! Now rhyme would be a perfect choice. It's the antithesis of science, and you two need balance."

Well, she was right. And today was perfect proof. Life needs to consist of facts *and* feelings. And don't forget faith. Facts, feelings, and faith. So here he stood with a treasured friend, confronting an odd cocktail of factors: the feelings of being ground in an atom-crusher by the American Congress; the fact he loved his work here and didn't really want to leave either MIT or his many colleagues; and faith—an element of his life to which he admittedly often paid little heed but nonetheless was central to his innate conscience.

"What is the matter, Omri?" Worry etched furrows on Francoeur's forehead.

Omri looked him in the eye. "Anton, I love you. I love Élise. I really love Élise's cooking!" They both chuckled. "But I must defer to another time, my friend."

"Oh, I'm sorry." Francoeur looked truly hurt.

Omri glanced around to ensure he could not be overheard. "I do hope, however, to dine with you again. Perhaps in Paris, if your government disavows the United Nations. Goodbye, my friend."

Omri stretched out his hand and Francoeur grabbed hold. As he did, Omri could discern the Frenchman was processing Omri's words. When the realization struck him Omri was indeed escaping, he offered a sad smile.

"Indeed, Omri. Indeed. I understand. And—" he paused, "Godspeed."

The two men exchanged warm hugs, then Omri hurried off, steadying his left hand so he could read his wristwatch: *4:41 p.m.* He had just lost three minutes, but Anton was worth the time.

5:18 p.m.

In Anacostia, on the southeast side of Washington, DC, the head of the United States Department of Homeland Security was meeting with her lead field operatives and the heads of the Transportation Security Administration, Customs and Border Protection, and Intelligence and Analysis. Seventeen men and five women sat around a long, oblong table in the largest conference room of the five billion dollar headquarters complex on the campus of St. Elizabeth's Hospital.

Shandra Constantine—tall, slim, stately, dressed in a pants suit with a high-necked jacket—ruled the room. She wished this meeting could have been held at seven or eight o'clock this morning, but these people had to travel this morning to DC from around the country. So be it.

"Our friends in Treasury are finally—let me repeat, finally—clamping down on the money flow," she said. "Their actions will help us immensely with Operation Cork, stopping the Jewish people *flow*. Jewish emigration is not only against international wishes, but now also against American law to emigrate to Israel. Besides being a boon to the Jewish majority in Israel, their exodus is a brain drain on this country—a drain the president and I want stopped. The word is *stopped*, not *slowed*."

Constantine's eyes narrowed as she looked around the table. These were her leaders. Besides the Customs and Border, Transportation Security, and Intelligence and Analysis directors, the others each controlled a region in the new task force created to prevent Jewish Americans from emigrating, even traveling, to Israel.

"When the United Nations voted a week ago to stop Jewish emigration into Israel, President Smith ordered Ambassador Snowe to abstain and not use our veto power; and so the resolution stood: UN Sanction 017-666."

Constantine shuffled some papers in front of her, then looked up again.

"Our friends at the United Nations and around the Arab world want to stop Jews from moving to Israel, and we intend to help. Russia is doing its part. The European Union is doing its part. Even South American countries, led by Brazil, by the way, shut down all air traffic to Tel Aviv."

Constantine gauged the reactions of her troops. Who was on board? Who wasn't? If this were the *HMS Bounty* and she were William Bligh, were there any mutineers like Fletcher

Christian among them? Loyalty played a part. Fear, also. And, yes, agreement. But sometimes loyalty and fear were more powerful motivators than principles and moral values. You could read so much in a person's facial expressions, or lack thereof.

"As you know," she continued, "at four o'clock this morning, I ordered that no Jewish travel outside the country be allowed. At this point, Canada still allows travel to Israel, so no Jews are allowed over the border where they can fly to Israel. Although Mexico is on board with the travel freeze, I have little faith in their ability to enforce the ban, so until further notice, I will allow no Jewish travel to Mexico either."

"But does the prohibition go beyond the written intent of the law?" asked Amy Durant, an African-American who worked out of Michigan, which had more than thirty-two hundred miles of Great Lakes coastline from which Jews could launch boats bound for Ontario.

Constantine leveled a harsh gaze on Durant and said, "An odd question for someone on the Canadian border."

"Just wondering," Durant said. "The law doesn't say to stop travel to countries not on board with the ban."

"No, but I do say. How else can we prevent Jews using that loophole?" Constantine glared at her underling. "Amy, do you have trouble with upholding the law?"

"Trouble with this particular law itself, ma'am. Seems pretty dictatorial for America … to me, at least. Controlling where people can and can't move?"

"We can replace you on this task force, Amy. I know a good desk position available. We could have you in Tallahassee in a week."

"Tallahassee?"

"That's in Florida, Amy."

"I know, ma'am."

"So, do you want the Tallahassee post instead?" Constantine watched the woman squirm in her seat. She knew Amy and her family had settled well in Lansing after several moves in the past, and her two children were ensconced in schools and church groups, her husband in a nice job at a local bank. Constantine made a point to know the details of her regional directors' lives.

Constantine didn't want to dismiss an employee who was both a woman and black; oh, no, such a move wouldn't look good. But she would, make no mistake. She'd heard people call her "The Guillotine" behind her back. At first she'd taken umbrage, but on second thought, she had decided the moniker fit her like a silk sock.

"Amy?" Constantine urged an answer.

Amy slowly shook her head. "No, ma'am. I'm happy where I am."

"And you'll devote your full attention to the task at hand." A statement, not a question.

Amy's eyes flickered. "Absolutely."

"Fine." Constantine again raised a manicured finger and caught the eye of every person before her. "Results, not guarantees, people. Not just our country's safety but the world's, is at stake. Lock down the borders and shut people of Jewish descent out of any transportation out of the United States, except for countries complying with the UN Resolution."

"Are we going public with our efforts?" asked a balding man to Constantine's right. "If so, we could engage the citizen-patriots in our mission."

"Samuel," Constantine said, "have you been watching or listening to the news today? The word is out, but—and I'll repeat, *but*—when someone's captured leaving the country, we want to be as quiet as possible about the detention. We don't want this to appear too … Machiavellian. Many people just won't understand the immense importance of this project. President Smith is holding a press conference at six o'clock today, we'll get on the Sunday talk shows, the vice president will interview with 'friendlies' in the media, we'll flood the country delineating the positives of the two actions:monetary stability in the Treasury Department's Project BankIt and emigration control in our Operation Cork."

"Um-hm," Samuel responded.

"Does everyone understand?"

Nods around the table.

"Think like a person who's trying to leave America," Constantine said. "If it were you, when would you travel? Where? How?"

"Nighttime," responded Russell Bedard, head of Customs and Border Protection.

"Correct. So, Russell, I want you to coordinate the drone program to scour the borders with Canada and Mexico during nighttime hours as well as day, using night-vision."

Russell nodded agreement. "I'm all over it, Madam Secretary."

Constantine looked down at the man to her right and said, "Damian, tell us what your people are doing."

Damien Pinto, head of DHS's Intelligence and Analysis Division, pushed his considerable bulk out of his chair and rose to his feet. He ran a hand across his balding scalp as if straightening a fine head of hair.

"On Monday morning, we'll be able to gauge how many Jews report to work around the country, which will tell us how many may be trying to escape to Israel. But that gives those who're intent on leaving an entire weekend to sneak out somehow. They may have gone to work today as a show to fool their co-workers into believing they're staying put, but it's a ruse because they'll flee as fast as they can after work. And they'll have more than two entire days! So we have to be *pro*active, not *re*active."

Constantine watched as Pinto hiked up his slacks and continued. "So we've compiled a short list of people very, very important to the country's future, a list we'll address with vigor, starting tonight. For instance, during work hours today we've had administrators calling Jews involved in projects, studies, what-have-you that are important to US interests. These calls might seem innocuous to the Jews, but they tell us these people are indeed at work, or not."

"These are not fools," said Bedard. "They'll know we've got an eye on 'em."

"So much the better," Constantine cut in. "Then, they'll know we're serious."

Pinto waved an arm in no particular direction and continued, "But even those who appear to be happy to stay in America, we'll continue to keep an eye on. For instance, Dr. Zohn is number-one on our list. You all know he's on the verge of perfecting nuclear fusion on a scale that will transform our energy resources—heck, the world. Well, he came to work this morning at MIT and was in his lab at the end of the day when our man contacted him. But we'll play it safe and, in fact, have feet on the ground in Boston ensuring he's still here."

Constantine interrupted. "Around the country there are ninety-six like Zohn who are prime assets to America—assets we will *not* lose. And we have an A List—a VIP Top Ten of Zohn and others. Damian's people are on them like Velcro, but we want your operatives in every division to have this list and be on the alert to contain these people."

"Damien," she said, looking his way, "pass out that list, will you? I want photos of these peopole at all the checkpoints leaving the country, at all the airports, marinas … everywhere."

Pinto passed a sheath of papers to his right and watched as the papers made their way around the table. Then he said, "Thanks for your help, everyone."

Waving her arm, Constantine gestured to everyone at the table. "We have a daunting task. If this vote by Congress had been taken in the middle of the week instead of three o'clock on a Friday morning, our task would have been a lot easier.

"So this weekend is not a weekend at all … for any of you or for anyone in your divisions who's necessary to cap Jewish travel outside the country. Get to your posts and call everybody you need. Spare no resources. Got it?"

There were nods of assent around the table.

"This," Constantine added, "is our chance to strut our stuff, right?"

A few half-hearted "Rights" echoed around the table.

Constantine scowled her disapproval of that attitude, then dismissed her charges, sat back in her chair, and exhaled deeply.

5:20 p.m.

Omri Zohn took one last look in the mirror. Looking back at him was Omri Zohn, twenty … twenty-five years younger. No more gray. He had dyed his beard and hair dark-brown and was happy with the results. Once outside, wrap-around sunglasses would do the trick.

He walked to his bed and triple checked his duffel bag, making sure the necessities were all there. A flash drive contained his research and a couple of the most important books he had written. Another flash drive held jpg and pdf files of photographs, his will, and other personal papers. A toiletry bag. The main compartment contained three pairs of underwear and socks, two shirts, two pairs of slacks, a windbreaker, a wad of cash, and of course, his Nobel medal.

Setting the duffel bag at the front door, he walked around the rooms of the house one last time, deliberately. He and Adina had built a life here and raised their two children here after moving from Israel.

Setting the duffel bag at the front door, he walked around the rooms of the house one last time, deliberately. He and Adina had built a life here and raised their two children here after moving from Israel.

He trod up the stairs and gazed into the master bedroom. On Adina's bedside table lay three items, a hairbrush, a bottle of nail polish, and a nail file, occupying the spot over the years since her murder. He had often polished the table top but always replaced those items in their exact positions.

Walking past Benjamin's bedroom, a guestroom, and Devorah's bedroom, where she'd grown into young womanhood.

Her whole life had been laid out before her. He pulled out a handkerchief to dab away the tears from his cheeks.

He entered his den, where the smell of leather saturated the air. Omri drank in the aroma. This was the room he'd most miss. His place of solitude where, without distractions, he could think through the latest problems in his research, catch up on his reading, and connect with his God.

Yes, they had lived, loved, and been loved here—until Adina and Devorah's death. This was a place, these were the memories he was leaving behind. He bowed his head and wept, then he blew his nose and squared his shoulders. He looked up at the front door and down at his duffel bag, then took two deep breaths. This was the moment. No turning back.

Thinking of his own parents and their daring escape from Poland, he wondered about his own flight. He just hoped his escape wouldn't be so dangerous. His parents had faced the SS, brownshirts, and neighbors-turned-enemies. He was facing … who? Homeland Security? Border Patrol? Other authorities.

He had to be alert and on his toes, not to mention invisible.

Seconds later, a bucket hat pulled down on his head, wearing sunglasses, carrying only the oversized duffel bag, and his hair dyed to his natural youthful brown, Omri closed his front door and quick-stepped down the short brick walkway toward the street.

"Omri? Is that you?" The voice caught Omri short, and the hair bristled on the back of his neck. *Mel! Not even out of my yard, and I'm recognized. Great.*

Omri slowly looked toward the voice, hoping his neighbor Mel Epstein wouldn't scream, or worse, laugh out loud.

"It *is* you!"

Omri shot out his right hand flat and motioned for Mel to keep his voice down. He pictured the many times Mel's wife, Hannah, a musical composition professor at the Berkee College of Music, had used the orchestral conductor's signal to lower her boisterous husband's voice. As her students obeyed, so did Mel.

Approaching the white picket fence separating their two front yards, Mel looked over both shoulders, then lowered his voice. "What on earth are you doing, dressed up like—?"

Omri placed a severe look on his face and locked eyes with his friend.

Mel read the look. "Oh!"

Omri could not stop a head-shaking response. "Time for me to go and you and Hannah appear to have decided to stay."

"True," Mel said with a shrug. "This too will pass, Omri. This too will pass. Clear heads will prevail. They must."

"Those were the famous last words of too many of our families—yours and mine, my friend, in times past. Too many times past."

"But this is insane," Mel said, something like torment shading his eyes. "Outrage will build."

"I hope you're right. If so, I may return."

"How are you leaving?" Mel asked.

"Best I don't say. The less you know, the better. But please tell no one. No one." Omri put his index finger to his lips.

"My lips are sealed," Mel said.

Omri checked his watch. Alarm caused his neck muscles to twitch.

"Give Hannah my love," he said as he and his old friend shared a good-bye hug.

—∞—

6:02 p.m.

Omri rose to hustle off the bus, headed toward Boston's North Station. Before leaving, he checked to make sure his cell phone, which he'd taped beneath his bus seat, was secure. Earlier, he'd put the cell on "Silent" and taped the phone there in case Homeland Security was tracking its GPS signal.

Walking toward North Station with an hour to kill, he decided to take a detour. He loved the North End of Boston and the hustle and bustle of Faneuil Hall, so he decided to take the short stroll there. When he reached the northwest corner of the famous rectangular shopping district, he stood next to an old-fashioned light post, straightened his sunglasses, and raised his eyes just enough to observe without being spotted by any surveillance cameras.

A woman stood on a short pedestal, her body and clothing painted green, looking so much like the Statue of Liberty. Another the gentleman, also green as a statue, unmoving and a bit unnerving, was dressed like firebrand Samuel Adams. And there was the little Discovery Shop he so loved because of the treasures inside, teaching children the sciences and the heavens. He wished he could walk through the shopping area and dine at one of the many Italian restaurants on Prince Street or Market Street, or grab a cannoli at Mike's Deli.

Omri continued to keep his head as low as possible so that no one would recognize him and no traffic cameras would be able to spot him. Assuredly, when the Department of Energy discovered he had disappeared, they would contact Homeland Security and then, watch out! Those people would pull out every stop to track him down and prevent him from leaving the country. He prayed any discovery would not happen until Monday. Then, no matter. He should be gone, leaving a lukewarm, if not cold, trail—enough as to not endanger Bunyan or anyone else in the new Underground Railroad.

Although others in his nuclear-fusion research team—especially those at Stanford University—could carry on the work without him, he was the government's prize, its Nobel laureate, the one the administration so much liked to push up on stage and shine the light on when publicizing just how much the regime was accomplishing for mankind. Four United States presidents had befriended him over the years. Photo ops at every turn. Where were they now? Why were they silent? Where was the shame?

Well, Omri thought, what will this latest fiasco do to the country? He shook his head. Unlike his colleagues at MIT who stood solidly against the Resolution, the Smith Administration had done such a stellar job of demonizing the Jews that the ban might actually unite the citizenry. How tragic!

So, he now fled from the government.

—∞—

When Omri arrived at Fanueil Hall, President Smith was walking to a lectern, fronted by the Seal of the President of the United States, for his press conference. He smiled slightly as he thought of stepping to a dais with a United Nations seal as the general-secretary in the near future. He quashed the smile quickly, wanting to look like a man troubled by the necessity of taking this drastic action against Jewish emigration, a man concerned, even distraught, that things had come to this.

Smith would make his points, take three questions from specific reporters friendly to his party, then leave posthaste.

He mentally reviewed his points. The Jewish state of Israel had been reprimanded dozens of times by the United Nations for humanitarian reasons and had not changed its ways. The Arab people had a long history of living in Palestine and deserved their land back. And letting Jews leave America would result in a "brain drain" the country's economic well-being could not sustain.

Smith had an obligation to protect the country—not just militarily but in every way. And so, like the decision or not, he would wholeheartedly support this ban on Jewish emigration. He might even fight back a tear if he could manage one.

One reporter would ask him, "By international law, countries who win land in defensive warfare have full rights to the conquered land. You've agreed in the past with President Obama's statement Israel should revert back to its 1967 borders. Do you still concur?"

He would answer, "Yes, I do. You're correct about international law, but is this righteous? The Jews have added the West Bank, Golan Heights, and Jerusalem to the land apportioned to them by the United Nations. Wars followed. I understand 'the spoils of war,' but is this a code we want to live by in the twenty-first century?

"If you and I get in an argument and a fistfight over a pretty woman and you win, does your victory mean you should get the pretty woman, no matter what?"

The next reporter would ask, "You've tried for years to bring peace to the Middle East. How much has Jewish construction in the Occupied Territories derailed your efforts?"

He would respond, saying, "We do not accept the legitimacy of continued Israeli settlement activity. Yes, the international law court has concluded these new Jewish communities are legal in the sight of the law. But tell me, how would you feel if a neighbor decided to build their garage on your back lawn? I would love to see my Israeli friends, led by their prime minister, finally take feelings into account in their negotiations. Isn't that how we all feel?"

The third reporter would then ask, "This is an extraordinary measure to take in regard to millions of Jewish Americans. How does this make you feel?"

He would reply, "Despondent, really. This is a sad day, but this ban on emigration must be carried out. And I hope all our Jewish friends and colleagues—those who, along with us, are striving to push our country to even greater heights—will agree, in the final analysis, this is the best for us, the best for America, the best for the land of Israel, and the best for the poor Palestinian people."

Over-and-out. Game, set, match. Walk away, don't look back, and absolutely and on pain of death, do not acknowledge any further questions.

Omri turned from one last look at Fanueil Hall and strolled northward toward the Charles River and North Station. A couple of minutes later, carried along with the crowd, he passed oversized images of Boston Bruins hockey players ten feet off the ground, winding up for slap shots, stopping on a dime from full speed, or snatching a puck out of the air in a goalie's glove.

Heroes, all. Omri enjoyed attending the games, cheering on these extraordinary athletes. There was no hockey in Israel. Even if there were ice and hockey rinks, the young men and women there were more concerned with staying alive, serving in the Israel Defense Forces, and protecting themselves and their families' lives.

Omri also loved baseball and going to Fenway Park to watch the Red Sox, though he'd never seen a game before moving to America. In fact, attending a game was how he'd met Bunyan Jackson, the big, left-handed first baseman who hit the long, towering home runs. Before the game, Omri, seated in a box along the first-base line and close to the rail, had became engrossed in a conversation with Bunyan.

When "Jacko" heard Omri speak, he guessed he was an Israeli. One thing led to another and they became fast friends. When CeCe died from cancer, Omri was at Bunyan's side. When Omri won the Nobel Prize in Physics, Bunyan made the trip to Stockholm to share the moment. They were an odd pair, for sure—Zohn, sixty-four-years-old, five-foot-ten, with the Semitic coloring and profile, narrow nose and neatly trimmed beard; and Bunyan, forty-three-years-old, six-foot-four, broad-nosed, clean-shaven, and a medium-dark range of the African-American shade spectrum.

Suddenly Omri was inside the cavernous North Station. Instructions on the wide cement floor directed people to the east, where a bank of elevators transported them to TD Bank Garden for Celtics and Bruins games and assorted other entertainment, or west to an open-air platform for a number of parallel train rails and docking areas.

Voices echoed as the masses hurried along. Few people paid attention to anyone else, but Omri was aware of the security cameras—always cameras—and made certain he kept his head bowed as he walked to the ticket counter for Amtrak's Downeaster rides. The departures sign confirmed what he already knew: the first northbound train left at 6:45 p.m.

He had twenty minutes to wait. Twenty minutes to remain incognito. Twenty minutes of hoping no one at MIT or the Department of Energy would call to check on him; or if they did, the possibility he was escaping his adopted country would not occur to them.

Omri didn't like anything less than total honesty and transparency. He required both from his students. He expected the same from his colleagues. But his freedom overrode such convictions.

What else was Omri to do? And how many other Jews were in comparable circumstances, almost compelled to flee by their ethnicity, multiplied by their indignation and exacerbated by America's lack of moral principles?

He handed a green-and-purple-haired girl cash for his ticket and walked, head-down, to a bench fifteen feet from the edge of the train platform. Setting his duffel bag on the empty seat beside him, he sat down. There he remained, flipping a pen between his fingers, from index to pinky and back, waiting for Train No. 681, which would take him through Haverhill, Massachusetts, to Exeter, Durham, and Dover, New Hampshire, and then into Maine through Wells and Saco-Biddeford, arriving in Portland at 9:10 p.m.

Ten minutes into his wait, Omri's eyes closed, his thoughts on the Western Wall in Jerusalem, when he was startled by a young woman's voice. "Dr. Zohn?"

Oh, my, again? With this dark beard and hair? With this hat and dark glasses? They must recognize my nose and high cheekbones.

Looking up to his right, he saw an attractive well-dressed blonde, with bright green eyes and well-exercised smile lines. Her accent identified her as Norwegian, Swedish, or perhaps Danish.

He had a split second—in scientific terms, a nanosecond—to acknowledge or deny.

If he said, "Why, yes," this might be a quick end to his escape. She could spread the word she saw "that Jew Zohn," dressed peculiarly as if in disguise and waiting for a train, headed north or northeast toward Canada. Worse still, she could rush to a police officer here at North Station and report him.

If he said, "Why, no, you're mistaken," he would pointedly end the conversation. or the diametrical opposite, open the door to a protracted tête-à-tête—something to avoid at all costs.

While thinking all this through, his tendency toward the truth won out before he could stop the words "Why, yes" from escaping his lips. *Oh, no!*

The lady tilted her head and bent toward him, curiosity evident in her eyes. "You don't want to be recognized, do you?"

Omri hesitated.

"I'm intruding." She straightened and took a half-step back. Had she read his mind? Was she thinking of turning him in to authorities? Should he try to keep her here to prevent his exposure?

Omri stammered. Since childhood he was a natural introvert, until his wife had gone to work on what she perceived as a defect, preventing him from becoming the man God wanted. Slowly, she transformed him into as much a people person as he could have ever dreamed. And so, here he was, not wanting to draw attention to the two of them, but not wanting to be harsh with this lady. And yet …

"I'm so sorry. Excuse me," she said, turning to leave. He looked up and followed her eyes. She was looking furtively about her. Could such a pleasant-looking woman be scanning the station for an officer? In an instant, he remembered the story of a German fraulein, a beautiful movie star, who was one of the most high-profile Jew-haters in the Third Reich. She had actually filmed a propaganda documentary calling Jews "swine too evil for a rubbish bin."

Omri's hand shot up, gripping her wrist as she took her first step.

"Please, dear lady, sit with me," he said.

She stopped. Her eyes posed a question. He released his grip and motioned to the bench, sliding to his left and pulling his duffel bag close to give her space to sit. This was his next moment of decision. He was terrible at poker, a characteristic that could lead to his downfall.

And so he said, "You're correct in both matters. I *am* Omri Zohn and I *am* trying to travel *incognito*. I'm hoping for a weekend away from Boston, away from university, just away to relax—with no work, no research, no colleagues."

She looked at his duffel bag. "You travel light."

He forced a smile. "Today, yes. Just for two days at the ocean in Maine."

"Aha."

Was that an "Aha" of belief or an "Aha" meaning she saw through him like a pane of glass?

"No research to challenge me; no textbook to write."

"Um-m."

Was this "Um-m" displaying she understood such a desire, or an "Um-m" that knew the mind of a scientist was always contemplating, never ever completely free from his work?

Again he motioned to the bench and again she stood firm, frowning as she scanned the station. Was she worried? Was she on the right side of history, like Anne Crouch, or the wrong side, like the silver screen star? Omri's neck hairs bristled. He prayed, his lips still but his mind calling up to the Lord to sway this woman to the moral right.

Finally, she said, "I'm waiting for my son, Darren. He's in college here and coming home for the weekend."

"Really? Where does he go to school?"

"MIT," she answered, "like you."

Oh, no! Lord, how could You do this to me? Of all times for such a coincidence!

Then he mentally slapped himself. He didn't believe in coincidence but rather God-incidence

Now, if the Creator could fashion the earth and, indeed, the universe, could He not maneuver people, time and space.

Omri looked up the woman and asked, "MIT? What's his name?"

"Darren Sørensen," she replied. "I'm Mette Sørensen." She offered a hand, her long, well-manicured fingernails, polished to match her red dress. "I'm so glad to meet you, Dr. Zohn."

He stood and grasped her hand in his. "My pleasure, Mrs. Sørensen. I'm afraid I don't know your son."

"He's just a freshman, so he won't be able to take any of your courses for a couple of years, I assume."

He nodded agreement. "Well, I look forward to seeing him."

Just then, the station's loud speaker blurted: "Now boarding Downeaster Train Number 681, dock number five."

With a sigh of relief, Omri said, "Ah, my train."

As he reached for his duffel bag, she said, "It was so nice to meet you. You know, when *Discover* magazine ran its feature on you after your Nobel Prize, I held onto the issue for months, not just because of your research but for your outlook on your place in history. Your humility stood out to me, Dr. Zohn. Do you remember what you said?"

"I'm afraid not." Omri squeezed and unsqueezed his bag, anxious to leave, to get out from the station's bright lights, from this cavernous place where voices seemed to echo even when spoken softly, but he did not want to be rude.

"I do," she said. "'God placed us here for a purpose, his purpose. Whatever our calling, whatever our accomplishments, they're penned in history by our Creator and he should get all the glory.' Then you held up the medal and said, 'This I share with him.'"

Omri smiled at the recollection. "My beliefs," he said. "Nice to meet you, Mrs. Sørensen. I look forward to seeing your son in class some day. A joy meeting you, but now I'm sorry, but I must go. Enjoy your weekend with Darren."

As he turned to leave, Mette Sørensen reached out and grasped his elbow. She leaned in to him and spoke only as loud as to be heard above the bustle around them. "I'm Danish, Dr. Zohn. My people helped your people escape the Nazi scourge. My great-grandfather hid more than a dozen Jews in his fishing boat during several trips out of his village. If I can help you, please, please let me do so."

Relief softened his tense muscles. Omri smiled broadly, then took her slim hand in his and kissed it lightly. He put his finger to his lips in a "hush" signal and said, "That's all I require. Perhaps you may help others in a more substantial way."

Unexpectedly, she wrapped her arms around him and whispered in his ear, "Godspeed."

Two "godspeeds" in the last three hours. God's presence was tangible as Omri stepped down the dock to board Train Number 681. Destination: Portland, Maine, en route, he hoped, to Israel.

Chapter Four

8:48 p.m.

Like toxic fumes, the CBS News broadcast spilled out of the radio in the Rosenbaums' SUV:

> In airports across the country, TSA officials report Jewish people are being turned away at ticket counters when trying to arrange flights to Israel or any country allowing travel to the Holy Land.
>
> This is the result of the Congressional vote in the early hours of this morning to adhere to the United Nations Resolution to ban emigration to Israel. The ban extends to non-American Jews engaged in what is deemed essential work for the U.S. government.
>
> Along the U.S.-Canadian and U.S.-Mexico borders, literally thousands of Jews have been detained.
>
> Here is CBS News correspondent Charles Rivers.

Jake, I'm standing at the U.S. Route 5 international border crossing from Bellingham, Washington, into British Columbia, Canada. We've spent the better part of five hours here and have witnessed US border agents turning away dozens of people. In fact, at last count, fifty-three vehicles—apparently most, if not all, of the occupants being people of Jewish descent. As they've turned to return to where they came from, we've been able to speak with several of them. One woman was succinct—and representative—in her exasperation. Well, let's call her feelings what they were: outrage.

"This is horrid!" An obviously elderly woman's voice crackled. "I survived Auschwitz. Auschwitz! I lost my father, little brother, aunts, and uncles in the September Campaign in Poland. My mother died at Birkenau. At least four cousins died in the killing fields of the Pripet Marshes. "All died in the camps at the hands of Jew-haters. For no reason, Jew-haters. What had my abba done to them? My eema? My abba was a shop owner; my eema, a seamstress. What was their crime? And now, all these years later, this? What is my crime I cannot visit the land of Avraham, Yitzak, and Yacob before I die?"

"Many see this as a modern kind of pogrom."

"The enemies of God's people will always come up with new ideas."A middle-aged man was speaking. "And our Congress, our president, agree with them? Shame! And shame on these border-crossing agents for complying."

"And so goes this historic day, at border crossings and airports all around the country. A crackdown, most assuredly, and one President Smith condones with reluctance."

From his press conference, Smith began to count off his reasons to support the United Nations, but Naomi slammed a fist down on the radio's power button, and the SUV was suddenly silent.

Ethan turned to see the exasperation etched on his wife's face. He knew what was coming, and sure enough …

"I don't want to hear his 'reasons,'" Naomi made quotation marks in the air. "I don't want to hear his voice. I don't want Congressional contortions to explain this."

"Okay, okay," Ethan said, trying to catch his wife's eyes while keeping track of the cars all around them vying for position on Interstate 26. "I agree. And we won't have to hear them any more—not after we get out."

"If my parents were alive …" Naomi's voice cracked and she went quiet.

"Well, I told you what Dad said." Ethan sent a furtive glance her way.

"I know, I know. If your mom were still with us, they'd have left as soon as the UN Resolution passed. But now, he'll wait to see if we succeed."

Ethan envisioned his father's face, always encouraging, imparting wisdom, considering Ethan his child even after he'd reached adulthood.

"And if we do, then he'll find a way to join us," he said.

"But what about Janey and Barbara? What about Etta and

Gloria?"

"Naomi, we've discussed this for hours. I thought we'd decided—and without doubt."

Naomi nodded. "We have. But that was a dream, reverie, us fantasizing. If we follow through and do this, we step over the line into … into …"

"Into reality?"

"Okay. Okay. There are dreams and there's reality. But this truly means leaving your dad, our jobs, our friends, our synagogue." She sighed deeply. "I'm not saying I'm changing my mind; I'm just—I don't know—reconsidering. I haven't said my goodbyes to Adelle, Sarah, Trish …"

She sighed, then asked, "Is leaving worth the risk, Ethan? I know you've been to Israel for business several times, but as a couple we've visited there what, once? Is going to our homeland worth leaving America? Are we leaving because we want to live in Israel, or because of our outrage that the UN and the American government would do this?"

"Because the government would do what, sweetheart? Betray us?" Ethan couldn't stop his voice from showing his anger, and he didn't want to. "Because the people who represent the citizens of America have betrayed six million of their own?"

He turned the vehicle down a ramp off Interstate 26. Silence fell for a full minute.

Finally, he said, "These are all hard choices, babe." He reached across and put a hand on her shoulder. "But do we want to live in a 'free' country anymore? Or a country with control over where you can and can't travel? That goes along with the United Nations and Arab countries just to get along? We've lacked courageous leadership for twenty, twenty-five years. America has no moral compass anymore. He turned left at the end of the ramp.

Naomi turned and look directly at him, then placed a hand on his forearm. "Okay, darling. I'm so sorry for my double-mindedness. You've convinced me … again. We do need to leave."

They approached a traffic light and even heavier traffic.

"I still can't believe this is the earliest evening train out of Charleston," Naomi said. "And look at the traffic!"

"It's Friday night—date night, party night," Ethan said. "At least we can feel safer in the dark."

"We could have come an hour early."

"I know. I know. I thought about coming earlier, but we've got to avoid suspicion, and I didn't want to be standing around, waiting. But I didn't expect traffic to be this crazy."

Ethan looked at the clock on the dashboard. "Gonna be tight."

"Do we look so Jewish that people would notice and think, 'escaping Jews!'?" Naomi hesitated, then added, "All right, we do."

Ethan shrugged and agreed—Yes, we do. Others may not, but we do. He concentrated on maneuvering around a stalled sedan at Ashley Junction to Railroad Avenue. The Amtrak train station was up ahead. Ethan flashed an uneasy glance at his watch.

He spotted the long-term parking sign and turned into the lot. He pulled a time slip out of the check-in gate and started to put the paper in the usual place, the unused ashtray, for safekeeping. He thought better. If he and Naomi were tracked and authorities checked inside the vehicle, they'd find the time slip and be able to deduce what trains they might have taken. He stuffed the slip into his pants pocket.

"Gotta hurry, babe," he said as he parked.

He stepped out, opened the rear door, and hauled out two

black duffel bags. Slipping an arm through each set of straps, he said, "I'll carry them. Let's go!"

After a couple of steps, he caught himself. "Oops!"

"Oops, what?"

"My baseball cap." He returned to the car, pulled out his cap, and pulled it down to his ears.He then clicked "Lock" on the key fob.

Off they hustled toward the train station, about a hundred yards away.

A minute later they were in a short line for Silver Meteor number 98, departing at 9:23 p.m. Ethan looked down at his watch: 9:14 p.m. At the counter, he paid in cash, grabbed a small time schedule for the train, winked at Naomi, and wrestled a duffel bag over each shoulder. They hurried to the platform and the front of the silver bullet-shaped train.

After stashing their duffel bags in the storage bin by the door, Ethan and Naomi walked down the half-full front-most business class car. Each pair of seats faced another pair, separated by a low table.

Ethan breathed a sigh of relief when he spotted two seats with no passengers across from them. Naomi sat by the window; Ethan nestled in beside her, feeling the protector, the sentinel at the outpost.

"Fourteen hours to Penn Station in New York City, arriving at 11:29 a.m.," he said, holding up the schedule to show her. "Then, with a one-hour layover, we catch Northeast Regional, train number 164, leaving Penn Station at 1 p.m. Another four hours and eighteen minutes and we arrive in Boston South Station at 5:18 p.m. tomorrow.

Naomi blew out a breath. She was exhausted.

Ethan managed a smile. "Finally, Downeaster train 687 leaves North Station at 6:45 p.m. and arrives in Portland at 9:10 tomorrow night."

"So we have plenty of time to get from South Station to North Station."

"No problem. We could walk the distance and have time for dinner at a restaurant in the North End. But we'll take a cab or the subway."

"Fourteen hours to New York, four more to Boston and two and a half to Portland? Phew!" Naomi squirmed in her seat. "My fanny hurts already. But a real dinner in the North End does sound delicious—if I can fight off the fear enough for my stomach to settle down."

Peering at the schedule, Ethan asked, "Do you believe we make twelve stops between Charleston and Penn Station?"

"An 'express' with a dozen stops," Naomi deadpanned. "Great."

"And," Ethan added, holding up his left arm so Naomi could see his wristwatch, "we're two minutes late leaving."

"You're depressing me. We have to think positive," Naomi said.

Just then, two women dressed in pantsuits and carrying briefcases slipped into the seats facing them.

"Oh, boy," Ethan whispered. "Cover up, sweetie. Start reading a magazine."

He pulled his baseball cap down over his eyes, leaned back, and pretended to sleep.

The fewer conversations, the less chance of being identified later. Who knew what lengths the government would go to stop them? The Defense Department had certainly shown enough interest in his research. He closed his eyes, reached for Naomi's hand, and squeezed gently, hoping to transfer some iota of reassurance.

—⁂—

9:01 p.m.

His body turned at an angle for optimum concealment, Omri stared blankly out the train's window. The lights of homes on the outskirts of South Portland whizzed by, but nothing registered. His thoughts were filled with one thing: The blood of my people. The blood of my family.

No, once more he settled on this as the right decision. No more second-guessing. No more looking back. What did the Lord say about looking back? Lot's wife was an example of what to avoid. For, as Sodom and Gomorrah were spiritually dark, so was today's America.

—⁂—

9:07 p.m.

President Smith finished his workday, judging he had escaped the press conference relatively untarnished. At least that's how his chief of staff assessed the early flash polls. Those who hated him would always hate him. Those who loved him would always love him. And he didn't have to run for election again, so the tenuous lot in the middle—not cowed by the intransigence of the right nor the lambasting assaults of the left—were of no consequence at this moment in the lengthy timeline of his career.

He and Theresa had eaten a rare meal alone—no foreign dignitaries, no guests, no chief of staff, no children who were both off at college—just the president and first lady. And though Smith had a sheaf of papers spread on the coffee table before him, his attention was on his wife at his side.

"Hal," she said, eyes aglow, "I've heard more than one commentator today declare you'd be a perfect secretary-general for the United Nations when your second term ends—and there are rumors the rule preventing that from happening will be changed."

Smith pushed himself back in the sofa and turned his eyes to his wife of twenty-two years. "Really? Who? When?"

"Wolf Blitzer and Bob Beckel. Late this afternoon."

"Aha." The sound escaped Smith's lips like a soft breath. "Well, appears our little 'talking-points' balloon is working."

Theresa flashed the smile that had won him over at Harvard when she had helped him win the student body presidency. "Your name should be at the top of the list even without balloons." She turned her shoulders square to him. "And without any agreements with the Arab League."

Smith nodded, but in reality doubted he'd get there without the Arabs. Voting for the ban on Jewish emigration to Israel was reaping benefits. He could see himself at the lectern leading the UN, traveling the world not as the United States president but, in effect, as the world's supreme leader. World leader exactly described the secretary-general since the UN had been given such wide-ranging control—from the World Court to global climate-control taxes, even powers of warfare instead of just peacekeeping.

He curled a crooked smile. "If I've learned anything from history, it's if you dream of being the leader of the world, not just a country, there's no better way than to disapprove of the Jews and Zionism."

"If you're angry with those stiff-necked, self-centered bullies, you're in sync with the rest of the world," Theresa agreed, her voice husky.

"Back when Chuck Hagel was approved as Secretary of Defense, with little debate and after all his anti-Semitic hyperbole, any poli-sci major could have guessed this day was coming, sooner or later," Smith said.

"Came sooner."

Smith leaned back in a leisurely pose, draping an arm toward his wife."Tessie, what do they call the wife of the secretary-general?"

"I've grown used to 'First Lady,'" she said, duplicating his smile. "I'll stick with it. And let America come up with another name for the president's spouse."

—m—

9:15 p.m.

As Ethan and Naomi continued their self-imposed nonchalance toward their neighbors, Omri was lifting himself from his seat on the Downeaster. A few minutes earlier, the train had stopped at the Portland junction and most of the people aboard had hurried off and to their cars in the adjacent parking lot on the other side of a chainlink fence, or to catch one of the three or four taxi cabs waiting in front of the lobby.

Omri wanted as few witnesses to his movements as possible. Wearing sunglasses at nine o'clock at night would only draw attention, so he waited a few extra minutes for the business class car to empty out. Only three people remained seated, waiting for the train to continue on to Freeport and Brunswick.

Omri pulled his hat lower on his brow, dropped his head, and sauntered to the back of the car, his duffel bag in place. Disembarking into the dusk, he began to walk up an eight-foot-wide asphalt ramp under a long canopy toward the railway station. Small lights along both sides of the canopy shone a dim glow on his footsteps.

He dared a cautionary glance to the end of the ramp and spotted a security guard standing at the entryway to the station a few feet ahead. Quickly he returned his eyes to the walkway and offered up a prayer.

Eight more steps and his prayer was interrupted.

"Sir?"

Omri lifted his eyes to the guard. Curiosity was etched on the man's face.

The guard hesitated; Omri swallowed hard. The man looked him over, head to foot. Thoughts were whirling. Omri wished he could read minds. After what seemed a minute, the man shrugged and said, "Have a nice evening."

Omri nodded and struggled to get out the words, "You, too."

—~—

Bunyan Jackson sat in his black Escalade, parked in the front row of the station's rear parking lot, facing the one-story brick building. A circular drive curled in front of the station, but the plan—which admittedly they had created when the necessity of escape was a dim possibility—was for Omri to walk to the SUV.

Bunyan thanked God he had chosen a vehicle with darkened windows all around. He'd bought this one in part because of the heavy tint. Although he enjoyed interacting with baseball fans, sometimes he desired privacy to be able to cruise through Portland without cars honking and people waving and hollering "Jacko!" at every red light.

He had even avoided the allure of getting a "Red Soxy" (as his wife would say) license plate like "Sox Rule" or "GameTme."

No. Tonight was a chilling time when privacy was priceless. Secrecy was vital. Concealment, precious. The optimum result? No one recognizes him, no one recognizes Omri, and no one sees Omri get into his vehicle.

Just then, Omri stepped out of the entryway and under the wide portico fronting the station. At least he appeared, by his size and gait, to be Omri. Bunyan double-honked his horn and, when the man turned in his direction, double-flashed his headlights.

Yes, he was Omri. He turned on his heels and walked quickly in Bunyan's direction, still keeping his head low.

A tap on his window startled Bunyan. He turned his head in response. A tall man wearing a Red Sox windbreaker stood close by, smiling broadly. "Jacko!" he exclaimed. "It is you!"

How could he see inside?!

The man bent down and picked up a boy, about five or six years old. "Danny," he said to the child, "here is the best first baseman who ever wore a Red Sox uniform, Jacko Jackson!"

"Wow!" the boy exclaimed.

Bunyan took a quick glance in Omri's direction. He was about fifty yards away. Fighting to maintain a calm exterior, Bunyan turned back to the man and punched the button to roll down the window. Planting a broad smile on his face, he said, "Why, hello! A member of Sox Nation, eh?"

"Since I was as old as my son here."

This man has the look of a doctor or lawyer and will certainly recognize Omri. Concealing his movements as best he could, he flashed his lights twice, hoping Omri would raise his eyes and notice something was awry.

Then he extended his arm and shook the man's hand.

"I'm Todd Duncan. This is my son, Danny," the man said.

"Glad to meet you, Danny." The child extended his little hand, and Bunyan engulfed it in his own. A glance toward Omri. Forty yards. Again he secretively flashed his lights twice.

"Hey, Danny," Bunyan said. "I've got a baseball or two in the back. How would you like me to sign one for you?"

The boy's face lit up like a lighthouse. "Sure, Jacko!"

Bunyan opened his door and anxiously peeked toward Omri. Thirty yards out. Omri, head down, was nearing the open gate to the parking lot which was surrounded by chain-link fencing.

Surely his friend would look up and notice the commotion around Bunyan's SUV.

Bunyan strode to the back of the vehicle and swung open the

rear door. Todd followed with Danny still in his arms.

Reaching into an athletic bag, Bunyan grabbed a baseball and extended his hand toward Danny. "This is a Major League baseball," he said. "You think some day you'd like to play in the Majors?"

"Sure would!" The boy, eyes wide open, put his hands together like he was holding a baseball bat. "Next year I'm playing T-ball!"

"Whoa! A great start, son. I'm sure your daddy'll show you all the ropes."

That drew a smile and firm nod from the father.

Bunyan glanced toward the parking lot gate. Ten yards out and closing.

Omri's steps on the crushed rock were audible now. Todd glanced his way, then took a closer look.

Bunyan coughed loudly, hoping to alert Omri to stay clear. Omri must have noticed because he suddenly veered away. Not too sharply! Bunyan nearly spoke aloud, thinking such a quick and drastic move might draw suspicion.

"Okay," Bunyan said, drawing Todd's attention to him. He tossed the ball in the air and caught it just as the silhouette of his friend passed ten feet or so behind the father and son.

Breathing a sigh of relief, Bunyan said, "Let's make this special."

He grabbed a pen from a sleeve in his athletic bag and wrote: "To my friend Danny, a future Red Sox!—Jacko Jackson."

He handed the ball to the child. "Oh, boy!" Danny exclaimed.

"You know, every summer I take a group of Little Leaguers to Fenway Park to see a Red Sox game," Bunyan said. "When you get to be ten or eleven years old, write me a letter, remind me of tonight, and I'll take you with me, with your dad as a chaperone." He looked at Todd with raised, questioning eyebrow. Todd nodded agreement.

"Wow, Mister Jacko! A Red Sox game with you would be aweful! I mean awesome. Awesome!"

"Shake hands, then."

The boy boldly shook his hand, followed by his father.

"Thank you, Jacko. You made my day. Heck, you made my year!"

Bunyan grinned. "Well, always nice to meet a fan."

Omri stepped through a line of cars in his peripheral vision, and meandered toward the back of the lot.

As the father and son strode off a moment later, Bunyan slipped back into the Escalade, counted fifteen seconds and double-honked the horn.

Two minutes later, Omri had rushed back to the SUV, tossed his duffel bag into the back seat and climbed into the front passenger seat. Both winded and exhilarated, he gasped for air and looked up, seeing the worried face of his friend.

"Bunyan." He breathed the name and extended a hand.

"Whoa!" Bunyan's eyes grew large. "Omri, you look twenty years younger. Great disguise!"

Omri waved off the compliment. "I was recognized before I got out of North Station!"

"No!" A look of worry.

"Are you sure you want to do this?" Omri asked.

"Never more sure, never more upset with my government," Bunyan said. "I was just reflecting on my great-great-great-great grandfather Tice and his escape on the Underground Railroad."

"And here I am, my friend," Omri said, "getting off an above-ground train and joining your Underground Railroad."

They came to a stoplight at a four-lane street in South Portland. Four vehicles were ahead of them. The right-hand turn onto two-lane Route 77 would take them the ten minutes to Bunyan's home.

"Tice had an exciting escape," Omri commented.

Bunyan nodded. "But our more immediate concern is your escape."

"And the Rosenbaums. I only wish their trip here weren't so lengthy. It's such a long trip by train, but, in the balance, we figure the train's safer than flying."

"Agreed." Bunyan glanced at him. "You had no problems, right?"

"One hiccup when the mother of an MIT student somehow recognized me. But otherwise I kept my head low, avoided traffic and security cameras as best I could, then found a seat by myself on the train."

"So what's the Rosenbaums' timeframe?"

"Plan B calls for Ethan and Naomi to take the first train north after work. If I'm not mistaken, they left Charleston a few minutes ago, will switch trains at Penn Station at eleven-thirty tomorrow morning, and arrive in Boston at five-eighteen. Then the Downeaster will get them here at nine-ten tomorrow night."

"We're losing twenty-four hours, but we'll still be able to get you out of the country before Monday."

"With no hitches." A hint of warning invaded the air, like a vulture circling above an unaware prey.

Bunyan shrugged. "With no hitches."

"Your ancestor had a man chasing him all the way. Hopefully that won't happen in our case."

"Hopefully," Bunyan said. "Here we are."

He turned left into a long driveway lit by eight-foot-high black wrought-iron lampposts at intervals along the way. The driveway ran through a small stand of sixty-foot-high pine trees and into an open area with an expanse of lawn on both sides. Though Omri couldn't see past the illumination of the lampposts, he knew the property well. He'd visited several times, including one memorable month-long vacation two years before, during which Bunyan had escorted him all along the stunning Maine coast until they reached the border between Calais, Maine, and St. Stephens, New Brunswick.

"If only I could get news to my brother and son I'm making aliyah to Israel," Omri said.

"Contact would be dangerous," Bunyan said. "I'd wait until your feet touch the ground there." He looked at Omri with a serious expression. "How is Ariel doing?"

"I'm afraid there may not be much time—perhaps a few months. He's in stage four."

Bunyan shook his head. "I'm so sorry, Omri."

"He's in God's hands." Omri checked his wristwatch. It was 9:47 p.m. They had almost an entire day to wait for Ethan and Naomi. An entire day to hope the Department of Homeland Security would not be looking for him. A day to hide—like a runaway slave.

Chapter Five

"You've got your usual room," Bunyan said as they entered the front door to his manse. "Why don't you take your duffel bag upstairs and come back down for a hot meal?"

"No-no-no," Omri said, holding up a hand in objection. "Don't bother."

"Listen." Bunyan put his hands on his hips. Sometimes when with Omri, Bunyan felt like he, not Omri, was the professor, giving the student the advice he needed. "I know you missed dinner in order to make the train, and I'm guessing you didn't get any food on the train to avoid being identified. Right?"

Omri shrugged.

"Lana's cooking up your favorite pasta dish. We'll have a late dinner together."

Just then Lana walked through the wide entryway. "Doctor Zohn! So nice to see you, sir." She smiled broadly. "The chicken's simmering."

"Lana, you're a gem," Omri said. "The aroma persuades me. I'd love a true meal."

Looking at Bunyan, she asked, "Shall I start the linguini?"

He nodded.

As Lana retreated, Bunyan turned to Omri. "Been living on frozen dinners, haven't you?"

Omri chuckled. "Frozen dinners are my nutrition salvation. I've no time to cook. Oftentimes, I forget about meals altogether. The nearer I've gotten to completing Sunny, the more the excitement has driven me onward."

"The whole world will be excited when they find out about Sunny."

Omri appeared tired, but his smile spread from ear to ear.

"Why don't you get settled in and come down to the dining room?" Bunyan said. "Linguini takes about ten minutes if I'm not mistaken."

As Omri started toward the stairway, he peered at Bunyan. "You're unsettled," he said.

"No."

"Yes."

"Well—"

"You're worried."

Bunyan shrugged.

Omri looked at him with reassuring eyes. "My friend, surely our Lord is with us. My prayer since I called you at three o'clock this morning was He would keep you safe."

"I'm not worried about me, Omri. And not just you, either." Bunyan rammed his hands into his pants pockets. "My concern is our country. Someone once said, 'Politicians are too concerned with right and left, not right and wrong.'"

Omri laughed.

"Well, the American citizenry has allowed this to happen," Bunyan continued. "We continue to check the box for 'the lesser of two evils' when often we think the best choice can't win. More often, the best man isn't even running."

Omri nodded agreement.

Bunyan continued, "When will we learn we've relinquished power, and those to whom we've surrendered control don't reflect our values and opinions or have our best interests at heart? Even if we learn the lesson, will our awakening be too late? I'm afraid that's a rhetorical question, and I don't like it."

"Well, *right* as in *righteousness* isn't determined by majority vote," Omri said. "That's now been established in both the United Nations and Congress over the past week. But, my friend, doesn't the New Testament tell you Christians not to worry, that fretting can't add a single hour to your life? And Joshua declared: 'Be strong and courageous. Do not be terrified; do not be discouraged, for the Lord your God will be with you wherever you go.'"

With that, Omri scurried up the stairs, duffel bag in hand, to wash up.

Ten minutes later, they settled down to a scrumptious meal. After Bunyan said grace, he watched with delight as Omri devoured Lana's chicken linguini. She had prepared a special sauce, substituting a magical concoction of curry and other herbs for cream, which Omni, as a practicing Jew, couldn't eat with meat.

When Lana checked in to see if they were finished, Bunyan said, "This sauce was surely dreamed up by the Man who made the manna that fed the Jews in the desert."

She smiled, then took way the dishes.

—₩—

Moments later, Omri watched as Lana returned, carrying a tray with a coffee pot and two demi-dishes filled with crème brûlée.

"Your favorite, Doctor," she said.

"You spoil me, Lana." Omri thought of the missed meal with Franceour and Elise and her plan for crème brûlée.

He caught Lana's glance at Bunyan.

Putting spoon to dessert, Omri looked at Bunyan. "You don't know how thankful I am for you. I know how much you're putting at risk by helping me and the Rosenbaums."

Bunyan tossed up his hands. "You'd do the same for me, I'm sure."

Omri smiled sadly and nodded. Might America come to that? Like the Christians who were imprisoned with the Jews in the Holocaust.

"Well, with God's help, we'll get you out of the country on Sunday."

Omri offered a look of consternation. "I wish we could be in touch with Ethan and Naomi. I'd like to know if all's well with them, where they are, if they've run into problems. But we just can't call because we don't know if the government is tracking our locations by the GPS on our phones."

"That's why Dan Callahan and I use encrypted PGP phones," Bunyan said. "Security."

"Dan and Margaret," Omri said, thinking of the couple who lived in mid-coast Maine, his next destination. "Seeing them again will be pleasant, even if it's just for a few hours."

9:05 a.m. Saturday

Henry Webster sidled up to the sedan parked in front of the three-story brick house on Tappan Street in Brookline, Massachusetts. He'd been here once before to visit Dr. Omri Zohn. Shrubs and a flower garden sported a plethora of brilliant colors and aromas.

He wouldn't admit his feelings to anyone, but Zohn's home was just one of myriad reasons Webster was jealous of the Nobel Prize winner. When around Zohn, a sense of inferiority covered him like a wet jacket—another good reason to resent the man. And the fact that Zohn seemed universally loved by his colleagues was yet another motivation for envy.

Webster stepped up to the entryway and rang the bell.

From inside came Zohn's voice: "I'm going to a North Shore beach this morning, then to the movies this afternoon. Please call back on Monday."

A recording on your door bell? I'd like one of those. He speed-dialed Zohn's cell phone.

"I'm relaxing today—at the beach and the movies. Try me again Monday." The quality of the call sounded tinny and inconsistent; in the background was a strange noise, sounding like a machine humming a tune.

Webster put his hands on his hips and twisted his mouth into a pucker. *A North Shore beach, eh? Where would that be? Salisbury Beach? Crane's Beach in Ipswich? Wingaersheck Beach in Gloucester? Parker River on Plum Island? Or a beach in Revere, Salem, or Marblehead? Or …*

Webster cursed under his breath, then he speed-dialed Constantine's office. The secretary connected him to his boss.

"Zohn's not home."

"Where is he?"

"Don't know." Webster told her what had transpired. "Strange that his car's in the drive, though."

"We'll do a camera check to see if we can spot him leaving Brookline by subway or bus."

"What do you want me to do?"

"Canvas the area. Ask neighbors if they've noticed anything out of the ordinary. Do what a cop would do trying to find a missing person, Henry!"

"Yes, ma'am." Webster ended the call and swore again. This time Constantine was the object of his derision.

Omri forced himself to stay in bed late, trying to fight off the anxiety of not knowing whether a search was underway for him or Ethan. Finally, at quarter past nine, he rose, slipped into light slacks and a short-sleeved shirt and stumbled downstairs to find Bunyan.

Sunshine flooded the entryway. Omri figured he'd locate his friend outdoors on the patio or closer to the shoreline. He was correct.

"Sleep well?" Bunyan was sitting in a chair on the patio.

"Like a lamb snuggling up to its mother." Well, this was true for the first few hours.

"Dr. Zohn," Lana called from behind him, "what would you like for breakfast? Mister Jackson had me buy bagels and lox just for you."

"Then bagels and lox is the order, Lana. Wonderful!" Omri rubbed together his hands. He looked out at the Atlantic. This felt like a resort in Haifa on the Mediterranean, complete with a good Jewish breakfast.

As Lana retreated to the kitchen, Omri shot a thank-you smile at Bunyan. "We've got less than twelve hours to kill."

"Chess?" Bunyan asked.

"You're on."

At the headquarters of the Department of Homeland Security, Shandra Constantine leaned forward in her chair, grabbed her telephone, and called special agent Joseph Conrad, her righthand enforcer. "There's one person I don't want to leave this country," she barked. "That's Dr. Omri Zohn. He's not home in Brookline."

"You know my team and I are at Logan Airport right now," Conrad said. "They just announced boarding for our flight."

"That's right! You're in Boston!" Constantine couldn't believe her good furtune.

She reiterated Webster's report, then added, "If he's at some beach, fine. Get eyes on him twenty-four-seven. If he's at the movies, fine. Do the same."

"We're on the case, chief."

"I'm texting you his address, so start there, then Boston and the North Shore. Check every security camera in the State of Massachusetts to find the man. If he's on the run, I want his butt here at HQ, ASAP!"

"I'll get the Boston people to use facial recognition and get every set of eyes in the division on computers to scour the area while we're doing the footwork." Conrad put his forefinger and thumb to his mouth and whistled. His three-man team, seated nearby, turned at the familiar signal, and he waved them to his side.

Constantine started to slam the phone down, but stopped halfway. Inspecting the new manicure on her long, slim fingers, she slowly settled the handset onto the end table. She would remain calm throughout. Demeanor. *It's all in your demeanor, my dear. A calm exterior can take a person a long way in this government gig. Fireside, you pompous pimp for the president, you think you're next in line? Move over.*

—~—

Ethan was stretched out in his seat, engrossed in a dream. He stood beside an enormous aerosol can nearly as tall as his six-foot height, waiting on the platform of a railway station. Naomi stood at his side. Brutish men, their muscles bulging in Nazi SS uniforms, beat nightsticks against their bare palms as they stalked back and forth, scowling and demanding that all Jews step to the edge of the platform.

Naomi looked fearfully at Ethan. He smiled, moved her gently in front of the aerosol can and pulled down on its actuator. A vapor from the can enveloped Naomi, and she vanished. Ethan slid into the spot where Naomi had stood. As he reached up to depress the valve, one of his colleagues from his company's research and development department, a tall, thin woman with blonde hair and blue eyes, appeared. Pointing at Ethan, she called out to an SS officer, "There's one!There's a Jew!"

"Ethan, honey." Ethan nearly shot out of his seat. He felt the cool touch of his wife's hand on his elbow.

"Honey, we're here. Penn Station. Right on time."

She raised her wrist so he could see her watch: 11:31 a.m. Penn Station in the belly of New York City.

Ethan shook his head, trying to shed every memory of the dream. He breathed a sigh of relief as the two women across from them rose and left hurriedly. In fact, everyone was in a rush, like they'd caught the city-that-never-sleeps fever.

Naomi turned to him. "Are we witnessing why the term 'a New York minute' was first expressed?"

"Yeah, by appearances, the equation is now sixty divided by half."

"Or thirty seconds."

"That'd be my guess, but I'm no expert. Remember, we've been living in Charleston the last seven years …"

"And a 'Charleston minute' is more like sixty *multiplied* by two …"

"Or two minutes."

"Class dismissed." Naomi grinned and kissed him on the cheek.

A minute later, they stepped down from the train and followed the flow of people off the platform and into a short tunnel that split left and right.

"Glad you wore your sneakers?" Ethan asked.

"You bet."

Ethan grabbed Naomi's elbow and pulled her to a wall just before she was knocked from her feet by two men in suits, carrying expensive-looking briefcases.

"Gee!" she said. "The term 'rush hour' must have originiated here, too."

"I think I'd call it '*race* hour.'"

Naomi grinned. "Well, they're leaning into the left-hand turn as if they're driving in the Daytona 500!"

Ethan couldn't help but chuckle. "Speaking of which, I do need a pit stop."

She elbowed him in the ribs.

"Okay, let's see where we need to go," he said, pointing toward directional signs at a T directly ahead of them. "We're looking for Northeast Regional, specifically train number 164, departing at one o'clock."

Spotting Northeast Regional directionals, they took the left-hand tunnel. In a hurry. "If you walk normally, you get bowled over," Naomi commented.

"Just like on the turnpike," Ethan said.

"Well, I want to get on the …"

"Ethan!" A voice came from several feet in front of them. "Ethan Rosenbaum!"

Ethan flinched; a snake-trail of fear ran up his spine.

A moment later, a ruffle-haired giant of a man, wearing a bright yellow T-shirt and blue- and-white-checked Bermuda shorts, stuck out a mutton-sized hand in front of Ethan. The human traffic seemed to part around his bulk, avoiding him like race cars skirting around a NASCAR crash, Ethan thought morosely, keeping to the racing metaphor.

Ethan forced a smile and shook the offered hand. "Jacob—Jacob Larson."

"What a small world, eh?" Jacob hiked the strap of his luggage over a shoulder. "Imagine meeting at Penn Station in the middle of, what, eight million people?"

"Yes, imagine," Ethan said. "Eight million people, each with a story to tell, according to *The Naked City*." Catching himself, he introduced Jacob to Naomi. "Naomi, Jacob works for the Defense Department."

"And, boy, are we excited about your husband's cloaking research." Jacob quickly put a hand over his mouth. "I didn't say that. It's supposed to be under wraps."

Ethan glanced at his wife, hoping she would read his body language. *Do not lengthen this meeting any more than possible.*

Naomi sported a winning smile, extended a hand and said simply, "Pleased to meet you, Jacob."

"So, are you catching a train right now? Am I holding you up?" Jacob said.

"Yes, we're in a hurry," Ethan said.

"Taking a long weekend, are you?"

Ethan hesitated, then got angry with himself for doing so. Why was he caught off-guard? As a scientist he should have been prepared for any possibility, any distraction.

"Or—" Jacob stopped and Ethan could almost see a light bulb go off in the man's brain. "Ethan, you're heading north. Are you? Would you?"

"Jacob, we—"

"The UN vote, the Congressional vote—" Jacob's eyebrows knit together. "Is this, are you—leaving, or trying to—"

"Jacob," Ethan looked anxiously about them and spotted a security guard who seemed to be paying special attention to people's faces. Was Ethan on a watch list? Could Homeland Security be that organized this quickly?

Ethan bent his head more toward Jacob and away from the direction of the security guard and tried to keep his voice low but, at the same time, audible above the hubbub. "Please, please tell nobody you saw us, Jacob."

Naomi put her hand on Jacob's forearm and looked with pleading eyes at him. "Please!"

"So you *are!*" Jacob suddenly shot a hand to his mouth.

Ethan's nerves seemed to ripple underneath his skin. He could sense his vocal cords tighten. He glanced toward the security guard, who had taken a few steps in their direction. He nearly flinched and knew when he spoke, the words would come out in a squeak. They did. "Jacob, my team and the folks at Duke will perfect the cloaking. In fact, the research is nearly done already. But I must—we must—"

"You must—go," Jacob murmured.

Ethan could see Naomi's grip tighten on the man's arm.

"But as a DOD employee, I must—"

"*Must?*" Ethan asked.

"Well, I—"

"Think, Jacob." Ethan implored, "We're two people who simply do not want to be denied ever seeing our people's homeland. We should be able to come and go, shouldn't we?"

"Yes, but the UN, the Congress—"

Out of the corner of his eye, Ethan could see the security guard's blue uniform. *Oh, no!*

He leaned in toward the man and coughed out hoarsely, "They succumbed to the Arabs, Jacob. They gave in to oil. They're afraid of angering them. And so—"

"So they went along with the Arab demands," Jacob finished.

Ethan tried to hide his exhilaration at Jacob's response. He breathed out a "Yes!"

Jacob patted Naomi's hand, which was still glued to his forearm, and then narrowed his eyes on hers. A tear was working down her cheek. Ethan prayed it would have an effect.

Just then, the security guard—tall, ruggedly built, young—pushed his way through the flow of traffic and stepped up beside the three of them.

"Any trouble here?" the guard asked.

Ethan, Naomi, and Jacob all looked at him blankly.

Ethan held his breath. His and Naomi's future lay in the hands of Jacob Larson—a man he would describe as an acquaintance, even a friend. But a trusted friend? No.

He breathed a prayer to God in whom he did not believe, but he had nowhere else to turn.

He shook his head, avoiding eye contact with the guard. Naomi also shook her head. Ethan could tell she was wound tight as a knot. They both turned their eyes to Jacob.

Jacob's lips tightened into a thin slit.

The next moment reminded Ethan of the lapse in time when his father's cancer specialist was about to reveal the results of the test on his brain tumor.

"No, sir," Jacob finally answered.

The security guard's eyes narrowed, and he put his fists on his hips, then nodded so very slowly the move was almost imperceptable. Ethan tried to guess what he was thinking. Maybe he deducted they were merely friends chatting in the midst of the rush. Or maybe he suspected something was afoul. Maybe …

"Okay, then. Move on, please." The guard started to turn away, then spun back and faced Jacob. "Guys your size kind of hold up traffic, you know."

Ethan caught Jacob's reaction. He could easily see Jacob was not happy at the insult.

As the security guard walked away, Jacob looked at Ethan. "Okay, my friend. I did not see you today. In fact, I haven't seen you in what—a month ago at the Pan American Scientific Congress in New Orleans, right?"

Ethan smiled broadly. He had to contain himself from grabbing Jacob in a bear hug. "Yep, you're right. The Renaissance New Orleans Arts Hotel."

"Godspeed, then," Jacob said. "Bon voyage, my friend."

"Thank you."

"Thank you," Naomi repeated, as she reached up on her tiptoes to plant a kiss on Jacob's cheek. Jacob beamed, then moved his bulk out of their way and waved them past him.

Ethan tugged on Naomi's hand, and they again joined the flash-dash-slash of the runaway New York herd. Ethan had once entertained thoughts of going to Spain to take part in the running of the bulls. Within ten minutes, as they pulled up at the Northeast Regional boarding area, he forever pushed such a notion out of his mind.

Joseph Conrad and his team arrived at Omri's home to find Henry Webster waiting for him.

"No one knows anything around here," Webster said. "I've asked 'em all. Nothing but reports of Zohn's—he made air quotes—'innate goodness,' his—more air quotes—'willingness to lend a helping hand'."

Webster pointed his thumb behind him. "Lady over there said just last year Zohn heard her cries for help from her house, ran in and delivered her baby girl. Ridiculous, fairytale stuff."

Conrad took measure of the man. *An odd duck, probably single and living with his elderly mother, couldn't get the truth out of a twelve-year-old even with a bullwhip.*

Turning to his team, he said, "Answers, guys. Someone here knows something. I don't believe MIT professors enjoy themselves at the beach. We'll send the Boston folks there, but most likely Zohn's on the run."

He pointed them to different homes, then slid past an astonished Webster to break into Omri's house in search of clues.

—~—

Their chess game at a standoff, Bunyan stood up and stretched. "I've got to move these bones."

"I'll join you," Omri said, rising also.

Bunyan gestured toward the expanse of lawn south of the patio. "I know we can't pass the time at the Portland Museum of Art or strolling the Old Port, so take your pick. The batting cage, the croquet lawn, or something new you haven't seen before … a par-three golf hole."

"You know my excuse for being so bad at golf," Omri replied. "There's all of one golf course in Israel, and it's in Caesarea, so I never tried the sport as a boy. And you've seen me swing a bat, proving beyond doubt there was no baseball in Israel when I was growing up, so my first game at Fenway Park was truly a first. By default, I choose croquet. I think I've beaten you once or twice."

Bunyan snickered. "Once or twice? I've changed all the angles and distances so I might be able to beat *you* just once! Somehow, math skills outweigh hand-eye coordination when croquet's involved."

Several minutes later, Bunyan lined up a croquet shot through the final side wicket while Omri looked on. A bright light flashed over Bunyan's shoulder. Looking closely, Omni saw the flash again, coming from an upper window in a neighboring home about a hundred yards away.

"Did you see the light?" he asked.

Bunyan turned to him, pointed an accusatory finger, and said: "Croquet etiquette says, 'A player may not attempt to disrupt another player while he or she is lining up, about to stroke, or striking a ball. The penalty is a free knock by the embattled player to his choice of the offending player's croquet balls.'"

Omri chuckled but responded, "Seriously, Bunyan, I saw a flash of light. Might just have been a window pane but also could have come from binoculars." He pointed. "Right over there."

Bunyan followed Omri's finger, and his jaw fell open. "The Marchand place," he said hoarsely. "Omri, don't panic. Act normal. We'll finish this game in two minutes. Keep your head low."

Omri looked down at the ground.

Bunyan pulled a cell phone out of his pocket.

"Who are you calling?" Omri asked.

"Lana."

"Why?"

Bunyan raised a finger to indicate quiet, then he spoke. "Lana, grab the binoculars from the den and hurry to look out the window. See if anyone at the Marchand place has opera glasses or binoculars and is looking our way. They're in a second-floor window. I'll wait."

He looked at Omri. "We'll see."

Suddenly Omri's fingers were shaking. After remaining so calm on the train, contemplating Psalm 91, he was surprised to suddenly lose that peace, the *shalom* of God.

"I don't know these people well, but we're not on the best of terms," Bunyan said, still holding the cell phone to his ear.

"Really?"

"They own a furniture business in Portland. When CeCe and I had this place built, they came by and made a big sales pitch for us to buy all our furnishings from them. We said we'd shop around, they took offense, and, well, they've been like a couple of icebergs ever since."

"And?"

"Well, I wouldn't be surprised—if they realize who you are—they would call the authorities just to make sure you're staying in the country."

Bunyan put the phone closer to his ear. "Yes?" A pause. "Really? Another pause. "Who?"

Looking at Omri, Bunyan slapped the phone shut and said, "We're wrapping up this game."

"Are these neighbors anti-Semitic?"

"They're anti-Red Sox. Isn't that enough?" Bunyan chortled, but Omri could read unease in his friend's face.

"Go ahead and hit your ball, Bunyan. I'll leave your path to the pin unobstructed."

"Pshaw! Unobstructed?" Bunyan said playfully. "If I didn't want to rush you into the house, I'd beat you playing backwards."

"You count chickens before they're laid," Omri said. "A miscalculation. But one I'll let slide this time."

Bunyan rammed his ball through the wicket and, with a sidespin, the sphere sailed toward the final two wickets, settling just a foot in front of them. Twenty seconds later, Bunyan tapped the ball through the wickets off the pin.

"Home run," Omri said.

"Game over. Time to retreat to the clubhouse."

Walking briskly back to the house, Bunyan said, "Lana says Horace Marchand was in the window. What I left out was I did hear Horace use an anti-Semitic slur once. Just one reason we went elsewhere for our furniture."

"Oh." The feeling of knowing someone hated you solely because of your race was too familiar to Omri. Far too familiar.

"That doesn't mean he'll call authorities. Probably didn't even recognize you. Heck, from a distance, I might not have, myself."

Omri heard a "but" between the lines.

"But we want to play it safe. We have a good many hours before the Rosenbaums arrive and we had best spend them inside, away from the windows."

"Agreed."

—ɯ—

As Omri and Bunyan walked back to the house, Trudy Marchand entered the master bedroom.

"Horace, what are you doing with my bird-watching binoculars?" she asked. "Checking out some half-naked sunbather in Jackson's yard?"

"No, that'll never happen with a Bible-hugger like him," her husband responded. "Just checking out what's going on over there."

"And?"

"Here's this big lug of a baseball player, known for jacking home runs all over creation, and he's playing this pansy game, croquet, with another fella."

Trudy shrugged her shoulders. "To each his own."

She turned to walk away.

"Hold on," Horace said. "This other guy looks vaguely familiar. I just can't place him."

She stopped and looked over her shoulder. "Familiar as in someone in town, another athlete, someone famous?"

"Not sure. Just familiar." Horace put the binoculars down on a small, round table by the windowsill and walked past his wife, landing a peck on her cheek on the way.

She stepped to the window, picked up the binoculars, and peered out the window. Darn. Jackson and his friend—famous or not—were gone.

—~—

Conrad expected pertinent information would be found in the den or bedroom. The den was the first room to the left. He scanned the room, full of floor-to-ceiling bookcases, all loaded with boring, brainiac, mind-numbing stuff.

His eyes stopped at the large mahogany desk. He took a seat and started rummaging through the drawers. An address book had to be here somewhere. Who doesn't have an address book? Or if they have one and are leaving? Then they'd take it with them.

Or shred it.

He leaned over the side of the desk to check the waste basket. Empty? Not completely. He reached in and pulled out an empty spiral binding. On the cover, in simple Helvetica type: *Addresses and Phone Numbers.*

The man had torn all the pages from his address book. Probably shredded it. Spotting a shredder nearby, Conrad went to it and lifted the cover. Empty.

He swore a string of expletives worthy of Constantine.

A warm noon sun beat down on Camden Harbor, glimmering over the cool ocean waters of an incoming tide. Dan and Margaret Callahan strolled down the gangway to their mooring with their grandson, Davey, and their golden retriever/border collie mix, Tack, who happily weaved left and right behind them, herding them to the wharf.

Dan took a deep breath of the salt air and declared this would be a five-star day. His best friend and wife at his side, and his teenaged grandson along too.

Davey joked, "Tack's herding us starboard and port, staboard and port."

Dan and Margaret laughed with him.

Behind them, bustling crowds strolled on the boardwalk, stretching from the innermost part of the harbor for about a mile seaward.

Margaret and Davey stepped aboard *Abby*, their twenty-four-foot Harrasty Argonaut, while Dan busied himself untying the rope from the wharf. Tack, obviously anxious to get underway, stood beside Dan and barked as if ordering him to "speed it up, Dad."

Dan ruffled the hair behind Tack's ears.

Dan tossed the rope on board, gave the boat a slight nudge away from the wharf, and jumped aboard. Tack, alighting next to him, hurried to the bow where he would spend most of the trip, pretending to be a hood ornament.

"Glorious!" Margaret declared, as she looked to the cloudless blue sky. "I'll step inside to the galley and put together some sandwiches."

"Good-o, my love. Davey and I'll make sure we don't cause too much of a ruckus out here. Right, young man?" Dan ruffled his grandson's longish red hair.

"Right, Grampa." Davey's smile was broad. "I can't believe it. My first time sailing *Abby* out to sea."

"No more pond! No more harbor!" Davey exclaimed.

"Sail her with authority, Davey," Dan advised. "*Abby's* smallish for the ocean, but she possesses real sea-keeping ability. She's an elegant sloop rig, our *Abby*—"

"Well," Davey said, "I love her brass, teak, mahogany, and oak."

"She's a real presence, for sure, even among the cutters of the rich and famous around this harbor."

Dan waved an arm at the slew of yachts, catamarans, and other sailboats plugging up the inner harbor. "Show her you're worthy of her captaincy."

"Sure will try, Grampa."

"It's 'first mate,' Captain."

"Right, first mate."

"Tack's second mate and your grandmother, well, she's the admiral."

Davey chuckled. "She told me you'd catch onto that by your fiftieth anniversary."

"Ha!"

With that, and a hearty double-bark from Tack, they were off the dock, out the bay, and heading north to the several islands that made this one of the most picturesque areas on the Atlantic Coast.

Several minutes out into the ocean, Margaret stepped out from the galley, holding a tray filled with chicken salad sandwiches, a bowl of chips, and glasses brimming with milk. She set the platter to the right of the wheel.

Dan said grace over the meal, then grabbed a sandwich.

He took a bite, then winked at his wife of forty-two years. "Perfecto, my dear."

"Sure is, Bubbe," Davey said, using the Jewish name for grandmother that Margaret had inherited because of her love for the Jewish people.

—ɱ—

Margaret looked squarely at her grandson, whose handsome face reflected the strong jaw and bright brown eyes of his grandfather. He stood taller than her, broader and more athletic than most boys his age, judging by the soccer and baseball games she and Dan had watched him play. In fact, he was already being recruited to play baseball by several East Coast colleges.

Old Smiley, she thought, recalling the pet name she'd given him as a baby. Well, he was nearly grown now, and this had to be the time.

She cast a look at Dan, and he returned an approving nod, adding, "Now or never, Maggy."

"Okay." Stepping closer to Davey, she said, "You're a young man now—almost ready for college."

Davey flashed a bright-eyed smile. "Yeah."

"And now, with your Mom and Dad in England for this next year while your Dad's on sabbatical, we may need you to grow up even more."

"What do you mean, Bubbe?" He turned to look at her, but she quickly motioned for him to keep his eyes on where he was sailing.

"Something serious. Grampa and I may need your help and at least your silence because—well, what we're involved in might turn out to be perilous."

Davey's eyes widened, and he swallowed hard. "What do you mean, Bubbe?"

Margaret and Dan spent the next several minutes discussing the Jewish emigration ban, then Dan said, "Davey, you know about the Underground Railroad that helped slaves escape the South?"

"Sure do."

"Well, we're involved in an Underground Railroad today. Or at least we're connected with like-minded people who foresaw something like this might happen some day. The day is here."

"Wow!" Davey's eyes grew wide. He took both hands off the ship's wheel and hugged Margaret, then Dan. "Boy, Bubbe, you and Grampa are something special!"

Margaret winked at Dan then smiled and motioned toward the wheel. "Hands on the till, Captain."

Davey quickly recovered and handled the wheel, but he remained wide-eyed.

Margaret lifted an index finger. "Davey, this remains between you, your parents, your grandfather, and me, Okay?"

"Mom and Dad know?"

Margaret nodded. "They do."

"This work is holy unto the Lord, Davey. Silence is critical. Grampa and I wanted you to know because you may see people come and go at our place. You mustn't mention this to anyone outside the family."

"Okay, Bubbe. I'll keep mum."

Dan put a hand on his grandson's shoulder. "We begin tonight, Davey. I heard from Bunyan yesterday before you arrived. If all goes well, he's bringing four Jews late tonight."

"Bunyan? You mean Jacko?"

Dan nodded.

"I love Jacko!"

A smile crossed Margaret's face. "Yes, this all has to do with Jacko. You know the story of his family and mine, the Chadwicks, being connected since our ancestors helped his great-great-great-great grandfather Tice escape slavery to Canada."

"Yeah."

"Many of us," Dan said, "will never experience the darkness of a black heart. But those slaves sure did."

"What about you, Grampa? In battle?" Davey asked.

"I've seen such darkness, but usually sparked by revenge. Like a soldier wanting to avenge a comrade's death in the battlefield. Dark words certainly came out of my own mouth in wartime. People say greed is the root of all wars. From my experience, I'd say hatred, pure and oftentimes vile, is more often the cause."

"Maybe what Tice experienced in slavery was akin to the emotions men carry with them in war," Margaret said. "He said he felt the sting of his foreman's whip. For a boy, imagine the trauma."

"And, so …" Davey offered, "today some Jews will want to escape America just like Tice and other slaves did back in the mid-1800s?"

"A lot of them, I think," Margaret said. "News reports say they're being turned back at border crossings all across Canada. And at airports, as well."

Dan tapped Davey on the shoulder and pointed. "Hey, Davey, skirt around this island up ahead."

"Seven Hundred Acre Island!" Davey pumped his fist, then adjusted the jib. "We're almost there—almost to Dark Harbor."

Margaret and Dan smiled broadly and, standing close, each put an arm over his shoulders.

Fifteen minutes later, they sailed into Dark Harbor on the southeast end of Isleboro Island. Davey looked around at other boats, hoping to spot a pretty girl who'd be impressed by his sailing expertise. Then he noticed a gleaming black Windjammer moored in the harbor with its famous pin-striped sails tied down.

"There's *J&E Riggin* up ahead!" he called out, pointing.

"What a sailing ship!" Dan said.

Davey pulled out his smartphone and snapped a picture of the schooner. "I'm sending this to Mom and Dad," he said, then as he punched a couple of buttons before putting the phone back in a pocket of his cargo shorts.

For the next few minutes, the teenager commanded the winds like a veteran.

"The guys are going to hear about this!" he boasted.

He heard Tack bark three times up front.

"Three's his 'hello' to people onshore," his Bubbe commented. "Apparently they deserve an extra bark."

"No, Bubbe. Three's him saying what a good job I did circling around *J&E Riggin*."

Davey's Bubbe smiled her approval.

As Davey steered *Abby* back toward Camden Harbor, Dan pulled a PGP mobile phone out of a duffel bag and punched in a number. After a half minute, he turned to Margaret and shook his head. I still can't reach Frank."

"Where could he be?" she asked.

"No idea."

"Who's Frank?" Davey asked.

"Frank Reid's the next link beyond us in the Underground Railroad," Dan said. "He's the final escape."

"How?" Davey asked.

Dan waved his arm around him. "You're looking at the highway, son."

"By boat?"

Dan nodded.

"Cool!" Davey pumped his fist. "That's so awesome! Like pirate Jack Sparrow outrunning the Queen's fleet."

"Right!"

•••••

The sun shone on the little pond where a hatch of flies had sent fish on a feeding frenzy. Sitting in a green Adirondack chair on the porch of his log cabin, Frank Reid stretched out his long legs and looked at the water just fifty feet away. But he barely noticed the action. He was deep in prayer and reflection. Since his arrival late Thursday afternoon, he had sought to achieve total isolation by turning off his cell phone and ignoring the radio.

This was a retreat to discover whether he should leave the church he'd attended for two decades. At the moment, he was reliving the Wednesday-night Bible study. Like he did then, he frowned and flipped through the pages of his Bible in search of Romans chapter nine. He didn't like what he was hearing from his new pastor in this adult Sunday school lesson. His talk reeked of anti-Semitism.

"God has given us, the church, great promises," Reverend Bob Masters said. "His promises are all 'yea' and 'amen.' When the Jewish people, as a whole, refused to recognize their Messiah, they lost their claim to Him. The church has supplanted the Jews, just as so many times in the Bible, the younger child supplanted the older. Jacob supplanted Esau. Joseph displaced all his older brothers. The Jews' promises are now ours.

When Frank asked, "Are you saying God gave up on the Jews and canceled His covenant with them?" Reverend Masters replied, "No. *They* canceled the covenant,". "*They* rejected their Messiah. *They* turned away from God's gift of salvation."

"But," Frank countered, "God's covenant with the Jews was unilateral. The covenant was *His*. Plus, unlike a contract, a covenant is based on what you say, not what you do. Therefore, no one else could break the pledge. Right?"

The discussion degenerated from there with Frank Romans 11:7: "I say, then, have they (Jews) stumbled that they should fall? Certainly not! But through their fall, to provoke them to jealousy, salvation has come to the Gentiles.'"

Frank had taken a deep breath. "You see, Pastor, I think the church has 'westernized Christanity so as to wipe the Hebrew nation out of scripture. But, the fact is, Gentile believers become part of Israel."

Reverend Masters took a step toward Frank and his voice rose. "Are you suggesting there should be no church?"

"No-no-no. I'm saying when it began, Christianity, as we know the Body today, was a sect of Judaism. Believers weren't even called Christians until Antioch. The faith wasn't called Christianity. Perhaps it still should be a sect today. I don't know. But in fact, the church *is* the fullness of Judaism."

Reverend Masters looked at his watch. "Folks, our time is up for this week. Frank," his eyes flickered over his congregant, "I'll look into what you're theorizing, and we can discuss this further."

"Thanks, pastor," Frank said with sincerity. "I think you'll find theorizing is not the correct word."

Reverend Masters' mouth twitched at the admonition. *Have I overstepped my bounds?* Frank wondered. And as he sat now on his deck, he wondered still.

Three forceful knocks to his apartment door drew Professor Anton Francoeur out of Simon Shama's *Citizen: A Chronicle of the French Revolution. So beautifully crafted*, he thought, *so … frightening.*

Three more bangs sounded. *Someone's upset, in a hurry, certainly misplaced their manners.*

"I'll get it, Élise," he called and opened the door.

Before him stood two broad-shouldered men, both Caucasian, both dressed in black pinstripe suits with white shirts and dark-blue ties. He looked at their shoes. Both wore black wingtops so well polished he swore he could see himself in the reflection.

He immediately thought of the perfectly matched Pinchons he'd seen in a horse-pulling contest a month before at the Barnstable County Fair. Yes, matched, not only in looks, but they seemed to possess the same attitude. This much was apparent from the identical sour expressions.

Either these men disliked their jobs, or they enjoyed them—and what they entailed—too much.

The man on the left held a badge in front of Anton's face.

"Qui est-il?" Élise asked, appearing from the kitchen.

Anton scrutinized the badge. "Homeland Security, ma chère."

"Agents Cross and Block," the man with the badge said.

As Élise came to his side, Anton looked up at them. "May we help you?"

Block keyed in on him and said, "You're a colleague of Dr. Omri Zohn."

Anton shrugged. "Yes."

"A close friend, we're told," Cross said.

"Yes."

"You know him well."

"Well enough to greatly admire him. He's one of the most honest men I know."

"I understand he's a coward," Cross said.

"Oh, I doubt that. He fought with distinction in the IDF."

"Tell ya' he did, did he?"

"No, I read about him in a magazine article."

Block cut in, "Can you tell us where this hero is?"

Anton wondered at the malice in the man's voice. "No."

"Have you spoken to him lately?"

Anton hesitated then, "Not really?"

"Not really? Whattaya mean?"

"Not since Friday."

"After the UN vote?"

"UN vote?"

"The Jewish ban, professor. Surely you're aware of the vote."

"Who's banned Jews?" *Let's see if they get the UN's inhumanity.*

Cross was having none of it. "When you saw Zohn, did he mention leaving the country?"

Anton took a step back and feigned surprise. "Leave the country? Omri? He's coming here for dinner Monday night, isn't he, Élise?" He cast his eyes on his wife, praying she'd pick up the baton.

"Ah, oui. Yes," she said.

Bright girl!

"Indeed," she continued, "I'm to cook a chicken chasseur with croissants and a crème brûlée. Omri would not miss his favorite, not on his life!"

Brilliant girl!

"And we'll top off the meal with his favorite coffee, Café Shachor," she added.

How I love this woman!

Block stepped into the room. Was this a violation of his space, Anton wondered. He didn't know these American laws. They seemed so odd with such things as gun-free zones inside military bases.

"You're in America as a fellow at MIT," Block said.

"Yes."

"As such, you're a guest of this country."

"A guest of MIT, more specifically." Anton narrowed his gaze on this man, guessing where he was going with this.

"As a guest of—this country—you're subject to being deported for any noncompliance with our laws.

"I suppose so."

"What laws?" Élise asked, concern edging her voice.

"Laws demanding you respond truthfully to inquiries from law-enforcement officers."

"Mais oui. But we do so," she said.

"I think not," Cross cut in.

"Nothing would make me happier than to extradite a liar to their country of origin," Cross said.

"Then, please," Anton said, "do your best. We're telling you all we know. If Omri's not coming to dinner, he hasn't told me so. He did not confide to me where he would be today. Such a beautiful day. He might be at the Museum of Science, one of his favorite places in Boston. I'd suggest looking there." He motioned toward the door for them to leave and to his surprise, they did.

Before leaving, Block leveled a sneer at Anton with enough venom to melt a lesser person than the son of Émile Bruno Franceour. Anton shut the door on their heels and turned to his wife.

"Ma femme bold." He smiled and pulled her into his arms.

Davey looked at his Bubbe and asked, "So, if the Chadwicks helped Jacko's ancestor escape into Canada, how'd the two familes stay connected?"

"Tice came back to Maine after the Civil War ended in 1865. He found my great-great-great-great grandparents, Abel and Elizabeth Chadwick, and their son, Caleb, who had become a close friend. He made his home nearby, starting his own family."

Boy, what a neat thing to be part of his family's history, Davey thought.

Just then, they arrived at the mouth of Camden Harbor, filled with all sizes of sailboats and skiffs racing across the waters. Davey stiffened and turned his attention to the challenge of avoiding a dozen potential collisions.

This aliyah stuff was all new to him, but he had to concentrate on sailing now.

Almost immediately, they passed a sleek, midnight-blue Catalina 470 named *Outward Bound*, heading out to sea. Tack double-barked at them. A man and woman aboard waved, and he double-barked again, his tail wagging furiously.

"I think he knows them," Grampa joked.

"He knows half the harbor," Bubbe said with a giggle.

Davey joined in, then pulled himself upright. Looking at Grampa, he asked, "Can I skipper *Abby* all the way in?"

Grampa chuckled. "I'm just the first mate. Why ask *me*?"

Davey mustered up his huskiest voice. "Well, then, first mate, man the mainsail until we get her moored."

"Aye-aye, Captain." Grampa saluted. Stepping to the mainsail, he sang out, "He gained a world. He gave that world its grandest lesson: On! Sail on!"

"Whose lyrics are those?" Davey asked.

Bubbe answered. "A man named Miller—about Columbus."

"So I'm like a modern day Columbus?" Davey asked. He pumped out his chest. "Gotta love it!"

—∾—

At 4:15 p.m., Margaret, Dan, Davey, and Tack moored *Abby*. They traveled straight to the farmhouse.

As they stepped inside, Dan's warm hand settled on Margaret's shoulder. "I want you to relax, sweetheart. Davey and I'll do a barbecue."

"Yeah, Can we make my favorite?"

"Okay," Margaret said, "but I'm making one contribution. I'll wrap some potatoes, carrots, and onions in tin foil, and you can cook those T-bones we bought yesterday. They'll spoil if we don't."

She looked at Davey. "That's what you meant by your favorite, right?"

His face beamed.

CHAPTER SIX

Ethan returned from the restroom to sit next to Naomi. This was one time he was thankful he was not famous and recognizable. He wondered how Omri had fared getting out of Boston and into Portland.

The train had passed Providence about a half hour before—right on time. Ethan checked his watch: 4:59. "Just fifteen minutes to South Station," he said.

Naomi smiled up at him. "Finally."

"We're about to embark on the home lap. I promise no more trains after tonight until—well, forever if you want.

"No trains in Israel?" she asked.

"There aren't any."

"What if we visit Europe?" she teased.

Ethan hesitated, then, with a hint of sobriety, retorted, "All of Europe has signed or is signing on to the UN Resolution. If we travel anywhere, it's going to have to be to whatever country has the guts to shun the UN."

"Canada."

"Yes, Canada. You can depend on them to oppose this type of ban."

"Australia, I bet."

"Probably. Gotta love the people Downunder. They've never been shy about rebelling against the world."

Resignation filled Naomi's voice. "Well, I would love to see a wallaby before I die."

"And a kangaroo."

"And a koala."

"And a platypus."

It was a game they played.

"And a numbat," Naomi said.

"And an emu."

"And a bilby."

Ethan knew he had more than met his match. "I kneel to your superiority, m'lady." He circled his right arm twice in front of him and bowed toward her.

"And I hadn't even pulled out my ringers," Naomi said with fake nonchalance.

"Ringers?"

"Yes." She smirked. "The spotted cuscus, sugar glider, and ever-popular Tazmanian devil—the largest carnivore of all the marsupials."

"Your degree in zoology serves you well."

"As do your engineering degrees."

"Touché."

Naomi's eyes moved beyond him. She had obviously seen the two men sitting diagonally across from them. Ethan had kept his eyes on them since they left New York City. She leaned toward him andwhispered, "You're taking all this in good humor."

"I have no humor about this," Ethan whispered back between gritted teeth. "I'm seething about this and always will. We had to mail good-bye letters to Dad and our friends and colleagues, for goodness sake. It's like going into witness protection. No phone calls or e-mails, so no one can catch us." His voice had risen and he quieted. "We shouldn't have to become felons to visit our peoples' homeland."

Naomi hung her head. After a few moments, she pushed a lock of hair from her eyes, and trying to change the mood, asked whimsically, "Will we have time to eat in the North End?"

"The North End, for sure. The train doesn't leave North Station until six-forty-five."

"Then we can stroll on past those food-court restaurants at South Station without paying them a glance."

It is so easy to love a girl so in tune with my feelings.

Suddenly the train jerked and began to slow.

"We can't be there already," Ethan said, craning his neck to look past Naomi out the window. They were obviously in the country, on an expanse of track between Providence and Boston where there were no houses. Ethan spotted a country road about a quarter-mile to the east.

The train now seemed to be coasting, the engine having lost its thrust. A minute later, the train came to a dead stop.A conductor stepped through the front door of their car, looking disconcerted and serious.

As if announcing a boxing match, he declared, "Ladies and gentlemen! Amtrak's Northeast Regional is the East Coast's number-one ranked train … in on-time performance and customer satisfaction. We're proud of her record. However, I'm distressed to tell you we're experiencing engine problems."

Ethan sighed, as did the entire carload of travelers.

"I'm afraid," the conductor continued, "we'll need to get buses here to take you to South Station."

This collective response was louder, more dissonant and dissatisfied. Ethan started to calculate the time. *Oh-oh.*

The conductor held up a hand. "Please, please. We're only ten to fifteen minutes out of South Station, and there are spare buses in the fleet right at the station, so they won't take long. Meantime, our mechanic is trying to fix the problem and if he does before the buses arrive, we'll simply continue on into Boston by rail. We apologize for the delay."

Naomi looked anxiously at Ethan.

"Stay calm," he said.

After about ten minutes, the conductor again appeared at the front of the railcar. "Our mechanic holds little hope he can rectify the problem before the buses arrive," he said. "It's an easy walk through the fields to the highway. In ten minutes, we want everyone to pick up your luggage at the back of the car and make your way to the road. The buses should arrive about the time we all get there.

Indeed, eleven and a half minutes later—Ethan was keeping time—seven Peter Pan buses appeared in tandem along the highway just moments after the first passengers reached the edge of the thoroughfare. Cheers resounded.

Several minutes later, Ethan and Naomi took a front seat so they could be first off upon arrival. Ethan checked his watch: 6:02 p.m. "Darn!" he said. He calculated if the buses could reach South Station in thirty minutes, the time would be 6:32, which would give them thirteen minutes to reach North Station. Thirteen minutes! And a Saturday in inner-city Boston.

Naomi frowned. "We're going to miss our connection, aren't we?"

"Not sure. You remember Boston traffic."

She lowered her head and released a deep breath.

"What we need is prayer."

"I'll leave prayer to you." He read the disappointment in her eyes, but that was familiar. He wasn't so certain a God was watching over them. If there were a Higher Being, he reasoned, He set the universe in motion, then let the sun, galaxies, and other rigamarole run. If a Creator existed, He was probably like a clockmaker and had moved on to create another clock or parallel universe, or some such thing.

"If we're late, maybe we won't be able to get away." Her shoulders noticeably dropped.

Ethan wrapped an arm around her and pulled her close. "Remember, sweetie, it's the weekend. Hopefully no one will know we're missing until Monday morning."

"Hopefully. But I keep thinking about synagogue. I was supposed to serve coffee afterwards, and they might be concerned we're not there."

Ethan searched the caverns of his mind for encouraging words. He was terrific at scientific problem-solving. With this stuff? Not so much.

Thinking of problem-solving, if they were late he'd have to figure some way to contact Omri or Bunyan to let them know. But the plan depended on simplicity—no contact with one another for the authorities to intercept or trace.

On the way into Boston, Ethan overheard the couple behind them talking about getting home to Danvers. "I miss our dogs," the woman said. Ethan knew Danvers was a suburb north of Boston.

He decided to chance the question and turned to face them. Appearing to be in their sixties, the two were the spitting image of one another—wavy grey hair; long, narrow noses; prominent chins; and bright blue eyes.

"I'm sorry, but I overheard you live on the North Shore. So you're going to North Station to catch a commuter rail?" Ethan asked.

"Yes," the woman replied.

"Can you tell me which is quicker to get from South Station to North Station … the subway or a cab?"

"Cabs are right outside South Station, but the subway's kitty-corner across the street too," the man answered. "During rush hour, a cab would be slower."

"Much slower," his wife added.

"But at this time of day? A toss-up," he added.

"Six of one, a half dozen of another," his wife agreed.

Placing a fist under his chin, the man said, "That is, a toss-up *if* you're familiar with the subway."

"If you're not," she said, "you could lose time when you switch from the Red Line to the Green Line at Park Street."

"That's right. Pretty confusing if you're not familiar with the system," the man said.

"There are three tracks there," the wife said, "and you might go to the wrong one …"

"And totally miss the next train to North Station," he said.

"On the other hand," she said, "you never know, if you're in a cab, some moron might cause an accident because he's eating or text-messaging while he's driving …"

"Or *she's* driving," the man added.

The lady elbowed her husband, then asked Ethan, "When's your train leaving North Station?"

"Six forty-five."

The lady looked at her wristwatch. "Gonna be tight," she said.

"Very tight," her husband agreed.

"Thank you," Ethan said and turned back to Naomi. "Did you hear?"

"Yeah. I think I'd feel safer in the hands of a cabbie than facing the possibility of getting on a wrong train in the subway. I also prefer to be above ground, especially when I'm someplace unfamiliar."

Ethan nodded. "We need to be out of here as soon as the door opens."

—ɱ—

Shandra Constantine gulped the last mouthful of her Coca-Cola—the straight-up caffeinated kind. After rushing home to her townhouse in a Loudon County suburb of DC, she had managed to grab only two or three hours sleep overnight. Today, she had finished a six-pack, keeping awake and alert.

The numbers of Jews turned back at airports and border crossings was piling up. There had been some arrests when the Jews had struggled with authorities. One smartaleck even showed up at Kennedy International Airport dressed in an IDF uniform, posing as an Israeli soldier, but the name on the uniform didn't match his identification. Ha! The fool. But, there was still no sign of Omri Zohn.

Conrad had checked in, having found no clues except a missing address book, which meant the dozen agents scouring North Shore beaches were wasting their time.

Constantine's technicians had examined every bit of traffic- and security-camera footage from Brookline, trying to catch a glimpse of Zohn going in any directon by any type of transportation. His car sat in his driveway, but word was he rarely used the vehicle, so this wasn't really a clue.

She was awaiting approval to examine his cell-phone use. She cursed the gods, all of them, especially the God of the Jews—Zohn's God.

She checked her expansive list of Jewish scientists and others of importance. Four out of five had been at their homes or places of work. A handful had been discovered trying to escape. Unlike "ordinary" Jewish citizens, these people had been placed under arrest and were being held in custody. The same fate would be Zohn's. Their jail would be no country club—no, siree.

Then there were the few Jews who were unaccounted for, so far. Zohn headed the names of missing malcontents. She read through the names of her A List: Omri Zohn; Abel Lischne, Benjamin Keith, Yael Ochsenstein, Abraham Rymer, Ethan Rosenbaum, Abigail Zimmerman, Tobias Urech, Nina Bader, Gabriel Reichenstein. Ten names in all. All brilliant. All PhDs. Men and women at the top of their professions—some of them, like Zohn, saluted the world over for their accomplishments.

Her intercom buzzed. Good news?

"What?" she asked.

"Treasury Secretary Blasted's on the line, ma'am."

This is odd. Blasted never called her, not since he'd placed a meandering hand on her forearm a year ago. A prince dare not go there uninvited! Blasted had barely escaped with his hand intact.

She gritted her teeth. "Put him through."

"Shandra!" Blasted sounded happy with himself. "I thought I'd call you personally, knowing how interested you are in getting the financials on your priority list of Jews."

"Yes?" She downplayed her interest. She couldn't wait to hear the figures, but she wasn't about to let him know just how much.

"I'll email all this to you but wanted to let you know it's coming."

"Anything big?"

"Well, Friday mid-morning, Dr. Zohn moved a large amount of cash—let's see, a million dollars."

"A million!? Where to?"

She heard a ruffle of papers, then Blasted answered, "The Jimmy Fund."

"What's the Jimmy Fund?"

Blasted cursed. "I thought the fund must be something he could withdraw if he left the country. But—"

"But what?"

"The Jimmy Fund's a children's cancer-research endowment at Dana-Farber Cancer Institute in Boston."

"Giving away a million bucks, heh?"

"Yeah, and another three hundred thousand to a scholarship fund at MIT."

"I didn't know professors earned so much."

"Well, he got the million from the Nobel Prize, and he holds a handful of patents on high-tech instruments of some sort—lucrative ones."

Constantine shook her head in consternation. "What else you got, Hank?"

"Ochenstein and her husband began investing heavily in several Israeli-based companies immediately after the United Nations' emigration vote. Zimmerman and his wife withdrew the bulk of their 401k, even suffering the penalty. Don't know what they did with the dough."

There was a pause, then he added, "Rosenbaum's wife took out a bucketload from their savings Friday afternoon—"

"Email all this to me ASAP."

Constantine hung up the phone and dialed an in-house number. Hearing the click, she said, "Sam, come to my office right away. We need to pull together agents to zero in on a handful of people."

She hung up. Rosenbaum. She rolled the name over in her mind. Again. And again. *Sounds familiar, but why, exactly?*

The moment the Peter Pan bus stopped under a canopy outside the western side of South Station, Ethan and Naomi were out the door. The older couple behind them both called out, "Good luck!" Ethan cast a smile in their direction before they rushed into the building. Voices echoed off the granite walls and high ceiling as they hurried past a Cajun Cajun, an Au Bon Pain, a Surf City Squeeze, and a half-dozen other fast-food restaurants. They maneuvered around scattered metal dining tables, a bevy of people milling about, over the marble floor, past an information booth, down a wide marble stairway, and finally, through heavy doors leading outside.

Several brown cabs sat idling, their drivers waiting for business. Ethan and Naomi shrugged off their duffel bags and slid into the back seat of the cab at the front of the line.

"North Station," Ethan said. "Our train leaves in …" he checked his watch, "thirteen minutes."

"Can't guarantee *that!*" said the cabbie, a petite African-American girl, wearing a Red Sox baseball cap.

"There's fifty extra bucks extra if you can," Ethan said.

She shoved the car into gear and peeled out. "I always love a good challenge."

A moment later, she yanked the cab into a U-turn, reversing direction. The highway was four lanes, and they were in the inner lane, heading west. The cabbie—her tag said she was Jailah—looked anxiously to her right and gave a hand signal to another cab driver in the right-hand lane. He honked twice and she swerved into the space he allowed.

Now they were behind two cars, facing a red light in front of South Station. Ethan looked at his watch. Twelve minutes and counting. He could feel his heart thumping against his chest, or was it the carotid artery throbbing in his neck?

Jailah revved the engine, impatiently tapping a rhythm on the steering wheel. She turned on her radio to wild, upbeat Latino music. Modern. With a thump. She half-turned toward them and, with a smile, offered, "I hope you don't mind. Gets me in the mood to razzle-dazzle."

Ethan shook his head. Whatever worked for this girl was fine with him.

The light turned green, and Jailah played toesy with the brakes and accelerator, jerking ahead a few inches and stopping, ahead a few more inches, then stopping. The first car drove straight ahead, but the girl driving the second vehicle, a fire-engine-red Mustang convertible, had apparently lost herself in her mirror, applying lipstick.

Jailah honked, hard and long. The girl seemed to jump in her seat, then stomped down on the pedal so hard she laid rubber and peeled right.

Jailah followed her onto Purchase Street, which ran parallel to Interstate 93, heading north. The traffic was moderate. She thought about taking I-93, but on second look, traffic there appeared heavier. No, Purchase was the best way to earn an extra fifty.

They wheeled ahead at an excruciating twenty miles an hour. Ethan could tell Jailah was glancing in her mirrors, looking for an edge, hoping to get past the red convertible, ever tapping to the music. She cranked the radio up a bit more, looked in the mirror to catch Ethan's eyes, and asked, "Too loud?"

He shook his head. *Just … go!*

At Congress Street they caught a green light. Ethan looked at Naomi and actually hoped she was praying. Instead, he found a look of fear. *Guess not.* When she prayed, she was never afraid.

He checked his watch. Eleven minutes.

Ethan recalled strolling the Boston Harbor boardwalk with Omri one summer day three or four years ago. They weren't far from here. You could walk alongside the harbor all the way up, past the Boston Aquarium, right through the lobby of the Boston Marriott Long Wharf Hotel, past Christopher Columbus Waterfront Park, and into the North End—probably faster than this snail's pace.

They came to a red light at Seaport Boulevard and waited. He looked at his watch—ten minutes—and wondered if they should jump out and run to North Station.

But when the light turned green, Jailah jumped the cab to the left lane, floored the accelerator, and cut back in front of the girl in the red convertible. She snickered, then sped ahead, weaving back and forth through traffic, missing a minivan by inches, a pickup truck by a foot. Other drivers honked in anger; more than one hoisted a royal salute, but they covered a good quarter of a mile until a red light stopped them at State Street.

Ethan looked to their right and pointed. There was the Aquarium hard against the harbor.

He checked his watch. Nine minutes.

Purchase Street turned to Cross Street. Just ahead, Atlantic Avenue, which hugged the harbor through the North End, merged from the right and traffic suddenly got heavier. Ethan stopped himself from cussing—a rarity for him even in the worst of times.

"Come on, come on!" he whispered.

"What?" Naomi asked him.

"Nothing," he replied. His right heel started twitching up and down on the floorboard.

The light turned green, and their lane started to move at a good pace. Ethan checked his watch. Seven minutes. They were close now, if he remembered correctly. To their left, running alongside I-93, were green walkways, paved with stones. A fountain flipped water into the air; a slight shore breeze wafted the spray westward.

Ethan turned to Naomi and pointed upward. "I-93 used to run on stilts about sixty feet off the ground, right where all that greenery is."

Naomi looked at him questioningly. He read her thoughts: *Why on earth are you thinking about such a thing? We're running out of time!*

She was right. He checked again. Six minutes.

There was Hanover Street! He looked left. Faneuil Hall! They were close and moving along smoothly. Suddenly Jailah slammed on the brakes and laid on the horn. In front of them, a young couple had decided to step out into traffic to cross the street, the man guiding a boy of about four years old and the woman holding the hand of a little girl who was having trouble keeping her footing.

Jailah turned off the radio, hurriedly rolled down her window, and cried out, "Pick her up and carry her, schmook! What's the matter with you!"

Ethan agreed with the sentiment, but Jailah shouted with force enough for the three of them.

A sudden a squeal of brakes and a loud crash of metal on metal rang out ahead of them.

"Oh, no!" Jailah exclaimed. She turned to face Ethan. "When's your train?"

Ethan looked at his watch. "Five minutes."

"We'll never make it now."

They could always hope the Downeaster would be late leaving the tracks. He fumbled with his duffel bag on the seat.

"What are you looking for?" Naomi asked.

"Our tickets. I don't want to be looking for them when we get there."

"Good idea, but I've got them." Naomi forced a smile and waved the two tickets in front of him.

Ethan exhaled sharply. Had he breathed at all since they left South Station? He didn't recall.

"Let's go," he said. "We're walking. Make that running."

"I'm sorry, folks," Jailah said. "If not for those stupid people and then this accident, we could've got there on time."

Ethan handed her a fifty and a twenty. "Good try, though. Thanks!"

They slid out the door, pulled their duffel bags over their shoulders and raced across the clogged traffic, onto the green, headed northeast.

"Only three or four blocks ahead!" Ethan said.

"Only?" Naomi made a face and not a humorous one.

Off they sprinted. Ethan soon wished he'd been more attracted to sports as a young man. At the Market Street intersection,their timing was perfect to catch the "Walk" sign. He looked to his right; Naomi was staying right with him. *Heck, she's in better shape than I am!*

He tried to read the time on his watch but couldn't focus on his wildly moving wrist. His guess: 6:42. If correct, they had three minutes.

When they reached Rose Kennedy Greenway, Ethan was so lacking in oxygen that he thought, *If I could focus, I'd wonder what a fascinating study of a woman Rose was.*

"Oh, there's a clock!" Ethan said aloud, though he didn't really mean to. It was a large clock like you'd see in a city park. 6:43.

Two minutes!

Ethan caught a second wind. *Yes!* He looked to Naomi, who was still going strong—in fact, ahead of him by a couple of steps.

Now the crowd was getting thicker. Must be a concert tonight! The thought struck like a body blow. Saturday night. Boston Garden. Of course. He shook his head in exasperation.

A slowpoke driver, a car accident, and now this. *If I believed in God, I'd think he was against us making this train, or perhaps even escaping. If.*

A half-block from the Garden, they reached a wall of people. Ethan and Naomi tried to sidlethrough them. The duffel bags made it thorny, and the obstinate nature of the crowd doubled the difficulty.

Stubborn Bostonians. In Charleston the crowd would part like the Red Sea for two people running in obvious distress.

But indeed they were in Boston and thousands of people were grinding their way forward to get into Boston Garden.

"What is this?" Ethan managed to ask a young woman with pink and green streaks in her hair.

"The Grateful Dead," she said.

"They're still alive?" he asked.

The girl shot him a lethal look.

Naomi, excited, grabbed his elbow and pointed. "Over there!" she said. "I think we can get through."

Ethan followed her direction. The crowd was pushing toward

the right side of the corridor, where stairways led up to the Garden, leaving an ever-so-narrow opening along the left-hand wall.

Naomi beat Ethan to the spot and, turning sideways, sidled quickly through the crowd.

Within a minute they were free and into the train-station area of the structure. They raced to the platform and looked at the Departures board. Ethan's head was spinning.

"There!" Naomi pointed. "Rail six!"

The Downeaster train was about forty yards away. They hoisted their duffel bags and dashed ahead. But as they drew near, the train started to move forward. Ethan looked down the platform for about sixty or eighty yards and spotted a man wearing an Amtrak uniform.

"Sir! Sir!" he cried out, gasping for air. "Can you stop the train?"

The man, an older African-American, wearing a weary look and a sad demeanor, replied, "Sorry, mister. If it's movin', it's gone. Couldn't stop the thing for the president. Well, maybe we could—for him, but nobody else, even the mayor."

Ethan dropped his shoulders and turned to Naomi, who stood behind him.

She threw up her hands. "What now?"

Ethan peered up at the departure board again.

"Hey, that's not bad," he said. "The next Downeaster leaves at eight o'clock."

"Wonderful," Naomi said. "Must be a popular line."

"Let's sit down." He motioned toward a bench on the platform. They peeled off their duffel bags and sat down, exhausted. People were all about them, but Ethan was oblivious. He needed to reach Bunyan and Omri to let them know they'd missed the train.

For security's take, they couldn't use cell phones. And they vowed only to use the satellite phones in emergencies and with the briefest of messages.

He unzipped a pocket of his duffel bag and reached for the satellite phone.

"What're you doing!?" Naomi asked, startled and worried.

"They're expecting us at ten past nine," he said. Looking up at the board, he added. "Now we won't get there until ten-twenty-five."

"Well, that's not life-or-death." She shrugged.

"We don't know. We don't know if anyone's looking for us. If they're smart they're looking for Omri right now, and if they find him they could find us as well. Besides, we don't want them waiting around the terminal for another couple hours with no clue."

He looked up and down the platform. There was no privacy here. He punched in a memorized number.

Bunyan and Omri sat at the dinner table, enjoying conversation and sharing concern for the night ahead of them. At the same moment that Bunyan's cell phone rang in his pants pocket, a small instrument in his other pocket vibrated, notifying him of an incoming call on his PGP cell phone.

"Oh, great. Two calls at the same time," he said.

He flipped open his cell while hurrying toward his bedroom where the PGP was stored in a side table to his bed.

"Hello."

"Bunyan! My God! Bunyan!"

He recognized the voice of Muriel Osgood, a close friend and member of his church.

"What is it, Muriel?" He reached his bedroom door. The vibration continued in his pocket.

"They've got Joe! Joe and, uh, two migrating birds."

Bunyan's eyes widened. "*Who's* got Joe?"

"The authorities. Border Patrol. One of their planes intercepted him trying to fly into New Brunswick and forced him back into Maine."

Muriel sounded on the edge of hysteria.

Bunyan went down on one knee to open the bottom draw of the side table.

"Muriel, you must remain calm. Think on Jesus. There's no fear when you're in His arms."

"I know, Bunyan. But … but…" Her voice trailed off.

"Just a moment, Muriel." Bunyan pulled a small wooden box out of the drawer, opened the lid, and pulled out his satellite phone.

"Yes?" he said into the satellite.

"Delayed. Ten twenty-five instead."

Bunyan didn't recognize the voice, but he understood the message. Before he could respond, the line went dead. Something moved in his peripheral vision, and he looked up. Omri was standing in the doorway, his brow furrowed.

Bunyan held up an index finger, indicating that Omri wait.

"Muriel, you still there?"

Through sobs she managed to speak. "Joe called from a police station in Calais. They've processed him, fingerprints, mug shot, and all! And they've got him behind bars along with his passengers."

Bunyan rubbed his cheek, thinking of his friend under arrest. This was no joke, no make-believe. The government was serious. Dead serious. Even targeting small airplanes like Joe's.

"Bunyan?"

"Yes."

"We may have an even bigger problem."

"Really?" He couldn't imagine what could be worse.

"I have two other birds needing to migrate."

"Two?"

"A mother and daughter. And I'm sure the authorities are on their way here."

Bunyan hesitated and looked at his watch. 6:50 p.m.

"The Cumberland Recreation Area is close to you," he said.

"Yes."

"Tell the 'birds' how to get there and to wait for me in the dugout of the first ballfield."

"Okay."

"Then clean up any evidence of them in your house. Dishes, glasses, unmade beds."

"Okay."

"Then pray, try to be calm, and call your son. William's a bright guy. Most important, he's a lawyer. I'll be in touch."

"Okay."

About to hang up, Bunyan first said, "Muriel, you're on your cell?"

"Yes."

"Crush the thing and throw it into the woods behind your house."

There was a pause, then, "Okay, Bunyan. Bless you."

"We'll be praying for Joe and the others."

Bunyan sat on the edge of his bed and turned to look at Omri. He shook his head in dismay. "Best-laid plans."

—∞—

A couple of minutes later, Omri fought to calm his anxiety as Bunyan drove away in his Escalade, leaving with the caution that if Omri accompanied him, he'd be placing himself in danger.

"In fact," Bunyan said as he climbed into his vehicle, "the Rosenbaums being late might be a godsend. Frees up time to get these two."

Omri nodded.

Bunyan had already told Omri how to contact the Callahans if something went awry.

—∞—

Early-August dusk was settling over Cumberland when Bunyan turned off Route One onto Tuttle Road and headed toward the village about four miles inland. On the one hand, he preferred darkness when picking up these people. On the other hand, in the dark, he might not be able to spot the smallish sign for the community park and ballfields off to his right. He'd been there three times—twice during its construction and once to dedicate "Jacko" Jackson Field, one of several area ball fields built with his donations.

He moved along the country road at about forty-five miles an hour. He saw Joe and Muriel's street on his right, so he knew he was close. He slowed down to watch for the sign.

Suddenly lights were flashing at him from in front and behind. For the oddest reason, a game against the New York Yankees flashed in Bunyan's mind. He'd rounded third base and was halfway to home plate, trying to score from second base on a single to right field, when the catcher caught a throw and stood waiting for him in the batter's box. Should he continue to the plate and try to bowl over the catcher, or try to retreat to third base and hope for a miracle like a bad throw from the catcher to the third baseman? Speed was certainly not his strength. But muscle was.

Bunyan hesitated and took his foot off the accelerator, then remembered the outcome of his race to the plate. (The catcher actually side-stepped his bull-rush, tagged him out on the shoulder, and threw out his teammate trying to reach second base.)

Again pressing his foot on the gas pedal, he looked away from the high-beam headlights and flashing blue and red lights heading directly at him. He was thinking through his statement to the police when the headlights flashed past him and turned down Joe and Muriel's street. Bunyan's heart went to his throat. Yes, these people were serious with a capital S. A few seconds later, the vehicle approaching from behind also turned down the street.

Bunyan blew out a breath of relief, then slowing down, he prayed, "Lord, watch over Muriel. Calm her with Your supernatural shalom—peace that passes all understanding. Give her son wisdom and discernment, Father."

He turned his attention to the park and the two wayward "birds."

Detecting the park entrance, Bunyan turned in and cut off his lights. Moments later, he walked around the cement-and-wood wall of the first-base dugout. Huddled together and leaning into the far corner of the dugout were two people. In the shadows of the oncoming night, Bunyan thought the woman to be in her early thirties and the child to be around eight. What looked like duffel bags lay on the bench next to them.

"Hello, mister." The little girl's voice sounded like a windchime outside Bunyan's home, sweet and sing-songy.

He smiled. "Hello, young lady. Are you Mrs. Rogers's friends?"

"Yes sir." She looked up at him. "Boy, you're *big!*"

"I've been told."

The woman spoke up. "Were those police vehicles heading to Joe and Muriel's house?"

"Appears so."

"I'm so sorry for them. If not for us—"

"Joe and Muriel signed up for this, ma'am," Bunyan interrupted. "They signed on for this of their own will. There's nothing for you to be sorry for."

The lady wiped a tear from her cheek.

"Is her son there with her yet?" Bunyan asked.

"She expected him to arrive about ten minutes after we left. But I don't really know."

"Well, I'm the cavalry she called. Bunyan Jackson." He held out a hand, "Please come with me."

The little girl jumped up and grabbed his hand. "I'm Daisy-Rain," she announced, waving a hand in the woman's direction, "and this is my mom, Ruth."

He couldn't help but smile at the child's exuberance. "When we get you safely out of here you'll have to tell me how you came by such a beautiful name."

Giggles spilled out of the girl like fizz from a shaken soda can.

Shandra Constantine sat on the comfortable chocolate-brown sofa in her office and rubbed her closed eyes. She hadn't slept more than a handful of hours since getting the call before sunrise Friday about the emigration bill being passed. She was exhausted, and her eyes felt like they'd been scrubbed with a Brillo pad. On top of this, she was I-could-eat-red-meat hungry. A sixteen-ounce prime rib, rare, with rosemary-and-olive oil, and her favorite shiraz would go down nicely now—if she had the strength to eat.

A knock at her office door roused her. Her secretary peeked her head inside. "Can I go home now, Madam Secretary?"

"Yes, Melinda. Order me a pepperoni pizza and stout before you go, though. From We the Pizza. Have Harvey bring it up here when it's delivered."

"Sure."

A few seconds later, Constantine's phone rang. She pushed herself up off the couch to answer the call. On the line was Melinda, telling her the president was calling.

After a moment with the chief of staff, she heard the distinctive voice of Harold Smith. He was his usual self—upbeat, the consummate politician, a boss who'd go to the mat for you. But if you were his enemy, watch out. She always strove to be on his good side. That's how she obtained the DHS post in the first place.

"Shandra!" he said. "Glowing reports coming in. By all accounts—and I'm not surprised—you're doing a fine job, winning the battle."

"We're trying, Mr. President."

"Everybody cooperating?"

"The other services, you mean?"

"Yes."

"We're well-oiled, sir. No complaints here. Even Hank's in top form."

"Hank was the best man at my wedding, Shandra. Be kind to him."

She chuckled to herself, knowing Smith was well aware of the prickly relationship between her and Blasted.

Smith continued, "Is there anything I can do?"

"No, Mr. President. We've got our end under control."

"What about your A List?"

Constantine lowered her head and pressed her index and middle fingers against her right temple. Great. Sleep- and food-deprived and now a headache. Probably a migraine. She cursed to herself.

"What'd you say?" Smith asked.

"Nothing, sir. Been a long two days. All our agents have been out straight, as you know. The count of Jews prevented from trying to leave the country is in the tens of thousands. Most were simply sent home, although a much smaller number have been detained in jails."

"Let them cool off a bit, then things will return to normal." Smith sounded confident. She'd never heard him appear otherwise. "Tomorrow, we're hitting the Sunday talk shows with both barrels. I've got a one-on-one with Ted Bissell on CBS."

"You can always count on the networks, Mr. President."

"Dan will be on NBC and ABC, Pete will hit two shows, and we're even giving Fox a go with Annette," he said, referring to the vice president and the speaker of the house. "I knew you'd be too busy doing the heavy lifting to do one of these, Shandra."

"You're right there, sir." She expelled a tired sigh Smith could surely discern at the other end of the line. She wanted him to appreciate just how thoroughly draining this assignment was, both physically and mentally.

"But back to your A List. How're you doing?"

She ran her finger down the names. Four more had been knocked off since Friday night: Abel Lischne, Abraham Rymer, Tobias Urech and Nina Bader. All staying put.

"We're down to six missing, Mr. President," she said.

"And they are?"

"The one you'd be interested in is Dr. Zohn."

Smith swore a word Constantine hadn't heard in years. She flinched.

"But we're inundating the Northeast with agents," she quickly added. "We'll get him, sir."

"Unless he headed west—the opposite of what you think."

"Oh!" Was the twinge she felt a punch to the gut or the ego? Smith could be right. Zohn could have fooled them all with a counterintuitive exit plan no one would have contemplated. She had to stop and think.

"What happens with our nuclear fusion without him?" Smith asked.

Constantine exhaled, wanting to get past this conversation and get her people checking westward escape routes.

"It goes on," she said. "He left a strong team in place, at other universities as well as MIT. But his absence would speak volumes to the country and the world."

"Volumes we want to silence," Smith said. "It'd be equivalent to Einstein skipping out of the country just before finishing the atomic bomb."

As if I don't know this, Harold! This isn't my first rodeo. For that matter, it's not my first manhunt.

"You know, Shandra," Smith said, "when we find him, we may have to muffle him."

Constantine knew she couldn't respond to his last comment, not positively at any rate. But after hanging up, she reflected on his statement.

"Muffle him." Are there any nuances to that remark? Any other ways to interpret the words other than what she was thinking? The president of the United States didn't just put a hit out on Omri Zohn. Did he?

Davey flew down the stairs wearing his Class A state champions T-shirt, blue jeans, sneakers, and a smile stretching from ear to ear. Tack followed on his heels, expecting excitement.

For me, yes, boy, but not for you. Sorry. He ruffled the dog's neck.

"So you and Alec are off to the Union Raceway," Grampa said from his seat on the couch.

"Sure am. Saturday night!"

"Kisses, then." Bubbe, sitting next to Grampa, set down a book and pointed to her cheek.

Davey leaned down and kissed her, as directed.

A horn sounded in the driveway. "That's Alec."

"Have a good time." Bubbe smiled. "And remind Alec to drive carefully. I've got angels watching over you two, but their presence doesn't mean you can be reckless."

"Will do, Bubbe. Remember, I'm staying at Alec's tonight."

"Okay, dear."

Wanting to trail along, Tack followed Davey to the door.

Davey kneeled and hugged him. "Not tonight, boy." Tack hung his head and walked back to lie down at Grampa's feet.

At 8:30 p.m., Bunyan arrived back at his home. He tapped a controller, opening the middle of three garage doors and drove in, parking between a Mustang convertible on his right and a Lexus sedan.

After closing the garage door, he hustled Ruth and Daisy-Rain into the house where Omri and Lana were waiting.

"Wow! That was exciting, Mister Jackson!" Daisy-Rain gushed. "Right, Mommy?"

"Yes, dear. Very exciting."

"Will Muriel be okay? I like her a lot. Will she?"

Ruth looked up at Bunyan for help.

"She's got a very bright son at her side," Bunyan said. "I'm sure she'll be fine, sweetie."

After Bunyan introduced everyone, they followed him through the kitchen and into the den.

He rested a hand on Daisy-Rain's head. "You must be tired, young lady." He turned to Ruth and said, "She should get some sleep. We're leaving in about an hour and a half to get you folks out of the country."

"Are we flying?" Ruth asked.

"Driving."

"Good. Flying didn't work out too well for the others."

"Federal agents are like bears hunting honey with this law," Omri said. "Too bad they've never been as possessed with keeping illegal aliens *out* of the country."

"Daisy-Rain," Lana said, reaching a hand toward the child, "let me show you up to a guest room where you can take a nap."

Daisy-Rain looked at her mother for approval and got it.

A few minutes later, they were seated around the living room. Omri thought of the nervousness he experienced when awaiting the results of an experiment. This was worse. He always hoped and prayed for the best, "thrilling triumph," but was prepared for the worst, "crippling disaster." Usually the results were somewhere in between.

He looked about. Would he reach Israel? Would Ruth and her sweet little daughter? Would Ethan and Naomi, who were leaving the country *not* for love of Israel but because their government had told them Jews no longer could emigrate there? Would his friend, Joseph Frank, a US senator, ever find his way out? And tens of thousands of others. Not long ago, they were told, "Your fortune stays here." Now they were being told, "You can't leave these shores."

He'd been watching the news while waiting for Bunyan to return and the outlook was gloomy, gloomier, and gloomiest. Roads, airplanes, and trains going out of the country were like big red bulls-eyes on a target, with Homeland Security and Border Patrol agents as the archers.

Motorists were backed up into oblivion. Airline and train passengers were less affected simply because a single body was easier to question than a car full of bodies.

While most reporters concentrated their reports on the necessity of America supporting the UN Resolution and the Congressional response—even talking to the requisite handful of Jews who were Arab apologists—a few were interviewing Jews turned away at these checkpoints. Some were hysterical, some terrified, and some dumbfounded.

Omri studied their faces and wondered how their appearances compared to the Jews who were hustled onto trains to Bergen-Belsen, Dachau, and Treblinka.

Omri shook his head in wonder. He'd grown up in an area Mark Twain, in 1867, called a desolation, "a silent mournful expanse." And yet, since God's people had returned to his land, despite constant lack of water, they had transformed the desert where a few nomads lived into one of the world's greatest producers of vegetables and flowers. *So, they now declare the land is better without us on it?*

His thoughts were interrupted when Bunyan brought in a tray with coffee cups and a carafe of coffee, with cream and sugar. "We'll be needing some caffeine tonight. We have a long trip ahead of us."

"Where are we going?" Ruth asked.

"We're picking up two more at the Amtrak station at ten twenty-five, then driving upstate to Augusta. We'll then turn east and head to a home near the coast, where I'll leave you. That's as much as I can tell you." Bunyan winked at Omri, knowing he was familiar with the Callahans.

Taking a sip of coffee, Ruth looked keenly at Omri and asked, "You look very familiar. Have I seen you before?"

"You may have," he said.

"Omri won the Nobel Prize in Physics a couple of years ago," Bunyan said. "My friend would never tell you himself, so I'll brag for him."

Bunyan glanced at Omri and continued, "I saw you on the cover of *Scientific American* a few months back, Omri."

"They made me look ten years younger," Omri said. "I'd like to know how."

"Besides dying your beard and hair like you've done?" Bunyan said with a chuckle. "They ought to train the people who snap driver's license photos."

"You always looked so menacing on your baseball cards," Omri said.

"Yeah, they make you choose—a half-witted smile or a scary snarl, like you could break the bat like a twig."

Omri chuckled. "I saw you break a bat like a twig on your thigh once."

"Fly ball. To the warning track in straight-away centerfield. Third out. Ninth inning. Sixth game. American League Championship Series." Bunyan spoke in staccato. "Who wouldn't have broken the timber?"

"Ahh."

"You played baseball?" Ruth said.

"For a few years, a decade or so ago."

"That's why you're so big!" the child exclaimed.

"I owe the size to my daddy," he said, "and to God."

"Yeah, God," she said.

Omri eyed Ruth. "What about you? What's your story?"

"It's all emigration, such a horrible thing and why we're on the run," she said, pushing back her long black hair. "My husband, Stanley, is already in Israel. He owns a software development company and does business there. Right after the United Nations vote, he called me, and we discussed what we'd do if America agreed to the ban. That's when we decided I'd escape with Daisy-Rain and join him."

"A smart man," Omri said. "Too many of us Jews are not so forward thinking. I guess many of us never believed such a vote would happen—could happen."

"We weren't *that* forward thinking," Ruth said. "But we did come up with an idea to easily carry much of our assets out of the country."

She pulled a small cloth bag out of her satchel and shook it in the air. "Jewelry," she said. "Mostly diamonds and a few rubies."

"Brilliant!" Omri said.

"Stanley's already found an apartment for us … in Tel Aviv." She offered a grim smile.

"Wonderful," Omri said.

"Now we've just got to get you there," Bunyan said.

At that moment, Lana walked into the room. "Well, she's sound asleep, the little princess."

"Dead tired," Ruth said.

"Not so tired that she didn't want me to tell her a story, but tired enough that she fell asleep in the middle of the telling."

They all chuckled.

"I hope she'll be able to sleep in the car," Bunyan said. He took a drink of coffee and looked at his watch. "Nine-o-five. We leave at ten o'clock. If anyone wants to catch a few winks, now's the time."

At ten o'clock sharp, with well-wishes from Lana, Omri slid into the front passenger seat, while Ruth and a half-asleep Daisy-Rain piled into the rear seat of Bunyan's Escalade. The adults each carried a tall travel mug full of coffee.A thermos full of steaming coffee sat in the console between the front seats. Twenty minutes later, they pulled into the Amtrak parking lot, in nearly the same spot Bunyan had occupied the night before. They had a clear view to the train station's entryway.

Omri's stomach felt like it was being tickled by a feather. His life had been so orderly—from his teaching to his research, even to the invitations to speak at various scientific conventions around the world. He always knew precisely how each week would progress. But this—this not knowing what the next *hour* held for him—surpassed discomfort.

And his wasn't the only future at stake. What of the others?

He'd grown close to Ethan since they first met, visiting him and Naomi at their home, sharing life stories with them, and, to a nonbelieving Ethan, pronouncing his own faith as best he could.

He and Ethan had emailed each other every couple of days and spoken on the phone every week or two. Ethan had become like a son to him. In fact, though the Lord had blessed him and his wife with but one son, Omri had dozens of what he called "quasi-children"—students who showed particular promise, applied themselves to their fullest, and went out and influenced both the micro-world of science and the larger world around them.

Ethan? His was a brilliant mind. Though ensconced in different branches of science, they each could listen to the other's questions and theories and offer helpful suggestions. The consequences of their friendship were far-reaching—personally and professionally.

And the Reminis? Clearly, their world had been tossed upside down. Separated from Stanley, they were leaving behind a full life. Neighbors, friends, colleagues, Daisy-Rain's classmates. And most of all, parents. What were the parents' emotions at this moment?

Had they checked on Stanley and Ruth, found them missing, and tried to track them down?

Bunyan tapped Omri's left hand. "Here come the people from the last train," he said.

Omri tightened his gaze on the entryway. An entire family of five, followed by several couples and a handful of individuals, exited, but none of them were Ethan and Naomi.

Then came a pause. No one else came out.

"No?" Bunyan asked.

Omri shook his head.

Without warning, a Portland police squad car squealed into the station, wheeling into the turnaround at the entryway. Two police officers jumped out; the one on the passenger's side drew a pistol.

"Omigod!" Ruth exclaimed. She was leaning forward in the back seat, looking between Omri and Bunyan.

"What's happening, mommy?" Daisy-Rain said, alarm filling her little voice.

"I don't know, dear."

Omri grabbed for the door handle to get out and rush to the station. The iron grip of Bunyan on his elbow stopped him. Omri looked at him. Pale light from parking-lot lampposts filtered into the car, but Omri could detect the warning in his friend's eyes.

He settled back in his seat. *Ethan and Naomi!*

"Don't know what's going on, but we can't get involved, or it could be trouble for everyone in this car," Bunyan said.

Moments later, a white vehicle screeched into the yard, blue lights flashing, a Cumberland County Sheriff's Department seal was centered the driver-side door. A deputy sheriff jumped out, drawing his hand weapon and hustling around the front of the vehicle.

"Oh, my!" Ruth said, then slapped a hand over her mouth.

"Mommy, what is it?" Ruth squealed.

Omri turned to cajole Daisy-Rain, clearly frightened to the brink of terror. She shivered and clung to her mother.

"Little one," he said, "whatever is happening, let's pray together. The Lord is in charge and will protect His people. Okay?"

She calmed a bit and still holding her mother by her waist, leaned forward and said in a subdued voice, "Yes sir, Mr. Omri."

Omri prayed briefly for God's supernatural protection and favor on the Rosenbaums and shalom to this dear child. Amens followed. A few seconds later, the lawmen emerged. The two police officers had hold of a manacled, middle-aged man with dark-hair. The sheriff's deputy, hefting two duffel bags over one shoulder, pressed an auburn-haired woman, also handcuffed, forward.

On the edge of his seat, Omri leaned ahead and squinted.

"Oh, no!" Bunyan said. "Is it them?"

Omri held up a hand, indicating to wait. He couldn't quite make out—"I can't tell for sure. Both have the same height, same build, same hair."

The officers pushed the man and woman down and into the rear seat of the cruiser. Seconds later, the two vehicles, blue lights turned off, laid rubber out the drive, turned right toward Congress Street and disappeared behind a Double Tree Hotel.

Omri's head felt like confetti. He rubbed his chin with his palm. *Those two must be Eth—*

Just then, a man and woman walked out the train station. Their heads were bent low as if they were avoiding a pelting rain.

But there was no rain. *They're avoiding the gaze of the police as well as security cameras. Ethan and Naomi?*

"Yes!" Omri exclaimed. "That's them!"

Bunyan flashed his headlights twice, waited several seconds, then flashed them twice again.

The couple, carrying their duffel bags like backpacks, noticed, then spun in the direction of the Escalade.

Omri breathed a deep sigh. His heart was liberated. But the feathery tickle? It remained.

Margaret and Dan sat on a glider on the back porch. Tack lay in front of them, front paws hanging over the edge of the porch, looking longingly toward the woods beyond.

"Wrong direction, boy," Margaret said. "You're looking east. Davey and Alec are *there*." She pointed to the right, south.

As if understanding, Tack jumped up, walked to the right side of the porch and lay down with his head on his paws. And whined.

"He's our second child, you know," Margaret said, smiling.

Dan nodded. "Yep."

"Today went like a breeze."

"'Like a breeze'—ha! Yes, and your grandson is some kid, isn't he, Maggie Chadwick?"

Margaret nodded.

They held hands, comfortable in each other's presence. Margaret looked sideways at her husband and admired his good looks. His full head of hair and rugged chin were what first attracted her to him. Later, she learned about his heroism in battle. Even then, someone else, not Dan, had divulged his courage.

No, Dan never revealed the events leading to his being awarded the Navy Medal of Honor and the Navy Heroism Medal.

Yes, he was handsome, but his heart was what had won her over. And his heart still held her in its grip. She looked up at the stars and mouthed a *thank you* to the heavens.

Dan smiled over at Margaret. The winsome young lady he'd met at an oceanside golf course while stationed in Virginia still made his heart flutter. He had admired her form in the foursome ahead of his. Later, after his round, he spotted her at a table on the clubhouse terrace, drinking a soda with some girlfriends. He approached her to express his admiration of her play and inquire where she had learned the game so well. That was the last day he looked with interest at any other woman.

After their marriage a year later, Margaret had followed him from post to post—Hawaii, Alaska, San Diego, and then to Naples, Italy, and Yokosuka, Japan—finding high school home-economics teaching jobs whenever they lived stateside. Along the way, they'd both found the Lord and brought a beautiful daughter,

Annie, into the world. And now, here Margaret was, still at his side, her hand in his.

In his retirement and his new calling to preach, he dealt with parish meetings of all sorts and served as counselor and encourager-general (or encourager-admiral, he'd say). Margaret stood alongside him, helping in all sorts of ways, both physical and spiritual.

All of this was fine with him.

"Look at the stars," Margaret said, looking up.

The heavens opened up above them, not one cloud dimming the view.

Dan said, "And God told Abraham, he would be the father of many nations, his offspring would number as many as the stars in the heavens."

"Then we believers must be part of that offspring, mustn't we?" Margaret added. "The Jews have always been few in number."

"Right. *Part* of, but not *instead* of—"

"Otherwise we wouldn't be carrying them on our shoulders to Jerusalem; someone else would be carrying *us*."

Dan laughed, then added, "The repercussions of Replacement Theology can get too scary at times, can't they?"

"God is unchangeable. Margaret squeezed his hand.

Dan leaned over, wrapped his arms around her and kissed her with passion. Suddenly, Tack was beside them, whining softly.

"He wants up," Margaret said.

"Yeah, and between us." Dan pointed his finger at the dog. "Sorry, pal. She's all mine right now." Tack barked, turned, and resumed his place facing south. Dan could almost see visions of Frisbee games in the dog's mind.

Chapter Seven

1:12 a.m. Sunday

A sliver of light flashed in Bunyan's rearview mirror. He peered uneasily into each of the Escalade's side mirrors to gauge its source, but the light was gone. A shiver touched nerves, traveling down his spine, jumping him to attention. The anxiety and fear, gnawing at his stomach since the train station, heightened by another notch. *Is the vehicle a cop, a trooper, the Border Patrol, or just another traveler?*

Bunyan tightened his grip on the steering wheel. He couldn't afford the possibility of being stopped for a driving violation, and at this time of night, every vehicle was probably considered suspect. He had to beware. Precious cargo. Illicit goods. Contraband. He knew his way, having visited Daniel and Margaret over the years, but some of the turns were easy to miss even in the daytime. True, the moon shone half-bright through thickening clouds, but the dim light was little consolation. Another twinge of trepidation tightened his thorax, and he knew if he spoke, his voice would betray fear, so he remained quiet.

From the back seat, Ruth said, "Bunyan, you can't know how much we appreciate your help."

"My duty to my God," Bunyan replied, "same as those many folks who helped my ancestor escape slavery. Many people back then didn't even consider a black person human. They were sub-human. Had no rights. Chattel."

"The same way the Nazis considered us Jews," Omri said.

Bunyan nodded and glanced in the mirror at Daisy-Rain, snuggled against her mother and fiddling with a handheld DS game.

It was too dark in the SUV to see the faces of his five co-travelers, but Bunyan figured anxiety was written on them—except perhaps Daisy-Rain. The prayers had worked. The word *whimsical* may not have been in the girl's vocabulary, but fancy was certainly in her spirit. He'd noticed as much in the few hours since he'd met her and her mother.

For the adults, Bunyan could only guess at the extent of their anxiety, the apprehension of leaving behind their lives and all they had with the trepidation of the unknown ahead. Imagine, being afraid of trying to leave your own country, even America, the land for whose freedom so many had fought and died.

He drove on across Maine's Route 17 toward the coast about twenty miles away, staying alert for the turnoff he had to make, looking for the little country store at the intersection with Appleton Road, Route 131. There he'd turn left and drive north along the ridgeline of the St. George River Valley and Sennebec Pond. Houses were sparse, and there were no streetlights to add light in the countryside, making spotting the landmark even more difficult.

Another flash of light in the rearview mirror. Two headlights! *Who else would be out this time of night?*

"There it is," Bunyan blurted impulsively as the little store came into view, perhaps fifty yards ahead. Not trusting his depth perception under the sporadic moonlight, Bunyan hesitated to touch his brakes. If those headlights behind him belonged to the law, he didn't want to inform them he was turning, so he downshifted, then downshifted again. The 403-horsepower engine groaned in response.

As he approached the turn, Bunyan turned off his lights. Daisy-Rain in the back seat gasped as all the inside lights went out as well. He yanked the wheel to the left and motored up the two-lane road only as fast as he could see ahead.

Thankfully, the road was straight, but Bunyan wished there were trees on either side rather than fields. To his left, about a half-mile behind, he could distinctly see headlights. He wondered if the moonlight allowed the driver to see his vehicle. He drove over a rise in the road, and on the downhill side, turned his lights back on and accelerated. Trees now hugged the road to the left and fields fell away to the right, down toward the river a half-mile away.

With the headlights back on, Bunyan pushed down on the accelerator. There hadn't been a twist or turn in the road since he came over the hillock, and he considered turning his lights back off. A bad feeling assailed him, an ache in his gut. His neck was beginning to stiffen. And his heart was beating too fast. Way too fast. He asked God for peace.

"Shalom, my friend," Omri said. "Meaning 'the peace of God, wholeness, welfare, safety, tranquility, perfectness, harmony'—oh, the word encompasses so much."

Bunyan nodded. "Exactly what I'm praying for. Peace. But, I'm concerned about the car behind us."

Omri swiveled to look through the rear window. "Oh-oh," he moaned. "I believe they turned up this road too. Headlights are about to come over the top of that knoll."

Mutterings of worry escaped the others in the back.

"Mommy, are you scared?" Daisy-Rain whimpered, her peace gone so soon.

Ruth cooed, "All will be okay, darling."

Bunyan pressed down harder on the accelerator. As he sped toward the little village of Appleton two miles away, he tugged at his coat and pulled a hand-sized gadget from his pocket.

He pressed the device into Omri's hand. "Take this GPS guidance system. If we break up, you need to get to that X that marks Dan and Margaret's house. Seventeen-fifty longitude, sixty-nine-ten latitude. Can you remember?"

"Certainly." Omri took the rectangular apparatus and peered into a blank display. "Plus, Ethan here is a world-class mechanical engineer."

"No names. Just a location, X. It's a big old farmhouse overlooking a long field that leads to a lake.

"How far from here?"

"Six or eight miles—Oh-oh." Bunyan's eyes locked on his rearview mirror. The headlights were eclipsing the hill, still probably a half-mile behind. They entered the tiny village of Appleton. Bunyan again turned off his lights. This time there was near silence in the vehicle; he thought he heard Ruth whispering prayers behind him.

Bunyan glanced at Omri and read apprehension on his face. Omri peered at the GPS device and nodded as if the contraption presented him no problem, then stuck the unit in his jacket pocket.

"Dan and Elizabeth don't know when we're arriving, just that we're to get there ASAP. I'm sure they figured tonight. I'm afraid the government has surveillance over all the cell phones, emails, and internet blog sites, watching for Jews trying to leave the country. So here's what you do when you get there."

Omri listened carefully to the directions. Then Bunyan turned to the people behind them. "Now stay calm, everyone."

Bunyan downshifted twice to slow the vehicle without showing his brake lights. He cranked the wheel to the right, drove over a short bridge, then sped up as best he could in the moonlight. The main road again bent toward the north; Bunyan followed until he spotted a small road, perhaps a driveway on the right, surrounded by forest. He turned again and flicked a switch to make sure the overhead light didn't come on when doors were opened.

"Everybody out! Take your duffel bags and coffee mugs," Bunyan ordered. "Hurry! Into the woods and hide!"

Looking at Omri, he said, "If this is just a simple traveler, then wait a minute after they pass by and hop back into the vehicle. If it's the law, well, you've got the GPS. Stay low. Stay in the woods. And get to the Callahans. Okay?"

Omri nodded and stepped out of the vehicle. The others grabbed duffel bags and mugs, scooted out in haste, and ran into the tree cover.

Bunyan watched from the driver's seat. Just as Ruth tugged little Daisy-Rain behind a bush, the vehicle following them slowed on the road. A searchlight flashed on! The light moved in a south-to-north arc, searing the darkness.

Bunyan swallowed hard, recalling the scripture, "What you fear most will come upon you." As the words ran through his mind, the searchlight caught the Escalade in its beam and froze. Bunyan bowed his head. *Father God, thank You for Your grace. Deliver Omri and the others, Father!*

The laser beam remained on the vehicle. To Bunyan, it seemed more intense every second. "Well, it sure isn't any ordinary traveler," he muttered. "Put on your game face, Jacko."

He flipped on his map light, reached for his *Maine Atlas and Gazetteer*, found map fourteen and pretended to study the roadways.

The car had turned into the driveway behind him, flooding the SUV with its headlights. A few moments later, a tap sounded on the window and a light shone inside. Bunyan cringed, then turned toward the light, forcing the panic from his face.

Over the years since his retirement, Bunyan's connection to his fans had helped him many times. He hoped the magic would work this time.

A man outside pressed a badge against the window. "Border Patrol. Roll down your window, please." Firm. Authoritative. No-nonsense. The officer kept one hand on his service revolver, a Berretta 96D, and with the other, scanned his flashlight through the vehicle. At one point, the light stopped for a few seconds.

Bunyan gulped. What had captured his attention? Did someone leave clothing, or coffee mug behind? Bunyan lowered the window.

"Yes, sir," Bunyan's deep voice rose an octave, surprising him in its obvious anxiety. He'd faced down Cy Young pitchers with the bases loaded and two outs in the ninth. He'd shaken the hand of the president after winning the World Series' Most Valuable Player award. He'd spoken to dozens of journalists at a time, with lights shining, flashbulbs popping, and microphones shoved in his face. Heck, he'd stood at home plate in front of a bevy of microphones and thirty-four thousand fans when the team retired his jersey number. But never in his life had he been so tense, so filled with a sense of dread.

Be anxious for nothing. Be anxious for nothing!

"You want to see my license or something, officer?" Bunyan asked the question but hoped the man would recognize him and say, "Aw shucks, Jacko, be on your way, will ya'? You're my favorite ballplayer, ever!"

"License, registration, and an answer."

Guess not.

"What're you doin' out here in the middle of nowhere at two somethin' in the morning?"

Bunyan didn't respond, just turned down the visor to get his registration, plucked his driver's license from his wallet, and, with hands shaking, passed them to the officer. The patrolman grunted and looked over both.

A moment later, he turned his attention to Bunyan and leaned toward the window. "Now answer the question, Mr. Jackson. Two a.m. Nowhere, Maine. You leave Route Seventeen and turn off your lights at the same time. Then you pull into this driveway in the middle of the woods and turn off your lights again."

The answer flashed in Bunyan's mind at that instant. "Alternator, officer. My alternator's failing." *Great answer, man. Home run!*

The patrolman stood up straight at the response. Bunyan could read the contemplation in his mind: *Yep, that could be a reasonable story.*

Maybe, Bunyan thought. Just maybe we'll get out of this. Maybe we'll *all* get out of this.

"Stay in the car, please, Mr. Jackson."

"Sure, officer."

Bunyan watched the man's silhouette as he retreated to his cruiser. Then he stepped out of the light. Bunyan heard the door open and pictured the officer sliding into the front seat behind the wheel. Bunyan snuck a glance out into the woods but couldn't detect any movement.

Squatting behind a clump of trees, Omri peeked between some branches. He could read the fluorescent "Border Patrol" lettering on the side of the SUV cruiser. The officer had turned on an inside light and was speaking into a transmitter. Omri wished he could hear the conversation.

He looked around at the others. Several feet away to his right, Ruth held Daisy-Rain tightly in her arms, patting the child's head, trying to calm her. Ethan and Naomi sat to his left, their heads bent toward the forest floor as if that might better hide them.

Omri guessed they were all holding their breath. He was. Naomi would be praying. Ethan, considering angles of escape, but perhaps, Omri hoped, praying as well. Some people prayed whether they believed in a god or not. Foxhole prayers. How inconsequential.

He thought for a moment of his younger brother in Israel, his children and grandchildren probably waiting and praying for Omri to escape from America. Oftentimes, the person living through the experience had an easier time than those at a distance who were praying for them.

The Border Patrolman slammed the door shut. Omri pulled his head back behind the tree.

Bunyan took a deep breath. His palms were sweaty. He wished he knew what was coming. Fastball. Curveball. Splitter. These he could anticipate. But what would this Border Patrol officer do, or ask?

"Mr. Jackson, turn on your ignition, please."

Oh, no. The engine's gonna start.

Bunyan turned the key partially. No sound.

"All the way, sir." The man sounded a bit surprised, then exasperated.

Bunyan turned the key all the way and the engine jumped to life.

"Turn on your headlights, please, sir."

Bunyan turned the knob for the lights, and they came on full-force. That neither the battery nor the alternator was dying was obvious. Meanwhile, lights came on inside the house about fifty feet away at the end of the driveway.

"I—I don't want to wake these poor people in the house," Bunyan said.

"Don't worry about them. Turn on the high beams, sir."

Bunyan did and they worked.

"Now turn on the inside bulb."

Bunyan did and the light worked.

"Now your left blinker."

Bunyan flicked the lever and the left-side signal lights began blinking.

"No problems with the alternator now, eh?"

Bunyan stammered. "I–I guess—Looks as if, uh—"

"Looks pretty suspicious and deceptive to me." The officer took a half-step back and his right hand gripped the handle of his pistol.

Bunyan shrugged. "I'm simply traveling, officer."

"To where, sir?"

Bunyan hesitated, then bristled. "Does my destination matter? I'm an American citizen. I'm not wanted for any crime. There's no law against driving at night—in Maine or anywhere else, is there? I find there's little traffic and traveling is easier at night."

The officer shook his head, then aimed his flashlight into the back seat. "What's that?"

Bunyan strained to look behind him and his heart leaped. It was Daisy-Rain's little DS game.

"Oh, that's, um, my, ah, my granddaughter's," he said. "She—she was playing with the game."

"When?"

"Last night."

"Last night and the gadget's still runnin'? Must be some battery."

The officer suddenly turned his back to Bunyan and shone his flashlight into the woods.

Bunyan could imagine the fear in the hearts of his charges, especially the little girl. Ruth was probably rocking Daisy-Rain in her arms, trying to quiet her, at this very moment.

The officer squinted into the darkness and took three steps off the driveway toward the woods. Bunyan opened the door and stepped out, not sure what exactly he would do.

Just then the front door of the house burst open and a large man with a shotgun stepped out. "Yo, there!" he hollered and began walking in long strides toward them, pointing the shotgun menacingly in their direction.

"Whoa!" the patrolman exclaimed. "Put the shotgun down, sir. I'm an officer of the Border Patrol."

"I'll put 'er down when I see your badge," the man retorted, quickly closing the distance between them. "What're you doin' in my driveway?"

"I'm questioning this fella." The officer shone his flashlight on Bunyan. "You know 'im?"

"Never seen—" The man, now just ten feet away, stopped and looked. He hesitated, then exclaimed, "Jacko! Bunyan Jackson, that you?"

"So you *do* know him?" the officer exclaimed.

"Well, don't *you*?" The man harrumphed. "Bunyan Jackson. He hit more jacks than any Red Sox player for years until his back—" He caught himself short and locked eyes with Bunyan on whom the officer was shining his flashlight. "How *is* your back, Jacko?"

Bunyan began to respond, but the officer cut in. "That's enough. I'm takin' you in for questioning, Mr. Jackson. Get back in your vehicle and follow me to headquarters. You didn't hit any home run tonight—" He paused for a moment, looked Bunyan over, and added, derisively, "Jacko."

Bunyan looked to the man with the shotgun, who simply shrugged. He glanced into the dark of the woods and reluctantly got back into his Escalade. *Lord, help Omri and the others. They're your people, Father, so please watch over them.*

Omri peeked around the tree and watched the two vehicles back out of the driveway and head south—the direction from which they had come.

He'd heard snatches of the confrontation, including the officer's final command to Bunyan. A twig snapped to his left, and Omri turned quickly toward the sound. The clouds continued to move along in front of the moon, transforming dim shadows into dark ones. He could barely discern Naomi.

"Yo, who's there?!" The man with the shotgun had stopped his retreat toward his house, hesitated, and stepped back to the edge of the driveway.Omri sucked in his breath. This man did not appear to be someonethey should to reveal themselves to—even if he weren't armed.

The man stood his ground and peered into the woods. Putting the butt of the shotgun to his shoulder, he took aim in their direction. Omri gasped. *He's pointing directly at Naomi!*

"Step out here, or I'll shoot!" the man called.

Naomi moved as if to stand up, but Ethan grabbed her elbow, put a finger to his lips, and motioned for her to squat back down low.

The man with the shotgun waited several seconds, then turned and hustled back toward his house.

"He's going to get a flashlight," Omri whispered. "Everyone, hurry. Directly away from the house."

Omri heard Ethan, Naomi, Ruth and Daisy-Rain scramble through the woods on either side of him, thrashing through bushes and between trees.

He heard Daisy-Rain yelp when she apparently stumbled and fell. "Hurry, child!" Ruth whispered hoarsely.

"Can I carry her?" he asked.

"No, thanks," she replied. "I'll take her."

"Ouch!" Naomi cried. Omri followed the voice and saw her push away a bramble bush she'd run into.

They'd put perhaps thirty yards behind them when a high-beam light flashed toward them from the driveway.

"Down!" Omri murmured just loud enough for the others to hear.

Omri's hip landed on a small boulder. Pain shot up his torso. He ground his teeth to squelch a cry. Ethan, now a few feet in front of him, tripped into a puddle of water, his satchel falling off his shoulder. He cursed.

"Sh-h!" Naomi warned.

Omri pushed himself up on his elbows, the weight of his duffel bag heavy upon him, and turned to see what the armed man was doing. Silhouetted by the porch light behind him, he was panning the woods with the flashlight. Apparently, he hadn't heard them.

Another form loomed behind the man.

"What is it, Bob?" a woman called.

"I dunno. Probably the Baylors' dog again, runnin' loose—little hellion. Hey, Jacko was just in our driveway."

"Jack who?"

"Jack who!? Aw, never mind."

"Well, come on back inside then. I just felt a sprinkle. It's startin' to rain."

"I'm lockin' up the garage first."

The woman returned to the house. The man took a few more steps into the woods and scanned it again with his flashlight. "Git out!" he hollered. "Mutt!"

"I'll keep the outside light on. Maybe the light'll scare him away," the woman said.

"Good idea," the man grumbled. Lifting his rifle to his shoulder, he turned and walked to the garage.

On the way he said, "Imagine. Takin' a hero like Bunyan Jackson into custody!"

Sudden downheartedness fell on Omri's spirit. *Bunyan. In custody. Because of me.* He shook his head in disbelief.

"Br-r, that water's cold!" Ethan exclaimed, interrupting Omri's thoughts. He looked at Ethan, who wiped mud from his chin with his shirt sleeve.

"At least I kept my satchel dry," Ethan said.

"Dry's good—knowing what's inside." Omri pushed himself to his feet. "But now they've got Bunyan."

What will the Border Patrol do with Bunyan? Maybe if I turn myself in. He pondered the hypothesis for a moment. So many variables were in play, each with values and unknowns and assumptions. Bunyan was willfully putting himself at risk for his own principles. If Omri gave himself up, he'd diminish that sacrifice—something he'd never do to his friend. But if he gave himself up, Homeland Security might not find Ethan, Naomi and the others. But *might* was one of the major unknowns plaguing this conundrum.

His thoughts flew to federal agents searching Bunyan's home, interrogating Lana, checking with nosy neighbors—

A small hand squeezed his index finger. Omri turned to see the dim image of Daisy-Rain. He thought he detected a frown.

"You okay, Mr. Omri?"

"Oh, dear one. I'm fine, just fine. Thank you for asking."

He smiled down at her and engulfed her hand in his. Then he looked up. Ethan was giving a handkerchief to Naomi, who patted at a scratch on her ear from when her face flirted with the bramble bush.

Omri released a deep sigh and rubbed his hip where he'd fallen.

"Bunyan can take care of himself. God's on his side," he declared with finality, asking God to truly implant this confidence in him. He squared his shoulders. He and the others must get to their destination on their own. He reached for the GPS instrument in his pocket and immediately exclaimed, "Oh-h no!"

"What's the matter?" Ethan asked.

As Omri held the instrument close to his face, a huge drop of rain landed on his forehead, blurring his vision for a moment. "I think I crushed it when I fell."

He pushed the tiny "On" button and waited. Nothing happened.

"Let me see," Ethan said.

Omri handed the apparatus to Ethan, watching hopefully as he scrutinized the casing.

"Dead in the water," he determined.

"Oh, Lord," Naomi said.

"Mommy," Daisy-Rain said, "are we lost? What're we gonna do?"

"We'll be all right, hon," Ruth patted her head.

"But—"

"We have God on our side," Omri said, squeezing the hand he still held tight. "Never fear, little one."

He looked heavenward and was rewarded by another larger-than-life rain drop, this one in his left eye. Omri lowered his head, rubbed his eye and noted, "Bunyan said we were four or five miles away from our destination. Maybe we can get there before morning."

"In this rain?" Ethan sounded doubtful. "And with no GPS?"

"Ethan," Naomi said, "did our people have GPS when they left Egypt?"

"No, and their trip took them forty years," he declared.

"Only because they sinned against God and doubted Him."

"Nevertheless," Ethan said.

Suddenly a lightning bolt flashed from the sky to the east, and a moment later a ball of sparks flared above the trees.

"Hey," Daisy-Rain said, pointing back toward the house, "the lights in that house just flickered and went out."

"Maybe they just turned them off," Ruth said.

"Did you say they flickered, child?" Omri asked.

"Yes. Then they went out," she said with firmness.

"I bet the lightning struck a power substation, knocking out the electricity," Ethan said.

"I'd say we follow 'the light by night,'" Omri declared, carefully stepping off with care in that direction, "with a little bit of our own light."

He pulled a cigar-sized flashlight out of his pocket and flicked it on. A well-defined beam of light lit up five or so feet in front of him.

"You say that's east?" Ruth pointed.

"Right." Omri pointed. "Good thing we crossed the river back there and won't have to swim. I *did* get a look at the terrain between us and our destination—a rural road outside a village called Hope."

"Ha! Appropriate," Naomi said.

"Curious, huh?" Ruth said. "And hope is exactly what we need."

"Right," Ethan said.

Omri chuckled, then added, "There's a body of water—Mill Pond—up ahead, then the road goes over a brook and turns into a dirt road, maybe an old tote road. Hopefully the path's walkable for people but not drivable for automobiles."

Abruptly, the rain became a cloudburst, and they could barely see one another.

Omri led the way, tenderly pushing branches out of his face so they didn't hit Ethan who walked behind him. The next hour they trudged through thick forest, sloshing through deep puddles here and there.

Daisy-Rain suddenly cried out, "Mommy! I twisted my ankle and it—really—hurts!" She winced in pain.

"Oh, no!" Ruth bent down for a closer look but was unable to see.

Omri turned back.Leaning forward, he pointed the flashlight toward the girl's ankle.

"It looks swollen," Ruth said.

"I *know!*" Daisy-Rain whined.

Ruth ran a hand through her soaking-wet hair. "You're too big for me to carry, baby. Are you sure you can't be tough and walk through the pain?"

Omri looked around to the others. "The child probably has a sprained ankle. We're all soaking wet. I think we should take cover and ride this out. Perhaps the ankle will feel better with a little rest. If not, we can take turns carrying her."

"But if we stop, we won't get there before sunrise," Ethan protested. "If someone spots us, we'll look pretty suspicious, five people wandering around in the woods, on foot but not dressed for hiking?"

Lightning flashed nearby again, followed immediately by a crack of thunder .

Daisy-Rain screamed, and Ruth hugged her tightly.

"That was close!" Ethan said.

"Too close—and we're in the midst of trees and tree roots. Not good," Omri said. "A professor friend of mine was standing on a tree root and—" he caught himself in mid-sentence, thinking of the child. This story was not meant for her ears.

"Okay, I agree with Omri," Ethan said. He looked at Naomi. "What do you think, darling?"

"Can we find a relatively dry spot and huddle up like a football team?" she asked.

"Yes," Ruth agreed, still cuddling her whimpering daughter, "then Daisy-Rain can sit in the middle of us all and rest that ankle."

"For a while," Omri said.

—∞—

Dan Callahan, dressed in red-plaid pajamas and a black robe, strode back and forth in the living room, checking his watch every minute or two.

"A watched pot," he murmured.

"What'd you say?" Margaret, wearing a flowered nightgown and dark-blue robe, looked up from her knitting.

"Three-thirty!" Dan said. "Where's Bunyan?"

"I'm sorry, dear. I don't know the answer any more than when you last asked—what, two minutes ago?"

The power had gone out a couple of hours earlier. They had lit several candles around the room.

Dan nodded toward the upstairs, where Davey was sound asleep in the guest room.

"Astonishing the thunder and lightning a teenager can sleep through."

Margaret smiled in agreement.

Dan looked again at his watch.

"'Which of you by being anxious can add a single hour to his span of life?'" Margaret quoted.

He stopped in his tracks and looked down at her. "Luke twelve, verse five."

"No one can pray and worry at the same time."

He paused and shook his head, "You've got me there. I don't know that one."

"Max Lucado," she said with a grin.

"Good old Max. Comes through whenever you need him. For me, the problem is *living* the Bible, not just *knowing* the words."

"They'll come," Margaret said.

"Yes, but I expected them hours ago."

"Plan B means ASAP. Maybe in this case, ASAP isn't so fast."

"I'm military, sweetheart. For me, ASAP is yesterday, or at least an hour ago."

Margaret lowered her eyes and shook her head. "You can take the commander out of the Navy but you can't take the Navy out of the commander."

"I know you're tugging my chain, but I checked the train schedules. Even if the Rosenbaums waited until after work hours Friday, which I expect they did, Bunyan should have gotten them and Dr. Zohn here by now. We'll be late getting them to Frank's."

"Bunyan would've contacted us if he were delayed."

"Not if he was on his way here and something happened."

"Perhaps the delay has to do with the power outage. Perhaps a tree fell across the road."

Dan considered the possibility. "Maybe so. I'm going to get in the truck and see if I can find them."

"Then let's pray."

The downpour tailed off to simply heavy. Omri's clothes clung to his soaked body; he knew the others were just as miserable. This was not one of those memorable, warm Maine summer nights. The rain possessed a chill as if it rushed down from the North Pole.

The thought of carrying Daisy-Rain trumped his misery. After the five of them had rested, they voted to move on. Again Omri took point, moving forward one baby step at a time. With flashlight outstretched, he headed toward the spot where the substation had blown. They'd seen no headlights of power-company trucks responding to the outage, so they had little by which to gauge their direction.

There was no finding the North Star in this storm. But if they could reach the road, they could walk eastward parallel to it and make their way to the Callahans' home.

He turned and shone the light on the others. Ethan, carrying Daisy-Rain on his back, brought up the rear. Omri shouldered Ethan's duffel bag as well as his own.

Daisy-Rain piped in, "Smells like Lici Bloom's house at Christmastime!"

"Balsam," Omri said. "Like a Christmas tree." He smiled at the thought of a long-ago Christmas day at Bunyan and CeCe's home, with a bunch of their church friends, singing and enjoying the wonderful aroma of the tree.

Wearing his US Open golf cap and LL Bean raincoat and boots, Dan climbed into his pickup truck, holding a travel mug full of coffee. He tossed a large full-beam flashlight onto the seat between him and Tack, who'd taken his prized spot next to his master. Margaret was staying behind in case Bunyan and his troupe showed up. If they did, Margaret would call him on his cell phone with the three words, "Home to roost."

The driveway spanned a good sixty yards and bent to the left around a thumb of evergreen trees. Dan drove cautiously, wipers at full throttle. The rain was so heavy the headlights, when on high beam, reflected off the raindrops and back at him. He turned the beams to low.

Once out of the driveway, he headed north. A minute later, he hung a left onto Route 105, heading west.

All the way back to Augusta, Bunyan had followed the Border Patrol officer, who fancied himself another Joe Friday of *Dragnet* fame—"Just the facts, sir."

Now he sat in a detention room of the Augusta Police Department, waiting. Waiting. They hadn't booked him or taken his fingerprints, but had simply placed him in a room with no windows and told him to wait. His request to make a phone call went unheeded.

Man, could his lawyer have a field day with this. He then considered the Patriot Act. Maybe not.

He bowed his head. What was happening to Omri and the others? Soon after he left, a tremendous thunder-and-lightning storm blew into the area. The deluge was so strong he had to slow to a crawl. For a fleeting moment, he considered trying to lose the Border Patrol agent, but then he imagined the six o'clock news—not the sports news but the news-news.

The anchorman said: "Authorities have started a manhunt for former baseball star Jacko Jackson near the coast of Maine."

That would sober up a hopeless drunk let alone a totally sober Bible believer.

Again he thought of his Jewish charges. They had no cover, but they did have the GPS. If only he could contact Dan and Margaret. Otherwise, the best he could do was pray. *Best? Heck, prayer is always the best you can do, Jacko.*

"We're there!" Omri exclaimed. He pointed. "There's the road!"

They stood at the edge of a mixed forest of balsam fir, pine and various other hardwoods. A level two-lane road, Route 105, Omri guessed, was but twenty feet away.

A bolt of cloud-to-cloud lightning lit up the area, revealing what indeed looked to be a power substation, surrounded by chain-link fencing, eight feet high.

Ethan, with Daisy-Rain on his shoulders, drew up alongside Omri. "If there's no power-company truck out, no one's driving along here this time of night." He set the girl down on the ground and worked his shoulders.

"We might as well walk on the road," Omri said. ""It'll be a lot faster."

"A lot," Naomi agreed, stepping to Ethan's side.

"Good idea," Ruth said. "And you can rest from carrying this little treasure." She put her thumb and forefinger to her daughter's chin. "How are you doing, honey?"

"I'm fine, Mommy. I think I can walk now."

Daisy-Rain took a couple of practice steps and declared herself "new as a baby."

Moments later, just as they reached the substation, headlights stabbed the night, approaching a knoll ahead of them.

"Off the road, everyone!" Omri ordered. They hustled toward the woods, Daisy-Rain stumbled at the edge of the asphalt and fell forward onto the gravel shoulder.

"Ouch!" she cried.

Omri turned back and awkwardly grabbed her into his arms, while trying to balance the two duffel bags.

"Here, let me take her." Ethan raised his arms toward Omri.

"No, no!" Omri said. "Run!"

The vehicle, a pickup truck, crested the rise and hit the flat straightaway, its headlights filtering through the rain and lighting up the spot where Omri and the others had stoodseconds before. Just as the outer edge of the beam reached him, Omri skirted behind a large fir tree. The others, several feet away, hunched down and crowded together.

The truck seemed to slow down as it neared them.

"This is like a big Christmas tree the Christians have!" Daisy-Rain piped in.

"Sh-h-h!" Ruth warned, "Quiet, sweetie. Like when we play hide-and-seek."

Daisy-Rain put a finger to her lips. "Sh-h-h." Omri set her down.

Suddenly, a few yards to their left, a young deer ambled straight out of the woods and toward the road. It looked toward the headlights, froze for two or three seconds, then sprinted across the road.

Inside the truck, Tack barked wildly. Dan thought he'd spotted movement up ahead, and Tack proved it. He slowed, leaned forward, and peered through the rapid windshield wipers and rain. Tack stood with his front legs on the dashboard, stretching his neck to look past Dan and out the side window.

At first Dan thought he'd seen a person or two on the side of the road. He felt a quiver of excitement.

"What is it, boy?" he asked. "What'd we see? Was it Bunyan on foot for some reason?"

But then a deer—either a doe or yearling, he figured—glared at him, its eyes neon green in the headlights. That explained the movement.

Tack backed off the dash and turned to look at the deer, barked twice, and jumped back up to the dash. He growled, but his tail was windmilling, so he wasn't being aggressive or afraid.

"Is there something else, boy?" Dan asked. "If there is, it can't be Bunyan and the others. No deer would be hanging around humans."

He patted Tack and then the seat. "Sit back down, bud."

Tack hesitated, but he didn't budge.

"Sit!" Dan said. Tack obeyed.

Glancing at the substation in the darkness, he wondered when the line crew would make it here. It always seemed the Hope and Appleton areas were last on the priority list when power outages occurred.

He exhaled heavily, shrugged his shoulders, and drove on, his eyes keen on perhaps spotting a fallen tree or branch on the road or Bunyan's vehicle off to the side.

—∞—

"Phew! Close call," Ethan whispered.

"You never know who's friend or foe," Omri agreed, his arm still holding Daisy-Rain tightly.

"Just like during the Holocaust," Naomi said, wiping wetness from her eyes. "Some neighbors were saviors and some were enemies, who a week earlier, smiled and waved hello."

"I thought those days were over," Ruth said.

"Think again," Ethan said in a sour tone.

Omri simply shrugged. He, too, had once thought those days were over—with the major exception of the Middle East, where in most places Jews were open game year-round. But here in America? He thought of the couples whose homes flanked his own, of his colleagues who were generally supportive.

"Maybe we should walk parallel to the road, rather than *on* it," he suggested, "just in case more traffic comes along.

—~—

An hour later, Dan walked into the house. The toll on his body was like one of those all-nighters in college, exhausted but ready for the upcoming test, yet somehow wishing he had just gone to bed and slept so he could awaken alert.

Margaret was asleep on the couch, a Bible in her lap.

Dan hung his raincoat and hat on a wooden post behind the door and stepped into the living room. As he draped an afghan over Margaret, she woke up. Her eyes asked the question.

His answer: "I drove all the way to Route 17. Only living thing I saw was a deer out on Route 105. No word from Bunyan, I take it."

"None," Margaret answered, "but God has spoken to me. 'Let not your heart be troubled.'"

"'Ye believe in God; believe also in Me.'" Dan finished Jesus's words from John 14:1.

He bent down and kissed her on the forehead.

"You can do better," she said, touching her lips with a forefinger.

He planted a luxurious kiss and smiled faintly. "Just like our first time."

"Yes." The word was one of satisfaction.

"Honey, if I'm preaching this morning, I've got to get some sleep," he said.

"What if they arrive while we're in church?"

"*We* won't be in church. You stay here in case they show, but I have to be there. There's no stand-in to call at this point."

—∞—

Eight o'clock Sunday morning came and went. The electricity was still out. Margaret fed Dan a make-do breakfast—a turkey sandwich and milk—before sending him off to church.

Arms crossed, she peered out the kitchen window over the back yard, the pasture beyond, and toward the lake a couple of hundred yards away. She tried to fight off the fear about which the Lord had been ministering to her. For the umpteenth time, she looked at her watch.

Bunyan, where are you? Why don't you contact us—somehow? If not on the PGP phone, a burner cell phone, or carrier pigeon? Something.

Patience was one fruit God was always working in both Dan and her. Even after walking twenty years with the Lord, patience still seemed to be a puny fruit. She shrugged in disappointment at the thought.

Tack's sharp bark from the living room interrupted her thoughts. Footsteps sounded softly on the porch. Her heart did a flip, and she spun, hurrying across the kitchen and living room toward the door. Tack stood with his nose near the doorknob and lowered his front legs—the border collie side of him on the prowl for sheep or, in this case, something suspicious. He released a slow, throaty growl.

Margaret sidestepped and peeked out the livingroom window. A young woman, with a child in tow, was standing at her door.

The woman, tall and slim, appeared to be in her mid-thirties. Her pretty face was exotic. Jewish, perhaps? Her eyes betrayed a measure of fear. The child, a skinny little thing with curly black hair down over her shoulders, was about seven or eight, she guessed, judging her against the ages of schoolchildren she had taught. They both appeared out of breath and were bedraggled and drenched, their hair plastered to their necks. Their faces and clothes were filthy.

"Oh, my!" Margaret exclaimed. *Get them inside, then ask the necessary questions.* She opened the door and ushered them in.

She read a tentativeness in the young woman, as though tension, like a rope, was strung tightly.

"Can I help you?" she asked.

"I do hope so," the woman replied, an edge to her voice. She swept her eyes toward the door and gripped the girl's hand tightly, drawing the child close to her side. She seemed to suddenly remember something, then looked quizzically into Margaret's eyes and blurted, "Hineni."

Margaret was taken aback. Her cheeks quivered and she almost lost her breath,. Could this be two of Bunyan's charges? The woman before her had tensed, her eyes widened. No, it was supposed to be Omri Zohn and a married couple. Nevertheless, Margaret had to reply. "Brucha habaha."

The woman was hesitant. "Todah."

Margaret could almost feel her own eyes light up at the Hebrew. She responded, "Bavak hasha."

The young woman released a heavy sigh of relief. Her shoulders relaxed and her lips formed a half-smile.

"Mommy," the word was a song on the little girl's lips, "she speaks Jewish!"

The woman patted the child's head, "Yes, Daisy-Rain. Yes, she does." She looked up at Margaret. "We all prayed we had come to the right place."

"All?" Margaret asked.

"Yes, there are others," she replied. "Bunyan was taken into custody in the middle of the night, and we've been walking ever since."

"And being carried," Daisy-Rain murmured. "I hurt my ankle."

Margaret had lost her breath at the mention of Bunyan. Now she spoke. "Bunyan's in *custody?*"

"The Border Patrol almost caught us. They had him follow them in his vehicle. We don't know where."

Margaret gasped. Her hand flew to her mouth. "Oh, my."

Then she narrowed her eyes on the woman, "How did you find us?"

"That's the miracle!" she exclaimed. "Like the Jews escaping Egypt. Our GPS was broken so we first followed the fire from a blown substation, then continued in this direction—"

"Then we saw the flame!" Daisy-Rain said.

"Flame?" Startled, Margaret shook her head.

"Yes!" the little girl chirped excitedly. "Hangin' from the sky right over your roof!"

"Father God!" The words escaped Margaret's mouth before she could catch them. He *is* alive! He *is* moving! He *has* included them in His plans!

"Where are the others?" she asked.

The young woman glanced toward the doorway and pointed. "Out in the woods. There are three others, waiting to hear from us. Praying this is the house. Dr. Zohn was to come first, but he feared if this were not the house, you might recognize him, and we'd all be endangered."

"Omri! Of course!" All she and Dan had known from Bunyan was he was bringing three Jews, not who they were. "Well, usher them in, dear. Usher them in!"

The woman hurried to the door, opened wide, and waved toward the woods.

Out of a knot of fir trees, the three others sprang forward and rushed to the house.

"Omri!" Margaret exclaimed and ran to meet him, throwing her arms around his neck.

"Margaret," he said in a voice as soft as a ball of cotton, returning the embrace. "Praise His name."

At that moment, the child gasped and Margaret turned to see why. The porch light and others around the house flickered on.

"Hallelujah!" Margaret declared.

—w—

"I ask you today, 'Where is your refuge?'"

Dan Callahan was always surprised at how his voice boomed and reverberated through the sanctuary of Mid-Coast Community Church. *No need for a lavalier here.*

More than two hundred people packed into the little sanctuary, even on a morning when, Dan had learned, lightning had struck the major Maine mid-coast switch yard, sending the entire region into darkness.

Yet, all these people had scrambled to church this morning, probably with stomachs grumbling. He fought off pride, knowing this was God's doing. He'd taken the reins as interim pastor a few short months before, and today proved he'd found his true calling after a career as a Navy officer.

Stepping down from the podium, Dan ambled past the front pews. He pointed to the second row, to a middle-aged man dressed in a plaid shirt and khakis. "Sam, where's your refuge?"

"My camp," Sam Philbert replied without hesitation.

Dan laughed. "Yes, and your bass-fishing boat with the three-hundred-horsepower motor."

"Yep," Sam said with a nod. A din of knowing chuckles filled the sanctuary.

Dan pointed to an older fellow who owned the region's best-known lumberyard. "And you, Carl, where's your refuge?"

"Anywhere I can get away from the phone," Carl Lawford said with amusement.

Dan smiled and swept a hand through his silver hair, then walked back the other direction. Then he pointed to a pretty young woman three rows back, her young daughter at her side. "Tina," he asked, "where's your refuge?"

Tina Belvoire hesitated, looked at her hands for a few moments, then up at Dan. "Well, pastor, I'd rather answer my refuge is my husband, Des, when he's not deployed with his Army Reserve unit to some other part of the world. When he's home, he's my refuge.

Dan stood up straight. "Aha. Then, perhaps my question should be, *Who* is your refuge?"

The ringing of Mel and Hannah Epstein's front doorbell was urgent, relentless. Mel looked up from his newspaper with pleading eyes.

Hannah, whisking eggs in a bowl for an omelet, shot him an exasperated look. "Okay, darling, I'll get the door. I have nothing better to do."

He nodded a thank-you. This was a serious story he was reading. The article revealed his old company had decided to cut ties with Israel, a connection Mel thought he'd made concrete before retiring just four months ago. He slapped at the newspaper, for the moment wishing the paper were the head of one Steven Foster, the company president. Why build a mechanical engineering firm into an international corporation just to pull the company apart?

Noises from the front door interrupted his thoughts. Men's voices. Hannah's panicked response.

Mel jumped from his seat and hurried down the hall.

"What is it?" he called. Eyeing two men in black suits, white shirts, and almost matching dark-blue ties, Mel shared a bit of his wife's fright. FBI, NSA, Homeland Security. Whatever they were, this was not good.

Dan's eyes scanned the congregation, "Okay, beloved, *who* is your refuge?"

"Jesus," was the resounding response, even from Tina. Dan refocused on the young mother. "Then, child of the almighty God, when Des is on duty, or when he's at home, you have an even greater refuge, eh?"

Tina smiled, nodded, and wiped away a tear.

Dan stepped back to the podium and grasped his Bible. "Our examples are everywhere, folks, from Genesis to Revelation, from the Old Testament to the New, from God's heritage people the Jews to God's church, Jew and Gentile alike."

There were murmurs of agreement.

—ɯ—

"What's this?" Mel Epstein asked, straightening himself to his full five-foot-eight.

The taller and broader of the two men, an African-American, smiled and held up a badge. "Homeland Security, Mr. Epstein. I'm Agent Black. This is Agent White."

Mel nodded to White, a thin blond-haired thirtyish fellow, and chuckled. "You must get a lot of jokes about that."

The men frowned as if they didn't catch the reference.

Then White said in a menacing tone Mel gauged as too severe for his poor attempt at humor, "We're here on serious business, sir. You might want to keep that in mind."

"We're sorry, officers—er, agents." Hannah looked at Mel with a twist to her mouth he knew meant, *Don't go getting us in trouble, mister.*

"What is it you want?" Mel asked.

"So," Dan said, "Old Testament or New, Jew or Gentile, man or woman, elderly or child—if I'm a believer in the Lord, then He's my refuge, my strong tower, my cornerstone, my protector, my provider—all I could possibly want for comfort and more."

Dan again stepped down to the level of his congregation.

"Another question, friends. Who are we to imitate?"

"Jesus," many people answered. "God," others replied.

"Uh-huh. So then, if He's to be a refuge for us, we're to be a refuge for others?"

Some people nodded agreement. Others were mulling over the question.

"Yes, sometimes physically, sometimes spiritually, but always a refuge," Dan said. "But how?"

He scanned the church, but no one answered, so he continued, "By possessing the love *of* God and love *for* God. If we love Him, we will do as He says, to love Him and to love each other as ourselves. We'll love the apple of His eye—the Jewish people. We'll love the sinner but not the sin. And, always, we'll love our fellow believers in Christ."

Dan looked at a friend and deacon, Hank Moran, hoping for a smile of encouragement. Hank gave him the first, and thereby the second.

—∾—

"We came by yesterday, but you weren't home," Black said. "You're friends with Dr. Omri Zohn."

Mel considered this a declarative sentence. Neutral. Non-aggressive. Non-accusatory. A simple statement. Said by another, it might even be construed as a positive vibe, as if "You know my buddy, Omri. Great!"

Mel peered at the man. Black knew the game; he'd played it before. But Mel had, too. In fact, based on what was called the Voila Jones Calculation, his engineering and software firm had helped develop instruments advancing the science of facial statement recognition, perfecting the biometric identifiers using a person's face, noses, eyes, mouth, and upper body. Used along with a person's articulations, this behavior matrix could predict their emotions and actions.

Black's face, his stance, the obvious subdermal tension were all a book. In his case, the book was all so obvious it could be a primer for beginners. Little nuance here except for the verbal expression, which was probably a practiced art by a veteran interrogator.

Black was on a hunt. An intense one. He was under immense pressure. If he succeeded, he would gain great honor and, perhaps, a promotion. His wife would applaud him. His children would be full of pride. If he failed, he'd be dropped down the totem pole of agentdom. No promotion. No honors. No applauding wife or bursting-with-pride kids.

Mel looked at White. He was along for the ride, learning, not expecting anything, really. Perhaps his brain was only half-engaged because he couldn't be a flunky and work for Homeland Security. Could he?

Dan picked up the pace. "I think believers all have an assignment in our lives. The general assignment is for each of us to be a refuge. The specific assignment is to be a refuge for whomever God gives us a heart."

Dan again stepped up to the lectern and pulled a newspaper from a shelf underneath. Holding it high, he said, "Did you read Saturday's article and photograph, on page A-five, about the synagogue in Portland being spray-painted with Nazi symbols?"

A few nodded.

"Why did this happen Friday?"

Congregants were in rapt attention. Someone in the back spoke: "Anti-Semitism."

"Yes," Dan said. "Anti-Semitism emboldened by the United Nations Resolution calling for an end to emigration to Israel, and the United States acquiescing to that demand. In response, some of God's church may be called to be a refuge to the Jews, much like Corrie ten Boom's family and others who endangered their own lives protecting Jews from the Nazis."

Dan drew a deep breath, stepped back up to the podium, set aside the newspaper and opened his Bible.

"Now stay with me here." Dan didn't want to confuse the issue. "Isaiah chapter fifty-eight tells us the fast God wants us to do is one done in humility, to loose the bonds of wickedness, to undo the bands of the yoke, to let the oppressed go free, to divide our bread with the hungry, and bring the homeless poor into our house, to cover the naked. He says, 'Then shall your light break forth like the morning and your healing shall spring forth speedily; your righteousness shall go before you, and the glory of the Lord shall be your rear guard.'"

Mel contemplated the situation. Omri was escaping; this much was sure. Black and White—with the president's blessing—wanted to catch him; this, too, was sure. Omri was one of the most kind-hearted men Mel had ever met, and he knew Hannah felt the same. She'd back him up.

These men? They didn't radiate compassion. They were giving sincerity their best shot, but even if that were true, sincerity wasn't necessarily a good trait. You could earnestly want to break someone's knuckles. You could honestly want to capture a Nobel Prize winner, a man who was national treasure for two countries. You could sincerely want to burnish your own star by spoiling the dreams of another.

In a world covering right and wrong with various shades of gray, this decision wasn't even close. Omri versus the government—

indeed, a government with the will to essentially build jail bars around Mel, Hannah, and every other Jew in America? No contest.

Agent Black stepped forward, looming over Mel and Hannah. "Dr. Zohn's not at home. We're sure you can tell us how to find him," he said.

Outward and obvious intimidation—like visitors' chairs being lower than the boss's. A non-starter.

"He said something about going to a beach for the weekend," Mel said. Hannah didn't budge—not a frown or a forehead wrinkle. Good girl!

"We've got men canvassing the beaches and hotels."

"Well, good then. I'm sure you'll find him." Mel stepped around White, extending his arm toward the door to lead them out.

Black and White didn't budge.

"Are you?" Black asked. "Are you sure?"

Mel was nonplussed. "I'm sure of this," he said. "If he wants you to find him, you will. If he's supposed to be found, he will be."

Black and White both frowned, questioning.

"Simple fact," Mel said. "If the Lord wants something hidden to be revealed, it will be. Rest assured, gentlemen, if your task is a righteous one, you'll fulfill your job. If not, well—"

Again, Mel motioned for the men to leave.

Black and White didn't budge.

This time White broke the moment. "Impeding a federal investigation is breaking the law. We could arrest you here and now."

"Listen here!" Hannah broke in. "Dr. Zohn's wife, Adina, was perhaps my best friend. Their children were close to our children, all their growing-up years. Even if we could help you, we wouldn't."

Hannah hesitated, then bristled, "Do what you need to do."

My Hannah! As she sidled up next to him, Mel wrapped an arm around her shoulders and drew her to him, hip to hip. His Hannah was not about to be bullied by these men. He knew she wouldn't allow her friends' names to be sullied without her protestations.

"I warn you, Mrs. Epstein," Black said, "if we discover—"

"This is our home, not some police interrogation room," Mel interjected. "If you discover anything and want to talk further, be certain to contact our lawyer."

He grabbed a pen and slip of paper from the telephone table next to him and wrote on it. "Here's his name and number." He handed the paper to Agent Black.

—~—

Dan looked up from the Bible. "This is a fasting time, I believe. A fasting time for your calling from God. A time to get your assignment. As the Lord is a refuge for you, what kind of refuge will you be to others? The world is white for harvest. People cry out for a roof over their heads, a comfortable bed to sleep in, a hot meal to fill their stomachs, even protection from evil governments—whether global or local. The bottom line in all these cases is for believers to be that refuge, then lead the lost under their shelter to the Great Refuge, Almighty God, Jehovah tsidkenu—the Lord our righteousness—Jehovah shalom—the Lord our peace."

Stepping out from behind the lectern and then down to their level again, Dan asked, "So, beloved, who is your refuge?"

"Jesus!" many called out.

"And what are you to be?"

"A refuge!"

"Then," he said, "do the prayer and fasting, take time to listen to His still small voice, discover your calling and assignment, and in doing all this, the Lord will watch over you this week. Go in peace but be watchful. Your time of being a refuge might be soon!"

Dan walked up the middle aisle to the entrance of the church to shake the hands of his brothers and sisters in Christ.

Chapter Eight

1:12 a.m. Sunday

At the moment Dan gave his charge to the congregation, Bunyan Jackson sat in an interrogation room at the Department of Homeland Security's Portland headquarters. He had been transported the one-hour drive south just after sunrise. The room smelled like Clorox. Surprising, since he'd always thought these places would smell like a locker room. He calmly intertwined the fingers of his huge hands.

"Jacko." A tall, thin black man in his thirties, entered the room. "I'm Agent Dennis Owen with Homeland Security."

Bunyan nodded acknowledgement.

Owen strode to the eight-foot-long table and took a seat opposite Bunyan.

"I cheered for you as a kid. I've been a Red Sox fan since I can remember. You were my Dad's favorite ballplayer."

This is a good start.

"I remember going to Fenway Park with Dad and Mom and seeing you hit a grand slam against the Yankees. Ha! Bottom of the ninth with two out and the Yankees ahead by three runs."

A really good start. Bunyan tilted his head and replied, "Yeah, I remember the game well."

"Yep, you brought Red Sox Nation a lot of great memories. Black men like my Daddy and me, someone to cheer on. Heck, I played first base 'cause of you."

Better and better. "Thanks."

Owen leaned far forward over the table, paused a moment, and then hollered in Bunyan's face, "So what are you doing helping Jews escape from this country!"

The man's fury shocked Bunyan back in his seat. Momentarily flustered, Bunyan thought, *Take a step out of the batter's box and take two deep breaths.* He did and it helped. He responded simply, "What do you mean, 'helping Jews escape'?"

"The DS game in your back seat, *Jacko*. You told the Border Patrol officer the device was your granddaughter's."

Bunyan stared at Owen. *All of a sudden this doesn't look like it's going to go well.*

"Fingerprints on that game match those of a girl named Daisy-Rain Remini. She's listed in the National Registry of Children in case she became lost or kidnapped."

Bunyan nodded.

"Kidnapped any little girls lately, Jacko?"

Bunyan shook his head.

"Find any lost girls lately?"

"No." Bunyan tried to look dumbfounded.

"So you'd be surprised to find out her father, Stanley Remini, has been in Israel on a business trip for two weeks now?"

"Don't know him." No lie there.

"When we discovered who those prints belonged to, we had officers check their home. Guess what, Jacko. Both the girl and her mother, Ruth, haven't been home since Friday morning."

"Uh-huh." Bunyan stretched out the two syllables. *I wonder if I could pass a lie-detector test on this one?*

"You know we have eyes and ears everywhere, Jacko. A matter of time—and probably very little of that, maybe minutes—before we can literally get a back-timed photo of them getting into your SUV."

Bunyan frowned, then stopped himself from doing so. *Gotta hide my feelings.*

"Were they alone in your back seat?"

"Listen, son, perhaps this girl you're looking for—Maisy May—is a friend of my granddaughter, Regina."

"First of all, it's Agent Owen. Second, it's Daisy-Rain. But you know that. Besides, your daughter and her husband and daughter live in Port Saint Lucie, Florida. The Reminis are from Albany, New York. Not quite the same neighborhood."

"Ah-h."

"Spill the info now, or the charges against you can be odious," Owen said.

"No info to spill, Agent Owen." Bunyan looked down at his hands and twirled this thumbs.

"Sometimes I wish we lived in the days of the rack." Owen spit out the words, then stood up abruptly. "I've had enough for now. Enjoy your day in the tiny little cell we've prepared for you."

"Don't I get a call to my lawyer?"

"No. We can hold you like this for twenty-four hours."

Bunyan checked his watch. "I've been under your control since about one-thirty this morning. So there's a bit of time left."

Owen straightened his back. "By then, we'll have gotten to the bottom of this. I hope we don't find out you've gone from hero to villain—Jacko."

Bunyan knit his forehead. "Do you really think people helping Jews leave the country are villains, Agent Owen?"

"More than villains, I think they're traitors."

"Traitors?" That threw Bunyan a bit. "Traitors for thinking Jews should be allowed to return to their homeland—the one place on this earth God set aside for them?"

"Sir," Owen's hands clenched the back of his chair, "I believe laws are made to be obeyed, not broken. First, none of us, no one, can leave this country and take our fortune with us. Second, the United States, in fact the United Nations, says there shall be no more Jewish emigration, from anywhere, into Israel."

"A decision you feel is righteous?" Bunyan pressed.

"Righteous?" Owen appeared confounded. "The law." Owen turned toward the door.

"Before you leave, Agent Owen, I have a question for you."

"Yeah?"

"Are you descended from slaves?"

"What's it matter?"

"Oh, something to ponder in regard to this whole Jewish thing."

Owen scowled, then stomped from the room.

He was in charge of the manhunt for Omri Zohn, and Joseph Conrad was used to success. Failure was for horseshoe players and college flunk-outs.

Conrad stood in the DHS Boston headquarters, seething at this "Jewish thing." He'd had to give away two tickets to the Washington Nationals game this afternoon, but he was glad for this—if he played things right, this particular challenge might lead to a career boost.

Conrad, who looked like Bruce Willis's twin, was known as brash, bold, cocky, and an all-around menace to those who didn't do as they were told. Stand in his way; watch out! His mouth twitched as he thought about Zohn. He'd find the good doctor.

This guy Webster from the Department of Energy? "Inept" was Conrad's description. Nor did the agents dispatched by Constantine have a clue. *Black and White seemed to be red all over*, he mused, chuckling at his wit. This was his mission, though he did need other feet on the ground. A man could get pretty far between leaving work on Friday and this morning.

Conrad picked up a photograph of the distinguished-looking, fifty-eight-year-old man with a Van Dyke beard and thought through the scientist's case file. Zohn, a widower, had a son and daughter-in-law who had emigrated to Israel a year ago with his grandson. *All the more reason for Zohn to want to escape.*

"We'll see about that, Doctor," he said, thinking of the accolades awaiting him when he caught the physicist. "Don't make any bets. This is my casino, and I'm holding the cards."

Conrad phoned his lieutenant, Nat Wallace. When Wallace's tired face appeared on the video-phone, Conrad said, "Fill me in."

Wallace yawned before speaking. "We've clamped down, sir. We've got people watching all transportation. Airlines, charter flights, private planes, subways, railroads, cars, taxis, buses, ships, yachts, you name it. People in the field are interviewing Zohn's colleagues, members of his synagogue. His face is plastered on every watchlist. We've examined his emails, tweets, text messages, phone records, and we're scouring his computers for personal contacts, plans, website visits, any clues at all. So far, no luck, but I *expect* we'll catch him."

"Strike the word expect from your dictionary, Wallace."

"Yes, sir. We *will* catch him."

"Get a couple of hours sleep, but only a couple. I suspect Zohn is fast-tracking out of the country, and I want his hide on my wall."

"Like the rhino from your safari. I get it, sir."

In an adjacent room, agent Russell Bedard, in control of aerial and satellite surveillance, was speaking to the agent in charge of the drone airplanes patrolling the United States/Canada border.

"Maine and New Brunswick, Denise. Pay full attention there. Canada didn't sign onto the UN Resolution, so my money's on that being Zohn's escape route, and I want our team to be the one catching him. A lot's at stake keeping this man in America."

Denise Richards smiled. Bedard liked her expression. The look foretold an optimistic response.

"I think I may have just discovered a breakthrough, sir," Richards said.

Bedard's eyebrow rose. "Y-yes?"

"I back-timed satellite imagery to late Friday afternoon—on Dr. Zohn's house."

She had Bedard's full attention. She pulled up the image on one of three monitors before her.

"We have Zohn leaving his house about five-forty, talking to a man, apparently a neighbor, and walking off, leaving his car behind."

Bedard stepped quickly to Richards' desk and stared at the screen. "Could you track where he went?"

Richards' face lit up. "He took a local bus."

"And?"

"A North End bus. One of the stops is Faneuil Hall, which is near North Station. All sorts of trains are coming and going from there—all of them to the north shore of Boston, or New Hampshire or Maine."

Bedard opened the palms of his hands in a questioning manner.

"He must've paid cash."

"Maine," Bedard said. "He went to Maine."

Richards typed on her keyboard and the North Station train schedule appeared on a monitor to her left. "Amtrak had trains departing for Portland at six-forty-five and eleven-thirty. At the time he would have gotten off the bus, he could have made the six-forty-five Downeaster to Portland."

Bedard called out to Conrad, "Hey, Joe, check this out!"

Conrad hurried to Richards' computer monitor, then ordered, "Get feet on the ground in Portland, armed with photos of Zohn. Then check security cameras, satellite, whatever you can for that arrival in Portland, Russell."

"Maine's a big state," Richards said.

"Right, but we've narrowed Zohn down from the entire United States," Bedard said.

Conrad took a step toward the door. "Call me when you have news."

Bedard turned to leave, and Richards hunkered down at her computer. He knew she loved this stuff. Loved the game.

—∞—

Shandra Constantine's phone rang. "Speak," she answered, curt and to-the-point, making obvious to anyone she wasn't to be disturbed with anything trivial.

"Conrad here, ma'am. We believe Zohn boarded a train to Maine after leaving his home early Friday evening."

Constantine's eyes widened and her lips curled. This could be a short hunt. Then she frowned. Maine was a big and rugged state, but she had the power to shut her down. She smiled again. Shut—her—down.

—∞—

Dan stopped his truck in the driveway and stepped out. Taking a couple of steps toward the front porch, he felt his spine tingle—not a scary prickle, but an expectant excitement.

Are they here, Lord? He glanced around the yard. Nothing. Around the woods. Nothing. He took a tentative step toward the house, then strode deliberately to the door, his heartbeat quickening.

As Dan stepped inside the house, he was taken aback. Omri, looking oddly much younger than the last time they met, another man, and two women sat in his living room—but no Bunyan. Everyone stood and Margaret walked toward him, looking calm and collected.

Tack lay at Omri's feet, the hair on the back of his neck smooth, not bristled. A good sign.

"Good news and bad," Margaret said. A mixture of cheerfulness and concern filled her face. "Our fish are here, plus two, but we think Bunyan's in custody, and we still haven't heard from him. In fact, they all just arrived on foot, because Bunyan was taken away in his car."

Dan bit his lip. "I see."

Omri stepped forward, extending a hand. Dan walked through the handshake and hugged him. "Glad to see you again, Omri. If only the circumstances weren't so ominous."

"Ominous, yes," Omri said. "We're very troubled about Bunyan."

Dan looked around. "Who are your friends?"

"Well, let me introduce my fellow outlaws," Omri said. He introduced the others, adding, "And Ruth's little girl is upstairs asleep."

Dan narrowed his gaze on Omri. "They certainly don't want *you* leaving the country."

"Certainly not," Omri agreed, "but I must, I must—before it's too late, before I'm in a barless prison from which I cannot escape. My son and his family are there. My brother is dying from cancer."

"I'm so sorry," Dan said.

Omri shook his head, "We just discovered this."

"Can't you get a travel exemption?"

Omri shook his head. "They feel I'm indispensable, but there are others here in America who know my work nearly as well as I do and can carry on. Honestly, the powers in control may not believe this, but America and her nuclear-fusion research will do fine without me. Brilliant minds have surrounded me."

Omri's so Jewish, a blind person could pick him out of a lineup by his accent and a deaf person by his appearance.

He turned to the others. "Of course, they don't want *any* of you leaving for Israel—either with your wealth or brain power."

Margaret squeezed his elbow. "Everyone's been able to take a nice hot shower, and I was able to find clothes to fit them all. They were dirty and drenched from walking the woods in the storm." Her eyebrows rose and fell. "I've got chicken pot pies in the oven, but they won't be ready for another half-hour. Let me get everyone some coffee and tea."

Dan removed his suitcoat and pointed to Tack. "Appears everyone's met Tack, and he especially approves of you, Omri."

Omri shrugged.

Turning to his wife, Dan said, "Let me help you with the coffee and tea, Maggie." He followed her to the kitchen. Tack stayed behind, obviously relishing the attention as hands scratched his neck and shook his paw.

In the kitchen, Dan reached for mugs while Margaret placed tea cups on saucers and removed tea bags from a tin container.

"The time's finally here," Dan said.

Margaret turned and faced him. "Yes, darling. We're living the aliyah."

The simple reply was filled with years of meaning, marking a point they both sometimes doubted would come before they died. Her reaction covered so much, especially a thankfulness to God for ending such a prolonged and often painful period of waiting.

For a number of years, God's "fishermen" had helped the Jewish people leave Russia and Eastern Europe, in particular, to emigrate to Israel. And who could forget their dramatic departure from Ethiopia? But now it appeared Jews were "in season" for the "hunters."

The kitchen door opened. Dan turned to see Ruth, a pretty young woman, enter.

"Can I lend a hand?" she asked.

"Of course, dear," Margaret said. "Come help with the tea tray while Dan carries in the coffee. I'll bring shortbread cookies for now and, in a few minutes, the chicken pot pie. You must all be famished."

"We sure are."

"Why are we flemished, Mommy?"

Dan and the women turned to see the child in the doorway. They chuckled at the sight of her little head bent in a questioning pose.

"Famished, sweetheart," Ruth explained. "It means hungry—and, young lady, yours wasn't much of a nap."

"Oh, I couldn't sleep. My tummy and my leg both feel empty."

"Your leg?" Dan asked.

"Yes." The girl's lips squeezed tightly together as she pointed to her right leg. "Daddy says it's hollow."

Ruth smiled. "Her daddy thinks his darlin' eats a lot for her size."

"Says I'm a little juggernut 'n need food for energy," Daisy-Rain said.

"This," Ruth said, looking at Dan, "is Daisy-Rain, and she surely is *sometimes* a little nutty but *always* a little juggernaut. Sweetheart, say hello to Mr. Callahan—"

"Dan, please."

Daisy-Rain reached up to shake Dan's hand and pointed to Margaret. "If she's Bubbe, you must be Zayde."

Dan recognized the Hebrew word for grandfather.

"Sure am," he said, "and as such, I think I should get a hug rather than a handshake, don't you?"

Daisy-Rain grinned and reached her arms up to his.

Margaret delivered the coffee and tea while Dan went to his den and pulled his PGP mobile phone out of a bottom drawer of his desk. He called Frank Reid, but again got no answer.

Dan emerged from the den, shaking his head.

"No luck?" Margaret asked.

"None." Dan looked at Omri, then the others, "We can't take you to your final destination until I reach him, and he's been unreachable since Bunyan called early Friday morning. You'll have to stay here until he contacts us."

Omri shrugged. "What must be, must be."

An hour later, their stomachs full, Ruth and Naomi helped Margaret in the two spare bedrooms upstairs, setting up three cots for the women and Daisy-Rain in one room and two for the men in another—cots they had bought in anticipation of this moment.

Downstairs, the men rested on a couch and chairs.

"I'm worried about Bunyan," Dan said.

"Me, too," Omri said.

"If Border Patrol or Homeland Security has released him, he would have contacted us by now. I'm going to check," Dan said.

He straightened up and walked down the stairway to the den and turned on his computer. While waiting for it to fire up, he opened the bottom lefthand drawer of his desk, lifted out a ream of paper, and picked up a "burner" cell phone kept charged by a hidden wire that ran through a hole in the back of the desk to a wall outlet.

No message.

When the monitor to his computer flashed on, he tapped on the email icon. Several emails, but none from Bunyan. Nothing with satellite, nothing with cell, and nothing with encrypted emails. Zero for three. A strikeout.

Now Dan was really anxious. He dialed the first three digits of Bunyan's secret cellular phone, then thought better. If Bunyan were indeed in the hands of the authorities, he didn't want his own call to be traced or triangulated back to their house.

Dan thought about his options, then prayed for God to protect their friend. He put the phone back in the drawer, returned the ream of paper, and closed the drawer.

When the women had finished upstairs, they joined Omri and Ethan in the living room.

Margaret looked at Ruth and Naomi, seeing their fatigue. "You two must be exhausted."

Naomi smiled and said, "Tired, but clean—"

"And smelling good, too," Ruth added. "Thank you so much, Margaret."

Just then Daisy-Rain raced into the room. She headed straight to Margaret and gave her a hug. "I love my dress, Bubbe." She backed away and twirled, holding up the hem of the garment in her right hand.

Margaret beamed. "It does fit perfectly, doesn't it, sweetheart? And it looks so pretty on you, matching your green eyes."

Daisy-Rain's face shined with delight. Tack wiggled up to her and barked as if to say he concurred.

Omri looked about him at the Callahan's comfortable home and property. He considered how much Dan and Margaret were risking—possible jail time and who knew what else—by helping him and the others escape.

Rising from his chair, he said, "We can't tell you folks how much we appreciate your help and the danger you're facing for hiding us."

Dan waved him off. "We've been praying to God to use us to help His people … when the time came. And here you are. You've come. This situation is actually an answer to *our* prayers."

"You're our Esther," Omri said.

"There are a lot of Esthers around the country right now," Margaret said.

He wondered. Were there really? How many people around America were helping Jews in their plight? How many were speaking up for them? Not the president. Not the majority of Congress. Were his friends at MIT a good sampling of the support out there, or not?

"You could tell me something, Omri," Margaret said.

"Anything."

"There's a lot of commotion about your work, but I don't really understand it."

"I'd love to hear too," Ruth said.

Omri grinned. He loved this stuff and had never minded an audience, as his beloved wife had pointed out on more than a few occasions.

"My favorite topic, but the explanation would certainly bore people to sleep," he said.

"No, no," Margaret said. "I'd love to hear. I may not understand, but I'll try to hang in there."

The others agreed.

Omri smiled and settled back. "My background is in nuclear engineering. First in Israel, then my wife (God bless her memory) and I moved here when we were both very young. I was right out of Hebrew University and came to America with a teaching fellowship to get my PhD at MIT. I've been working on this research ever since. The US Department of Energy and US Defense Advanced Research Projects Agency got wind of what I was doing and awarded me research grants to further pursue it even while I continued teaching at MIT."

"And this 'it'?" Margaret asked.

Omri rubbed his hands together. He missed his whiteboard. Heck, he missed his blackboard. "This 'it,' Margaret … This 'it' is sonofusion."

Ruth tried to pronounce the word.

"No, it's *so-no-fusion*," Omri corrected, "using sound waves to produce nuclear-fusion reactions."

"My team and I have actually developed an inexpensive tabletop device that accomplishes this."

"But nuclear-fusion reactors have historically required large, multibillion-dollar chambers," Dan said.

"Historically, yes, but my little tabletop creation—I call her Sunny—can be built at a tiny fraction of that cost. Tiny. Sunny generates nuclear reactions by creating tiny bubbles that implode with tremendous force."

They all sat on the edges of their chairs.

"The magnitude of this discovery is enormous. For the first time in history, we're able to use simple mechanical force to initiate conditions comparable to the interiors of stars."

"That is over the top!" Dan exclaimed. "Think of the clean energy!"

Omri lit up. "Oh, clean energy's only one result. Think about this in terms of security, or immensely strong materials, or investigation of deep space. We've been exploring ways to create a new class of low-cost, compact detectors for security applications that use neutrons to probe the contents of suitcases. A colleague is working to build a prototype machine to cheaply manufacture new synthetic materials and efficiently produce tritium, which is used for applications ranging from medical imaging to watch dials. And a friend at the University of Colorado is using this research to develop a new technique to study various phenomena in cosmology, including the workings of neutron stars and black holes."

"You say this sonofusion is desktop size?" Margaret asked.

"Amazing, eh?" Omri put his hand on Dan's mug of coffee. "May I?"

"Sure, just don't burn yourself." Dan smiled.

Omri placed Dan's mug atop his own. "Sunny's a clear glass canister about this height. Inside the canister is a liquid called deuterated acetone, which contains heavy hydrogen. The acetone is bombarded with a specific frequency of ultrasound that causes cavities to form into bubbles that are about sixty nanometers—or billionths of a meter—in diameter. That's billionths, with a *b*."

Appreciative nods passed around the room.

"The bubbles expand to a size large enough to be seen with the naked eye," he continued. "Then, within nanoseconds, these bubbles contract with tremendous force, returning to roughly their original size. The reaction releases flashes of light. Their contraction causes extreme temperatures and pressures comparable to those found in the interiors of stars.

"We estimate temperatures inside the imploding bubbles reach ten million degrees Celsius and pressures comparable to one billion earth atmospheres at sea level.

"At this point, deuterium atoms fuse together the same way hydrogen atoms fuse in stars, releasing neutrons and energy in the process. A major positive with Sunny is, whereas conventional nuclear-fission reactors produce waste products taking thousands of years to decay, ours will decay to non-dangerous levels in a decade or two."

A collective breath escaped those listening. Omri handed Dan his mug.

"And because of your knowledge in this research, the government will especially want to prevent you from leaving the country," Margaret concluded.

Omri nodded, then added: "But I have several colleagues around the country who can carry on my research without missing a heartbeat. Well, maybe one or two heartbeats."

Omri motioned toward Ethan. "But you must know about our friend here and his research. More fascinating than my work."

"Sounds impossible." Dan looked at Ethan.

"The good doctor exaggerates," Ethan said with a shrug.

"No-no," Omri objected. "Tell them, Ethan. Tell them."

Joseph Conrad stepped back into the office he'd commandeered, holding a mug of coffee in one hand and a thick folder in the other. He checked his watch and read aloud, "Twelve-o-five." He sighed deeply.

Agent Denise Richards, who had traveled with him from DC to Boston, spotted him and jumped from her chair. "Sir! Sir!" she called.

Conrad turned toward her. "Yes?"

"Ninety percent sure Zohn's in Maine."

A chill of exhilaration ran up his spine. The hunt!

"Security cameras caught him getting off an Amtrak in Portland. "He's disguised to look younger, but we've got a near-certain ID. He walked out of range of the cameras, but we spotted a black Escalade leaving the lot shortly afterward."

"Got the license?" Conrad asked excitedly.

"License number 317-502. Owned by a Bunyan Jackson of Cape Elizabeth."

Conrad snorted. "Of course. Jacko, three-seventeen lifetime batting average, five hundred and some-odd home runs, a Hall of Famer despite a bad back ending his career early. Now he's turned 'aider and abeter.' Whaddya say?"

"I say we make up for OJ getting freed."

"Where'd they go from the Amtrak station?"

"I've got them driving through Portland and over a bridge to South Portland, but once they leave the city, we lose them."

"What about satellite?"

"It was a 'burp' time when they left so one satellite had just gone overhead minutes before and another didn't fly over for three minutes."

"Put out an APB for that Escalade, code red."

"Yes, sir."

Conrad quick-stepped to his office and speed dialed the Portland DHS. *Ah-h, satisfaction. Just like a good cup o' Joe.*

Dan picked up two casserole dishes of chicken pot pie, while Margaret carried a large basket of hot biscuits. Omri opened the door from the dining room for them. The rest were still upstairs.

"Do we go to New Brunswick from our next 'station'?" Omri asked.

"Not with Homeland Security and the Border Patrol as vigilant as they are now. No, the coast is your last stop in America."

"You'll leave from the pier of a friend of ours," Margaret said.

"That is, we hope so. We've been unable to contact him." Dan looked at Omri and the others and added, "We only know one or two contacts bringing you here, one or two contacts to take you to. The extent of our knowledge—"

"In case someone gets caught," Margaret interjected.

Dan nodded. "If Bunyan's in custody, or otherwise out of the mix, our one remaining contact bringing people here will be one other couple."

"But—" Margaret began, but was interrupted by the back door swinging open. Davey entered the kitchen like a whirlwind.

"Bubbe! Grampa!"

"I thought you were having lunch with Alec and his folks," Dan said.

Davey waved toward the door and said, "Alec, come on in."

Alec Staples stepped inside and bent down to pet Tack, who had run to the door to meet them.

Oh, no. Dan caught his breath. He considered his options, then turned to Omri and whispered, "You're an old colleague of mine from the Navy. I was a captain aboard the *USS Cauldron.* You're my old-time admiral."

Omri squinted at Dan. "With this accent?" he murmured.

Dan hesitated, then, "Yes, the American and Israeli Navies had a special high-level exchange program. Remember?"

"I'll try my best."

More complications. The Peter Principle was playing out. First, Congress. Then, the Border Patrol. Then, the storm. Now, Alec.

Dan tossed up a prayer. *So many wrinkles, Lord. You'll have to iron them all out!*

"I figured you'd be having chicken pot pie, and you know how much Alec loves it," Davey said to Margaret. "Don't mind, do you?"

Margaret cast a furtive look toward Dan. He glanced to the ceiling and then heard footsteps bounding down the stairs. They were all coming down for the meal.

Omri look at Dan with an unspoken question: *Do you trust this boy Alec into your confidence? Could their secret be kept?*

Dan nodded approval to Margaret and, after a pause, she answered, "No, of course not. We'd love for you to join us, Alec. I'll just set another place."

"Come on into the dining room, Alec," Dan said. "We've got other company too, Davey. A surprise visit from an old Navy pal of mine and his family."

—∾—

Omri hustled to the living room to inform his fellow escapees of Davey and Alec's presence and the ruse they had to pull off.

"You're all my family," he said. "Ethan and Naomi, you're my nephew and his wife; Ruth, you're my niece."

"How 'bout me?" Daisy-Rain said. "Who'm I?"

Omri chuckled. "Why, darling, you're your Mom's daughter, a role you play very well."

Daisy-Rain giggled, making all of them laugh.

"We're all here as a surprise visit on our way to the coast—say, Mount Desert Island."

"Mount Desert Island," Ethan repeated. "But can you pull off being an old Navy admiral?"

Omri smiled. "Well, I used to sail as a boy."

"Yeah?"

"Well, the biggest ship I ever commanded was an eighteen-foot Aussie skiff, and my ocean was Hachoola Lake in the north of Israel."

Ethan chuckled.

"Guess what we called her."

"What?" Naomi asked.

"*Escape*."

They all laughed except Daisy-Rain, who didn't fathom the discussion.

"Sweetheart," Ruth said, patting her head, "just be your beautiful self, but don't mention Daddy, okay? No mention of Daddy."

What was happening? Without warning, agents unlocked his cell and rushed Bunyan to the interrogation room. He hadn't slept but a few winks all morning, unable to fit his oversized body on a tiny cot. *Beds made for wee people*, yawning and rubbing his eyes as he sat waiting—for what, he didn't know.

The door flew upon, and Owen, a manila folder in hand, stomped into the room. He glowered at Bunyan.

Bunyan offered up a "Good morning."

Owen ignored the greeting. "My hero, my nemesis," he spat out, slamming the folder down on the table.

Bunyan stared at the folder and waited for Owen to continue. The hair on his neck bristled.

"Do you know a Doctor Omri Zohn?"

Bunyan hesitated. If only he'd had more time to plan this. What could have gone wrong? Ah, the pickup at the station.

"Well?" Owen asked again, impatiently.

"I know the name, of course." Bunyan looked down at his big brown hands and prayed silently. He prayed all five in his charge had reached Dan and Maggie's home safely. He prayed Dan and Maggie were working swiftly to move them on. He asked God to help him maintain self-control in this grilling and not let slip any harmful information.

"By name only? Never met the man?"

Bunyan pursed his lips and shook his head.

"You own a black Escalade, license number 317-502."

"Yes."

"Were you driving the vehicle Saturday?"

Bunyan shrugged. "I suppose. Where?"

"Jacko, do you know the sentence for harboring and abetting a fugitive?"

"What?"

"Dr. Zohn is a fugitive trying to escape the country."

"Escape? Was he in jail?"

"No."

"Then how can you say he's escaping?"

"We believe he's intent on going to Israel."

"So, the government's into mindreading now? You take a special course, did you?"

Owen glowered at him.

"Perhaps he's just on a trip, a vacation maybe," Bunyan offered.

"We've gone over the law, Jacko. Jews can not legally emigrate to Israel. They can't simply travel there because we don't know whether they might stay once they get there."

"Then if he's not in Israel, he hasn't broken the law, and he's not a fugitive, right?"

Owen's eyes flickered, but his expression revealed he was getting exasperated.

"Listen, if we discover someone's making a bomb with the intent to blow up a bridge, he's breaking the law even if he has yet to plant and detonate the bomb. Intent is the key. If you go to a post office with a rifle in your hand intending to kill people, such an act today is a criminal offense. Again, intent is the key. If you travel out of the country planning to go someplace unlawful for you to go, your intent makes you guilty."

"That seems a strange interpretation of the law. Again, you have to be able to read a person's mind."

"We read his actions!"

"But if I intend to hit a pitch out of the ballpark but swing and miss, my intent is meaningless."

Owen's chair screeched across the floor as he bolted to his feet. "You're wasting my time, Jacko. Cameras monitored Dr. Zohn leaving the Amtrak station in Portland and your Escalade leaving moments later. The Escalade drove to South Portland, where we lost track of it. Were you going to your home in Cape Elizabeth?"

"Did I say I was driving the Escalade then?"

Owen hesitated.

Bunyan took advantage of the moment. "You can't see the driver of my Escalade on that footage, can you? Listen, Agent Owen, I've got lots of friends, and I allow any and all of them to use my stuff. They're in and out of my house all the time. Hitting cages, golf holes, a croquet lawn. We have great fun. Sometimes they use one of my vehicles. I don't drive the Escalade much. For all I know, someone borrowed and returned the thing. I've got a four-car garage, and I don't always look to see what's there and what's not. My '67 Mustang convertible is actually my vehicle of choice in the summertime.

"Now," Bunyan continued, "since you don't know the driver of the car, I demand to be released. You've had me for thirty hours and with no phone call."

Owen stared at Bunyan. A bewildered look? Determined? Whatever, a scowl followed. Then Owen breathed heavily and asked, "What were you doing driving in the wilderness of Maine in the middle of the night?"

"Well, I wouldn't call mid-coast Maine a wilderness, but if you must know, I was intending to spend a couple days' vacation. I'd rather travel distances at nighttime because there's no traffic."

Owen's eyebrows raised, and his lips curled into a "gotcha" smile. "There was no luggage in the vehicle."

Got this covered, bub. "I travel light. And you know one of the nice things about being wealthy? Being able to buy clothing wherever you are. I do on occasion. Rockland, Belfast, Mount Desert, they have clothing stores. Check it out."

"You haven't been a smart aleck until now, Jacko. Don't test my geniality."

Darn. "Sorry, Agent Owen. This incarceration must be getting to me."

"This incarceration will be for a lot longer than a day if we find you're complicit in Dr. Zohn's escape—and the escape of this Ruth Remini and her daughter."

"There you go with again with this escape charge. May I go home now?"

"We're going to enhance those camera shots and find out who was behind the wheel, Jacko. Don't be leaving town on any more trips." Owen knocked on the door and a uniformed DHS officer responded.

Owen pointed a thumb at Bunyan and addressed the officer. "Process Mr. Jackson out of here, will you, Joe?

The Callahans had an overflowing dinner table. Seven of those people were nervous, struggling not to divulge any secret information.

Omri looked over the table and decided to get things rolling. Might as well commit full-throttle. Stifling his Israeli accent as best he could, he asked, "So, are you young men taking a couple of weeks off at the end of the summer before starting school?"

"Yes, sir," Davey said. "I'm going back for my senior year in high school in two weeks, and Alec here is off to college."

"Yeah, he's just a kid." Alec chuckled.

"Where're you going, Alec?" Ruth asked.

"Down in Massachusetts—at MIT."

Omri couldn't stop a guttural cough at the mention of his university. Everyone looked at him, and he sputtered, "Oh, my! A smart boy, then."

An embarrassed smile filled Alec's face.

"And your major? Have you decided?" Ethan asked.

"Well, I'm not exactly sure yet, but I think I want to be a physicist and work on nuclear fusion."

Oh, my! Omri lowered his head and considered feigning sickness in order to leave the room. The boy could very well recognize him. This might ruin the whole escape—for him and everyone else!

After a moment, he recuperated and said firmly, "Admirable, young man. Admirable."

Davey looked directly at Omri. "You're a real admiral, sir?"

Omri nodded.

"But your accent's foreign."

"I came to the US as a naval liaison from my country, and later became a citizen and joined the Navy."

Davey appeared to mull over the response, then asked, "Was Grampa a good captain?"

Omri looked at Dan, who winked back at him as if saying, "Weave your magic on this one."

"I think he must have been the very best, son."

"Didja sail the seven seas?" Daisy-Rain piped up. "Seven seas" seemed to trill off her tongue.

"You know about the seven seas?" Omri asked.

Daisy-Rain puffed up with pride.

"Well," Omri said, "I think between Dan and me, we've seen at least half the world."

"Did you see the southern half?" Davey asked.

"North, south, east, west. Oceans all have their own personalities, Davey." Omri looked at Dan as if suggesting the statement were true. He wanted to hand off the ball to a real Navy man.

Dan picked up on it. "Yes sir, they've all got their own character—calm, dangerous, spotty-on and iffy-off."

"All put in their place by the good Lord," Omri said.

"Ah, you're a Christian!" Davey exclaimed.

Oh, boy. Omri considered the question, sat back for a moment and looked directly into the boy's eyes. "Davey, the Lord God of Abraham, Isaac, and Jacob is my God." He looked at Dan. "He's yours, too, isn't he, Captain?"

Dan smiled and nodded.

"Please, everyone," Margaret interrupted. "Dig in and eat before the food gets cold."

Omri detected a hint of anxiety that too much talk of the Navy and old times might expose the hoax. He took the cue and dug in.

"Well, despite my wife's surety, I, for one, have a hard time believing in God—or a god," said Ethan.

Omri looked at his friend, not surprised but suddenly emboldened to speak to the issue. "I've never understood this about you—nephew," he said. "As an engineer, those you call 'fathers of your discipline' believed at least in a Grand Designer."

"Who would that be—uncle?" Ethan asked.

Omri envisioned himself as an actor on stage—a Shakesperean play, perhaps *Much Ado About Nothing* with an exposé on honor, shame, and politics. He gathered his thoughts. "Why, Sir Isaac Newton wrote a million words of theology. He clearly believed the Bible and the prophecies contained therein."

Ethan's brow furrowed, and Omri took advantage of the hesitation. "I have two others, and perhaps more closely related to your science, nephew."

Ethan shot him a questioning look.

"Polarization of light," Omri said, raising an eyebrow. "David Brewster and Augustin-Jean Fresnel."

"Really?" Ethan said.

Omri nodded, took a sip of sparkling water, and added, "*And* George Gabriel Stokes."

"Fluid mechanics," Ethan said.

"Again—correct. The list is long. In physics alone, the list of Christians includes Galileo, Philoponus, Bradwardine, Grosseteste, Faraday, Maxwell—"

"Okay, okay. I get the picture," Ethan said.

"I'd say!" Dan chimed in.

Omri shrugged. "I'm really surprised that some, like the late Carl Sagan, can look at the universe, which is so astounding, and not see the hand of an Intelligent Designer. Here is little earth, snuggled into a cozy spot, the one particular solar system where we have the best position in the universe from which to observe what is happening out there in the vast, explosive cosmos."

"All I have to do to believe in God," said Margaret, "is look at a nut on the ground and know that it could grow into a massive tree!"

"Just that!" Omri said.

Ethan shrugged, "I guess."

"You should *know*, my boy, and I believe you will—in God's time. In God's time—but sooner than later, eh?" He smiled.

—∞—

Lana Mancini fumbled with the plastic tie around the end of the loaf of bread. She couldn't keep her fingers from shaking. What was happening with Mr. Jackson? He'd been so vague when he and Dr. Zohn drove off. He just said he'd be back late this morning. And here it was, afternoon.

Had the authorities caught them? He should have, could have been home by now. Should she make arrangements for dinner? If so, for how many?

The doorbell snapped her to alert mode. She set the loaf down on the island countertop and walked quickly past the stairway and to the front entryway, a heavy solid-oak door with a stained-glass-type window in the center.

She opened the door, and a woman's hand pushed a badge in front of her face.

"Agent Morales," the woman said. "Homeland Security."

She pointed to her partner, a skinny, very tall redhead. "He's Agent Murdoch."

Lana stammered "Y-y-yes," then asked, "Are you looking for Mr. Jackson?"

"No, we have him in hand," Morales said.

"In hand?" This did not sound good.

"He's under interrogation down at the Portland headquarters."

"Interro—?"

"He's being questioned about his role in the plot."

"Plot?"

"The attempt to help Dr. Zohn get out of the country."

"Dr. Zohn?" Lana's spine was shaking right up to her neck. *This is a horrible thing!*

"You know Dr. Zohn, don't you, Ms. Mancini?"

Lana hesitated. How did they know her name?

"Don't you?" the woman repeated.

Lana tried to maintain control. Why not admit she at least knew him? "Why, yes," she managed.

"Saw him just yesterday, right?"

"Yesterday?" But Lana knew she could not admit this.

"*Ayer. No te hagas tonta,*" Morales said in fluent Spanish. "Don't play stupid with me."

The bright hallway around her shrunk to a confined space, and Lana hated confined spaces. Claustro-something-or-other, people said. The foyer ceiling, normally twelve feet high, dropped to just above her head. The walls once distant were tight to her shoulders.

Lana couldn't contain the shake in her voice. "No. Not yesterday. Not for several months, perhaps last year."

"Are you familiar with jail?" Morales said.

"Jail?"

"*Cárcel,*" the agent said, continuing in Spanish. "I'm sure you have them back in Ecuador. It's where they put criminals. Where we put people who impede our investigations."

"Impede?"

"You're trying my patience." Morales stepped closer. Her breath was mint-scented, quite unlike her attitude. "Answer my questions and answer them truthfully."

Just then, Agent Murdoch moved toward the staircase.

"*Cómo se dice?*" she blurted, then caught herself. "Where do you think you're going?"

Murdoch pulled a document out from an inside pocket of his suit coat. "A search warrant," he said. "My passport to the house."

"And speaking of passports," Morales said, turning back to Lana, "do you have one?"

"I'm legal," Lana stammered. "I have my green card!"

"Green cards, yellow cards. Your card will mean nothing if I say it doesn't. We'll deport you back to your Third World village before you can blink."

Terror clung to her like a vice. Lana cried, "But millions have come to this country illegally, and I'm legal!"

Even as she realized her fear and took stock of the dread, Lana grasped the knowledge Morales was not just an agent of Homeland Security. She was an agent of fright.

Querido Dios, she prayed. *Dear God, calm me down, give me wisdom, show me the right answers. And protect Mr. Jackson and Dr. Zohn. Gracias!*

A certain peace enveloped her, a sure knowledge the Lord had heard. She looked at her hands. They'd stopped shaking. She stood straight and looked about her. The ceiling had lifted, the walls had receded, and, oddly, Agent Morales didn't seem so menacing any more. She was someone's little girl, perhaps someone's mom. She looked at Morales's left hand. Yes, a wife too. A mere mortal like her. A person for whom to feel compassion. And Agent Murdoch? What was there to discover upstairs? Nada. Nothing.

Lana allowed a wide smile to sweep across her face. She was in the hollow of her Lord's hands.

"And what are you smiling about? The thought of being reunited with your old friends south of the border?" Morales sneered.

Lana remembered a game she played as a girl. Each child would take on a character not their own. The boys loved to play American cowboys and gangsters. The girls tended towards heroines like Evita Peron and Menchu Tum. Agent Morales might just as well be playacting. The sneer. The scowl. Beneath the bluster was a child of God, though she wasn't acting like one right now.

"You were a beautiful child, I can see," Lana said.

Morales reacted like someone had lightly tapped her on the cheek. "What?"

"A lovely child," Lana said and pointed at her. "Puerto Rican, right?"

"Yes, and so what?" Morales sounded affronted.

"Oh, nothing. Just thinking." Lana shrugged.

"And my father entered this country legally too," Morales said.

Lana shook her head and said in Spanish, "I didn't mean to imply otherwise. But you get my point. If you can call my legality into question, perhaps someone else, somewhere else can do the same to you—some day."

Morales took a step back, frowned, then pointed her forefinger at her. "You're avoiding my questions! What happened with Dr. Zohn?"

Lana replied, "You'll have to ask Mr. Jackson. I've been on a short holiday. Mr. Jackson is a wonderful boss. He gives me a month vacation each year and pays my airplane fare to Ecuador and back twice a year. Sometimes, out of the blue, he'll say, 'Lana, you look like you could use a rest; take a couple days off.' That's what he did this time."

"So, you say."

"Sí. Yes."

"And when did you get back to work?"

"Esta mañana. This morning."

Just then, Agent Murdoch came down the stairs. He looked at Morales and shook his head.

Morales motioned for him to continue the search downstairs. He stepped toward the living room.

Morales returned her attention to Lana. "If we discover you've lied to federal agents, I will personally return here, click some handcuffs on nice and tight, and haul your Latino butt to the darkest corner of the dreariest jail cell they've got in this place. Maybe some place even worse. Maybe all the way to San Quentin. No more Mr. Nice-Guy Jackson. No more mansion on Cape Elizabeth. No more plane flights home to Ecuador. No more days off on the beach."

Morales's eyes darkened, but Lana simply flashed an impish smile. "Okay." Secure. No fear. God's kid.

Morales called out, "Come on, Carl. We'll canvass the rest of the neighborhood."

As they walked out the door, Lana grabbed hold of the little cross hanging from her neck. *"Gracias, Dios. Gracias."*

—∾—

Dan turned to Alec. “How’d your race go last night?”

Alec sat forward. “Finished first, Mr. C.”

“He lapped everyone but Jason McCoy,” Davey declared.

“Whoa! That’s impressive!” Dan said.

“What do you race?” Ethan asked.

“An old 2005 Pontiac GTO.” Alec’s eyes brightened. Dan knew the young man was in his element. “Not pretty, but she’s fast. Four hundred fifty-one horses, six-speed, ten-point-nine-to-one compression rate. Goes from zero to sixty in four-point-six seconds.”

“It’s got a Corvette engine,” Davey said, “and Alec’s dad has her souped up so she’s faster than an M3 or a Z4M. He replaced the factory bumpstick with an s-cam and installed a long-tube header and exhaust system so the engine exhales more efficiently.”

Alec’s voice rose, as did a broad smile, as he added, “Leaves Sam Thomas’s Mustang in the dust.”

“You shoulda’ seen Sam’s girlfriend, Glenda, turn red when Alec lapped him,” Davey chortled.

“Well, we’re proud of you, Alec,” Margaret said. She ruffled his curly short-cut hair like she had ten years before when he was eight years old and told Dan he could fix his “bad-soundin” lawnmower. “We’d love you even if the others had lapped *you*.”

Alec smiled. “Thanks, Mrs. C.”

“We’ll get to the next race, son,” Dan said. “What now, the Regionals?”

“Yes sir, in one week, just before I leave for college.”

“And he’s gonna spit dust in everyone’s face,” Davey predicted.

Alec punched him in the arm, good-naturedly. “Don’t make promises, Davey,” he said seriously. “What did God say about pride coming before humiliation?”

“‘The fall,’” Davey corrected. “‘Pride cometh before the fall.’”

“Yeah, that.” Alec punched him again and laughed. “Maybe I’ll forget to put fuel in the tank or something and be left at the starting line.”

“Yeah, ha!”

“Yeah, ha!”

“Four hundred horses,” Ethan cut in. “What’s the rear-wheel torque?”

“Four hundred nineteen,” Alex answered.

“Whoa!” Ethan said. “I wouldn’t want to be chasing you!”

Alec smiled and shook his head slowly. “No, you wouldn’t.”

Everyone laughed.

—∞—

Agent Owen’s ear was growing red as he listened to Conrad rant over the phone.

“I don’t buy his story,” Conrad yelled.

Owen could envision the scowl on Conrad’s face.

“Jackson was no more going to the coast for vacation than I’m going to Hawaii,” Conrad fumed.

The temperature was rising, Owen thought, and he wasn’t even in the same room with his boss. This was a moment to seize if Owen wanted to rise up in the ranks of Homeland Security. Fail? He envisioned a post somewhere in outer Alaska.

"We've got agents scouring Jackson's house and checking into all his phone and email contacts in that part of Maine, sir. If he's part of a group of some kind, helping Jews out of America, one of those contacts should pan out."

"I'm flying up myself to take charge of the operation first hand," Conrad hissed. "I'll be there by three o'clock, three-thirty."

Darn! Is that sulfur I smell? Owen set his jaw and shook his head, then hung up the phone and opened the door to his office. "Thompson!" he called.

A short, balding man looked up from his computer.

"Any luck?" Owen asked.

"I think maybe."

"Maybe?"

"Jackson sent an email to an address up in the midcoast around Rockland or Belfast very early Friday morning and again on Saturday. But the recipient's server was down."

"Who's the recipient?"

"Don't know yet."

"What'd the message say?"

"Don't know. It was encrypted."

"Encrypted email? Who does that? We've got him. Come with me. We're bringing Jackson back in for questioning."

"He's barely out the door."

"Doesn't matter."

—∞—

"So you know about engines?" Davey asked Ethan.

Ethan thought over the question. How much could he reveal? What must he leave unsaid. And, of course, Omri was the one who pushed the issue as he often did when they were together.

"My nephew," he said, "is an electrical and computer engineer and is doing some intriguing research."

Ethan shot him a look he hoped would send a chill or two down his spine. *Uncle-schmuncle.*

"Tell us about it," Margaret said.

I guess I'll let her rip.

"First," he said, "I've had lots of help from others in the UK, Japan, and here in the States, especially Duke University."

He eyed Daisy-Rain. "Did you see any of the Harry Potter movies, sweetie?"

"Well, they came out before I was born, but I've seen 'em on Blue-Ray." Obviously Daisy-Rain felt much more than the eight-year-old she was.

"Remember the invisibility cloak?"

"Yep."

"We can do that now."

"No way!" the child screeched.

"Yes, way." Ethan grinned. He could sense the sudden rapt attention around the table. "And we can make things undetectable by thermal technology."

"Thermal—"

"Satellites and airplanes that can tell where living creatures are down below.

"Wow!" the boys responded.

"How on earth does that work?" Dan asked. "In layman's terms, please, Ethan."

"To make an object vanish before a person's eyes, a cloak has to simultaneously interact with all of the wavelengths, or colors, that make up light, and this has always been the problem. Until now, cloaking has only worked in two dimensions and only at a particular microwave frequency."

"You mean you put it in a gigantic microwave?" Daisy-Rain's mouth went wide as she spread her arms as far as they could go.

Everyone joined Ethan in a laugh.

"No, little princess," he said. "The technology is difficult to explain. Let's just say, the design calls for tiny metal needles to be fitted into a hairbrush-shaped cone at angles and lengths that force light to pass around the cloak. This makes everything inside appear to vanish because the light no longer reflects off it."

"You must be talking about super-minute materials," Dan said.

"Metamaterial," Alec interjected.

"Right," Ethan said, impressed with the young man's knowledge. "In order to be manipulated, light has to be much smaller than the wave length of light being used. Light has unique properties that derive from its physical structure, not its chemical makeup."

"This is way over my head," Margaret said.

"Me, too," Ruth shook her head. Others groaned in agreement.

"Think of a mirage in the desert." Ethan spread his hands as if holding a large globe. "The sun heats the air above the desert and creates a temperature gradient. So when light from the sky comes down, the graded refraction bends the light. When it enters your eye, you see a mirage appearing like water. Okay?"

Everyone nodded. Nevertheless he could tell not everyone understood.

"Instead of creating a temperature gradient that only partially reflects light, the silicon-silica mix creates a physical gradient that instead makes light do a complete U-turn, exiting in the same direction it entered."

"Ethan," Omri interrupted with excitement coloring his voice, "take them to the next level."

Ethan nodded and made eye contact around the room. "Aerosol spray cans," he said.

"Spray cans?" Margaret repeated.

"To quote our little friend," Dan said, "'no way.'"

"Yes, way." Ethan smiled and raised his index finger. "We've converted the technology from a sheet or blanket to a mixture that can be used in a spray can. But with the spray, the effect only lasts a few minutes.

"Nanotechnology," Omri said. "A wonderful thing."

"Nano …" Ruth hesitated.

"Nanotechnology," Ethan said. "The study of the control of matter on an atomic and molecular scale."

"I'd love to study nanotechnology at MIT," Alec interjected.

Omri and Ethan exchanged glances. "I'm sure you will, Alec, if you want," Ethan responded. "MIT has some brilliant minds."

After everyone finished lunch, Alec hugged Margaret goodbye, said his farewells, and hopped onto his four-wheeler, driving through a wooded path to his home a quarter-mile away.

Everyone else went into the living room to wait for word from Frank.

Dan, sitting in his favorite leather chair, leaned forward and looked seriously at his guests. He knew they were anxious to leave. Who knew what was happening with Bunyan, or whether the feds were looking for Omri. He had to keep them otherwise occupied.

Finally, he spoke. "I'm curious as to why you all want to go and live in Israel."

"Daddy!" Daisy-Rain cried out in delight. "Israel's where my Daddy is."

"Yes," Ruth said, "Daddy's there, waiting for us."

Margaret, sitting beside Dan, said, "It's awful it's come to that. What about your friends here? Your business? Your other family?"

"We've talked about emigrating to Israel for years. To be honest, we just never had the guts. This decision forced our hand." Ruth shrugged. "As for friends and family, we hope they can somehow follow us there, if they wish. Many have no desire to go. Life's much easier here in America, not always worrying about rockets, or some madman—or woman—setting off a bomb on a bus, a restaurant, or in a school.

"As for the money, some of the assets from our business are already in Israel. But most of it, we'll simply have to build up again. We've done it once. Stanley's a brilliant businessman."

"They call him a whiz!" Daisy-Rain declared with a proud smile. "My Daddy's smart—'cept I beat him at 'Sorry' every time."

Dan couldn't hold back a chuckle. "What about you, Ethan? Naomi?" he asked.

"Never in my life have I wanted to leave our home and our life here," Ethan said. "I've always loved this country. I fought in

Operation Enduring Freedom in Afghanistan. I don't much care for religion, and I don't care at all about the Middle East.

"But," his voice rose, "when my country—for whom I offered up my life—tells me what I can't do, when America constrains me from a freedom everyone else has, I feel like I've been stabbed in the back. When this happens, I declare, Enough! I revolt because I am revolted."

The big man took a deep breath, and Naomi put her hand on his and cut in. "Wherever my husband goes, I'll go. If he said, 'Pack your bags, we're going to Outer Mongolia,' I'd simply pack warmer clothes and put on my woolies."

Laughter greeted her words. *I wonder how many Jews feel this way. Like the Jews in Europe of the 1930s, do you think?* Dan considered how he'd feel if Uncle Sam told him he couldn't travel to Ireland, the home of his great-grandfather Callahan. To him, Ireland was precious, a little like Israel is to the Jews.

"What continues to bother me," Naomi went on, "is my grandfather Kaplan was the lone survivor of the Holocaust from his family in Czortkow, Poland. He came to America in 1946 on the *SS Marine Perch*, the second 'quota' boat to arrive here. He escaped to America. Now I, his granddaughter, must escape from America."

The shame of it. Dan shook his head.

Silence reigned for a while, then Omri spoke to Naomi. "Your family is the epitome of the 'wandering Jew,' with no place to rest his head … for long."

"What about you, Omri?" Dan asked.

"Me? I was born and raised in Israel, which explains my—ah—minor accent." He laughed. "Israel's the home of my parents. Where I grew to adulthood. Where I was prepared for my studies, first at Hebrew University, and then Technion-Israel Institute of Technology, before coming to America and MIT.

"For years since coming here, I've walked the narrow streets of the Old City of Jerusalem, in my mind. I've again hiked Mount Tabor and Mount Meron, in my mind. I've stepped into the Dead Sea and floated atop its dense waters, in my mind. I've sat at my favorite restaurant on the shores of the Galilee in Tiberius, eating the same fish our ancestors caught and ate there some three, four thousand years ago. All in my mind.

"Yes, I've visited my family there on occasion, but for only a brief few days at a time. Mostly my teaching and research have kept me at MIT and lecturing around the world.

"My son, Benjamin, moved from Columbus, Ohio, to Haifa thirteen months ago with his wife, Sharon. They took my grandson, Elijah. Since then, I've longed for Israel more than any time in my life. The blood of my people is on that land. And now my wife and our daughter are there as well."

Omri sighed, then added, "This is a dream for me. I wish I'd done so when my dear wife was alive, or even a year ago and avoided this nonsense."

There was a hush in the room. Despite all the places he'd traveled, Dan always had a home port. What was life like to reside only where the world said you could?

Margaret spoke up, "Well, Dan and I wish you all Godspeed. We'll do our best in the underground railroad we're connected to."

Dan scanned the room and said, "No telling what Homeland Security is up to right now. I can't contact Bunyan. But I know with a certainty he has not revealed us to the authorities."

"We should include him in our prayers," Omri said.

"Thank you," Margaret said. "He's very important to us." She cast a worried look at Dan. He hoped his half-smile somehow consoled her.

Stepping into the family room, Alec noticed his father was on the couch. His Dad had been ill since the previous night, right in the heat of the championship race.

"Geez, Dad, you gonna see the doctor?"

"I got a call in to him, but it's Sunday. He's probably out on the golf course."

"Can I get you anything? Juice? Toast?"

"Naw, your Mom got me all set before she headed out to work. Thanks, anyhow."

Of course. Mom was always on the ball.

The television was turned on and, just then, an announcement drew Alec's attention to the screen.

A *Fox News* talking head—*man, is she pretty!*—was speaking. "The US Department of Homeland Security believes one of the nation's most prominent scientists may have been kidnapped."

A photograph appeared in an inset behind the anchor lady. Alec's eyes widened.

"Eminent physicist and Nobel laureate, Dr. Omri Zohn is the lead scientist in a world-changing project, using sound waves to produce nuclear-fusion reactions."

The screen went full-face to Shandra Constantine. *Don't like this person. Do not.*

Constantine spoke into a gaggle of microphones, "We believe a foreign power may have kidnapped Dr. Zohn—"

Alec straightened up and pointed. "I just saw—"

"What?" his father asked.

Alec stopped himself. This man, Dr. Zohn, was at Davey's house. The Callahans were straight-up people. Christians who really lived it, unlike so many others he knew. Mr. C. was a pastor and a great guy. Mrs. C. was like a second mom to him. They wouldn't kidnap anyone. Something was wrong with this picture. Weirdly wrong.

On the television screen, the pretty lady was saying, "If anyone has seen this man, they're requested to immediately report it to authorities. Here is the hot-line number—"

It can't be.

"What is it, son?" His father's eyebrows rose.

"Aw-w, nothing, Dad. I gotta go. See ya'."

In an instant he was racing out the door and jumping onto his four-wheeler. He had to reach Davey and get the scoop.

Once again, Dan slipped away to his den and pulled the PGP cell phone and small laptop computer out of their hiding place.

He again called with his message to Frank Reid, then started up the computer and sent it again as an encrypted message. Decoded, it read: "Releasing 5 trout into the pond today. Waiting for your OK."

Then he called Frank's "burn" cell phone, let it ring once, and hung up. He'd wait for a response before moving out. But his anxiety increased with every passing minute.

Chapter Nine

Owen figured the DHS jet carrying Conrad was approaching the Portland jetport at this moment. He needed to nail Jacko now while the matter was still in his hands.

Jacko was in the interrogation room again. Owen stood on the other side of the long, narrow table, peering down at him. He remembered Jacko's grand slam against the Yankees and how he'd leapt out of his seat, cheering. This guy was fearless. He could try a vicious scowl, but he knew it wouldn't work with Jacko. Better still, he was ready to throw the fastball-hitting Hall of Famer a devastating curve. *Ha!*

Finally, he asked, "Who did you send an encrypted email to?"

He studied Jacko's face. Did it reveal fear they'd found the message, or relief they couldn't decipher the memo?

The heavy metal door burst open and Thompson peered in. "Daniel and Margaret Callahan, sir."

"Callahan, huh?" Owen caught Bunyan's eyes in his own. "Midcoast, you say, Thompson?"

"Yes, sir," Thompson replied. "North Hope, just inland from Rockland."

"Not *on* the coast?"

"No, sir."

He had Jacko locked in his grip now. "You say you buy your clothes when you get there, Jacko. So, the Callahans are your clothiers?"

Bunyan shrugged. "Longtime family friends."

"Family friends?" Owen chuckled as if he didn't believe a word. "Callahan. Sounds Irish to me."

"Your only friends are black, agent?"

Owen harrumphed and shot a sideways glace at Thompson, a white man. He glared at Bunyan. "So they're old pals you tend to just drop in on in the middle of the night."

"Sometimes. This time, though, I just sent them a message telling them I was coming."

"Encrypted?"

"Yeah. Just for fun. Dan was a Navy SEAL before rising to captain, so I like to keep his little grey cells exercised."

Owen had to admit the explanation made sense, in a strangled kind of way. But nothing else did.

"What did the message say, Jacko?"

Bunyan shrugged. "Don't remember specifically. Just informed them I was coming, I think."

"Uh-huh."

"Maybe I told them the approximate time."

"Uh-huh. About two in the morning."

"This is inane, agent—frivolous. Why not just let me return home? I was enjoying my freedom … brief as it was."

"I think I'll wait until we question your Irish friends, the Callahans."

Owen smirked, hoping the comment would jar Jacko out of his safety zone. Nope.

—∞—

Owen stalked out of the room and pointed to a woman sitting at a nearby desk. "Marie, have them fire up the copter to take us to Rockland. Then call Rockland and have them get two Escalades to the helipad to meet us," he peered at his watch, "in an hour—three-thirty-five."

Owen figured Conrad would arrive at the DHS helipad about then, perhaps a few minutes later. Owen needed to appear proactive, ahead of the game.

Pointing to three men who were manning desks nearby, he said, "Sam, Juan, Adelius, we're off to Rockland. Bring your sidearms."

—∞—

When the photo of Omri Zohn flashed behind the anchor, Bunyan's neighbor Horace Marchand shot forward in his chair and pointed at the large-screen television.

"That's him!" he said. "The man I saw next door playing croquet with Jackson!"

"Well, then, he's not kidnapped, is he?" Trudy replied, lying on the couch. With a laugh verging on a snicker, she added, "And I wouldn't call Jacko Jackson a foreign power."

"Obviously Constantine's wrong. The guy seemed to be calm, relaxed, and enjoying himself."

"This is a national story, Horace. What'll you do?" She sat up now and put her book down on an end table.

"Let me think. Let me think." Horace tapped his temples with his forefingers.

A full minute passed.

Finally, he broke the silence. "If I call Homeland Security, several things could happen."

"Yeah?"

"It's possible they could use my name in announcing Zohn's been discovered. Could be good for business."

"Not to mention at the country club, my garden club, the Chamber of Commerce, Kiwanis Club—"

"Right," Horace said. "On the other hand, if this guy's actually trying to escape from the country like so many others, I'd be linked to his capture."

"What's wrong with that? With being a hero?" Trudy asked, frowning.

"Mainers love Jackson, adore him. They'd tar and feather me for being a snitch and getting their man in trouble. Besides, how many potential customers oppose this emigration ban?"

"True. And some of our best customers are Jews." Trudy leaned forward and, with her elbows on her knees, propped her chin in her palm. "A conundrum."

"Wrapped in a riddle."

"Hidden in a Chinese box." Trudy chuckled at her borrowed wit.

This, must be what a pedestrian feels like in the middle of a crosswalk with traffic revving up. Should I leap forward or run back? "So, do I keep mum, call anonymously, or what?"

"It won't be anonymous for long, not if you tell them where you spotted this Zohn guy."

"Right." Horace lowered his eyes. "Maybe losing some business wouldn't be so bad, maybe worth the harm, just to get Jackson in trouble with the law. Maybe a call wouldn't be so bad at all."

Shandra Constantine fidgeted with a pen as she spoke to Joseph Conrad who was on a secure telephone, flying to Portland. It still steamed her that nineteen Border Patrol section chiefs, not her, had been given tactical control of the two hundred and fifty helicopters and fixed-wing aircraft in their sectors. The largest law-enforcement air force in the world and should be hers to control. Hers!

The Border Patrol's northeast sector chief, Stanley Gowen, was a nit-picking little weasel who made even her lead agents jump through hoops to get planes. He controlled his little part of the country like his personal fiefdom. He'd been a royal discomfort, even to her, in releasing helicopters to various DHS personnel. And now Gowen had kept Conrad, who was higher up the food chain than him, sitting on the tarmac for fifteen minutes, waiting for approval to take off from Logan Airport in Boston.

"Gowen's head's rolling for this!" she hissed.

"A good head-rolliing is in order," Conrad agreed.

Constantine grabbed a Harvard Crimson letter opener and drove its point into a photo of Dr. Zohn that was on her desk blotter—right into his head.

People will do anything to deflect blame. In this case, Conrad could accuse Gowen if Zohn wasn't caught. Sometimes fifteen minutes could equal a lost fugitive. In the end, it was her head on a platter or her competence being honored.

Not to mention the Department of Energy truly felt Zohn's research couldn't proceed without him.

Constantine slammed her phone onto the desk. *Morons! Why do I have to deal with airheads?*

—m—

Immediately, Constantine's secretary buzzed her.

"Yes!" Constantine wanted to strangle somebody. Might as well be her secretary. Put a thundercloud over Little Miss Sunshine.

"Mister Pinto is on the line, Madam Secretary."

"Better be good news," Constantine groused, thinking perhaps it was. Damien Pinto was head of DHS's Intelligence and Analysis division. "Put him through."

"Dr. Zohn's been in touch with another person on your A List." Pinto always dismissed formalities. Constantine liked the quality.

She moved forward to the edge of her chair. "Who?"

"Ethan Rosenbaum."

"Go on."

"Zohn called Rosenbaum shortly after three o'clock the morning Congress took the vote."

"Do you know what was said?"

"No. Couldn't have been much."

"Oh?"

"Yes, the call lasted about three seconds. And guess what?"

"Damien!"

"Sorry. We discovered Senator Frank called Zohn a few minutes before Zohn called Rosenbaum."

"Find Frank!"

"We have. He and his wife were about to board a plane headed to Montreal. Thought his Senate credentials could get him out of the country."

Constantine let go a guttural chuckle, then asked, "Has he been grilled about Zohn?"

"Says he knows nothing."

"Get him to headquarters. I'll personally plant the fear of God into him." *Oh, to blast a senator with the lightning rod of the law!*

"Meanwhile, we haven't been able to track Rosenbaum."

"Find out in what ways Rosenbaum could get to Portland. Perhaps they're trying to leave together."

"Yes, ma'am."

Constantine hung up without a goodbye and dialed the Oval Office.

When President Smith picked up the line, the crisp voice of Shandra Constantine greeted him. "We've got three more corralled, sir. Only three more to go."

"Yes, and?"

"Remember the movie *The Fugitive?*"

He hadn't thought cutesy was in Constantine's entire world, let alone her personal character. He pictured Tommy Lee Jones and Harrison Ford. "Yes."

"I promise a better result."

"Good." Smith hung the phone on its cradle. He pursed his lips. *As a cat hunting a mouse, having all the modern tools at your disposal certainly helps the search.* That included some human tools as well. Dogged, even ferocious, Constantine was one of those. He wondered if he had a place for her at the United Nations. Surely so.

Homeland Security Sectional Chief Amy Durant sat in her Lansing, Michigan, office, staring at the knots in her mahogany desk and praying silently. Midafternoon on a Sunday and here she was, enforcing a law that made her physically ache in pain.

She'd been reading a sectional report on Operation Cork.

Because Canada hadn't signed on to United Nations Resolution 017-666, the United States wasn't allowing Jews to cross the border. If allowed, they could catch a flight directly into Tel Aviv. She and her husband had once taken an Air Canada flight from Toronto nonstop to Israel.

Those governments around the world in agreement with the Resolution were preventing Jews from leaving their countries and entering nations from which they could travel to Israel.

In her section alone, US agents at the borders had stopped and turned away one hundred forty-three Jewish people at Michigan's border crossings into Canada; another ninety-three were turned back at the border in Wisconsin and twenty-eight in Montana.

The national report showed DHS had accounted for seven of the ten Jewish VIP "priorities" and were closing in on two others. Most of the Top 100 list had been accounted for as well.

Amy studied a photograph of her husband and children, smiling out at her. Jesse was such a supporter of her career, taking his trade as an electrician and following her from post to post. They had hoped to settle here in Lansing. Director Constantine's threat to ship her to Siberia—well, Florida—weighed like an anvil on her mind.

Mental torment, but a spiritual kind of anguish as well. Since she was a teenager, growing up in Rockville, Illinois, she had a love for God's people and his nation Israel. Her Assembly of God pastor had instilled that in her. She recalled his preaching on God parting the Red Sea, sending manna to feed the Hebrews every morning, shooting water out of a rock. *Great stuff!*

"When they needed it, God would do something they couldn't even conceive," Pastor Earle said one morning. "Look at the miracles in the Old Testament and those in the New.

"Who would've thought God would split the Red Sea or pour water out of a rock? But then who would've thought a certain Jew by the name of Jesus, or Yeshua, would turn water into wine?

"Who would've thought," Pastor Earle continued, "Elijah would make the widow woman's little jar of oil replenish and reload enough to feed friends and neighbors? But then again, who would've thought, with five loaves of bread and two fish, Jesus could feed five thousand—make that fifteen or twenty thousand, counting women and children?"

All around the church a sea of hands rose toward the heavens.

"Who would've considered the possibility Elisha would raise the rich woman's dead son? But then who could envision Jesus raising Jairus' dead daughter?"

"Hallelujah!" Amy's dad had called out.

"When dark looks darkest, when no salvation, no rescue, is in sight—when all seems impossible—something, yes, some *thing* will happen, and you will know God's hand was at work.

"Old Testament, New Testament … God is the same!" Pastor Earle's voice rose. "In the Old Testament, he provided sacrifices for Israel's sins—sacrifices of goats and bulls. In the New Testament, he provided his Son as a perfect and everlasting sacrifice for all of our sins—a sacrifice once and for all, one that need never be repeated because the Lamb, the Lamb was without defect!"

"Amen!" the congregation stood and applauded the Lord, raising hands and voices.

Pastor Earle had made certain his congregation knew the importance of blessing and praying for the Jewish people and supporting a tiny little nation surrounded by countries wanting to destroy it. And he left no doubt God's hand was still upon "the apple of his eye."

—~~—

Amy knew Israel was not obliged to return the territories she had gained.

She also knew Jordan was created as the homeland for the Palestinians, but the controlling Hashemite king never had allowed such a habitation.

She believed modern-day Israel—despised by much of a jealous world—deserved to live! While Arab-controlled countries didn't allow the few remaining Jews living there to vote, Israel not only permitted Arabs to vote but allowed them seats in her governing body, the Knesset.

She knew it was to their everlasting shame many Christians did not rise up against Hitler and help the Jews during the Holocaust. In fact, the Roman church was complicit, helping Nazi leaders escape to South America and the Mideast after World War Two.

She took it as a personal umbrage when Secretary of State Condoleeza Rice declared there was no difference between Israelis trying to defend themselves from a jihadist Palestinian society and the white Southern bigots who oppressed African-Americans because they were black.

She knew at the Annapolis peace conference in 2007, President George W. Bush complied when the Arabs insisted Israeli representatives be prohibited from entering the hall through the same door.

She mourned when President Barak Obama demanded that Israel revert to the 1967 borders—boundaries that had provided no security at all.

These Presidents and other world leaders didn't even register that Christians were systematically exterminated in Muslim lands. They never condemned the slaughter of Buddhists in Thailand or Hindus in Pakistan. No one internationally—at the United Nations or elsewhere—ever stated the fact that, unlike Islamist terrorists, Jews never ran around slaughtering in the name of HaShem nor did Christians in the name of Jesus Christ.

Now the nation was in a new era, and if there were any changes, they were for the worse. Amy was grieved to her very core on learning her own country was acquiescing to the Arab-controlled United Nations in demanding that Israel not grow its population and give back the land the Arabs had used as launching pads for attacks on the tiny country over many decades.

Amy pulled her lipstick compact out of her purse and looked her reflection in the tiny mirror. "And how do *you* stand?" she asked herself.

Chapter Ten

Sitting at his desk in the den, Dan prayed, asking the Lord to be quick about His work. *As if He doesn't know.*

Omri and the others had brought their duffel bags downstairs. Everyone was waiting in the living room for the all-clear signal from Frank Reid before heading off to his house.

Suddenly a melodious noise sounded on Dan's computer, a message prompt. Frank! As he read Frank's reply, the phone rang on his desk, and he snatched the headpiece.

A voice, scrambled to disguise the speaker but obviously fraught with tension, said, "If you have guests, get them out—now!" The line went dead.

The hair on his neck bristled, and he felt an adrenaline rush that reminded him of naval battle.

Dan leapt from the desk. "Maggie! Get everyone out of the house!"

He reached the living room. "The spring house," he said, pointing to the field beyond the back yard.

Davey jumped to his feet and declared, “I’ll take them there, Grampa!”

Dan looked firmly at Davey. Involve his seventeen-year-old grandson in this? Then he recalled his own father fought in World War Two when he was seventeen.

“Okay,” he said. “Grab your duffel bags, everyone, and follow Davey. Quickly!”

Omri and the others scurried to the kitchen where their bags lay.

On his way out the kitchen door, Davey flung Ruth’s duffel bag over his back.

Dan watched as urgency spurred them all on. Ruth grabbed hold of Daisy-Rain’s little hand.

“Hurry, but be quiet as a synagogue mouse,” Ruth warned.

Daisy-Rain giggled.

“I’m serious!” Ruth said in a hoarse whisper, putting an index finger to her lips.

Daisy-Rain’s eyes grew large. “Okay, Mommy.”

In moments, all the guests were out the door and following Davey through the back yard.

From the living room, Margaret called out, “Dan, I think the law is here! A big black SUV is coming down the driveway.”

Dan looked toward the heavens and offered a prayer for protection.

Davey knew the spring house well. He'd used the structure as a sort of clubhouse for him, Alec, and other friends over the years.

Beyond the mowed lawn was a small pasture of meadow grasses and hay standing as tall as two and three feet. The lawn and meadow all gently sloped away from the house. In the distance, the waters of Moody Pond shimmered.

"There." Davey pointed to the three-foot-high, gray spring house, perhaps six feet square, sitting between a rambling wild lilac bush and several spindly ash trees. The place was partly hidden behind a burning bush. As Davey reached the spring house, he took the duffel bag off his back and fell to his knees. Ethan and Naomi were right behind him; Ruth and Daisy-Rain dropped to the ground behind the Rosenbaums.

Are the authorities right this moment coming around the house, searching for us?

Three steps into the meadow grass, Omri stumbled and fell to the ground, his duffel bag flipping him onto his right hip.

He stifled a cry. A tendril of fear trilled up his spine.

"Part the Red Sea, Lord," he whispered hoarsely, "and leave my enemies behind me."

He chanced a look back toward the house, about fifty yards away. No one was out back yet.

Hands shaking, Davey lifted a flat rock and searched for a hidden key. *Here!*

He tried to place the key in the padlock on the door, fumbling once, twice. His trembling hands were betraying him! He'd opened this padlock a hundred, two hundred times. *Stop shaking, fingers!* His heart throbbed in his chest. This was a netherworld worse than shooting a free throw with the game on the line.

A wave of nausea began to rise up, but he pushed the feeling back. *Focus!* After what seemed an eternity, the key slipped into the lock. One flick to the right and the padlock opened. Davey turned to the others and took a fleeting look over the meadow grass to the house beyond. No movement outside, but Omri was behind them all. He was struggling to move forward on his belly while dragging his satchel beside him.

"In here," Davey murmured. "Stay low."

Ethan, his burly body kneeling on the ground, hustled Naomi, then Ruth and Daisy-Rain inside.

Davey shook head to toe. How much time did they have? How close were the authorities? Should he go back for Omri? Could he? He remembered Bubbe's tales of Grampa's bravery. *I have those genes!*

Without further debate, Davey crouched low and dove ahead, straight into a bramble. *Ouch!* When he was younger, he stayed with his grandparents for a month every July. Dozens of times, he and his friends had played hide-and-seek back here on their knees in a maze of tall grass. That had been great fun. This, not so much.

He and his buddies had tossed every rock they'd bumped their knees on out into the nearby woods, but brambles were another story.

Keeping his legs and arms moving, Davey reached Omri and grabbed the duffel bag. "I'll take this," he said. Even then, he moved faster toward the spring house than the older man.

Looking out from the door of the spring house, Ethan and the others urged them on, madly waving their arms.

—m—

Strength, Lord! Omri prayed. *Give me strength and speed. I'm so slow!*

When Davey arrived at the spring house, he tossed the duffel bag inside, then kneeled, holding the door open.

With what seemed a supernatural burst of energy, Omri dove into the little structure. Davey slid in behind him and shut the door.

After being out in the sun, the spring house was dark as a dungeon. The others were obviously all inside and had crawled backward to give him and Davey enough space to enter.

All around him, the people released their breath, probably their first breath since getting here.

"That was *fun!*" Daisy-Rain sang the statement.

"Sh-h-h," Ruth warned.

Omri wiped perspiration from his brow. A thought flashed in his mind of Jews, crowded into railroad cars with no light or room to move. How did they survive such long trips?

Beside him, Davey said, "I'll get us some light from the back side." He crawled to the wall facing away from the house. A moment later, he flipped up a vent and a narrow slice of sunlight turned the darkness to dusk.

Somehow the tiny bit of light was enough to encourage Omri and the others.

—~—

Like a well-practiced hand on deck, Davey then made his way to the front. There he felt along the wall and, finding what he wanted, pulled out a knot in a plank of the wood siding. *Voilà! A view into the world!*

He put his right eye to the knot.

Just then, a large African-American man dressed in a black suit, stepped around the corner of the house and stared intently about the back yard.

"There's a man in the back yard," Davey reported, whispering just loud enough to be heard. Then, like a broadcaster calling play-by-play in a baseball game, he announced, "He's slowly walking around. He's putting his hands on his hips. Now he's walking closer to the field."

He doubled down to a lower-key whisper, like a golf announcer when a golfer prepares to putt. "He's walking in this direction. He's folding his arms. He's looking out here."

"Where would we go from here?" Ethan murmured.

"We're too far from the woods," Davey replied. "He'll see us if we run."

"But if he comes this way, we should all run in different directions, shouldn't we?" Naomi asked.

"No," Omri said quietly. "Just pray, dear ones."

"You sound like our rabbi," Daisy-Rain chirped. "I'm one of his dear ones."

Omri reached for her and patted her head. "Yes, you are, Daisy-Rain," he murmured, "so believe Elohim will protect you, that He'll hide us all."

"Okay." The little girl sighed sheepishly.

"Hey, he just kicked my soccer ball into the field," Davey said, wishing he could jump out there and give the man a piece of his mind, the creep!

"Whew! He's walking back to the house."

Another communal sigh of relief met his words.

Davey brought his eye away from the hole.

"Here," he said, pulling out another knot hole closer to the door and yet another one further away. Ethan and Ruth moved to the two spots.

Naomi grabbed Ethan's elbow and asked, "What do you see?"

"He's nearly back to the house."

"Now he's stepping up onto the back porch," Ruth added. "He's turning around and looking back out here again."

Ruth ducked and several of the others had to stifle laughter.

"Mommy," Daisy-Rain whispered, "I don't think he can see you through the knothole."

Ruth smiled a smile Davey had seen often from his mother when he'd said something witty. Something about moms and their kids.

"Now he's going inside," Ethan said.

At that moment, the cell phone at Davey's belt sounded with the words from Red Sox announcer Joe Castiglioni: "It's strike three! The Boston Red Sox have won the pennant! Can you believe it!"

Davey swiftly pulled the phone from his pocket. He recognized Alec's number on the display. "Alec," he whispered, "I can't talk. I'll call you later."

"Davey," Alec said, "I just saw the admiral's picture on television. Homeland Security says he's a kidnapped scientist!"

"Kidnapped?"

"Kidnapped. I know they're wrong. What's going on?"

Davey whispered ever so softly, "I can't tell you right now. You've gotta stay away from our house, though."

"Where are you?"

"In the spring house."

"The spring house!"

"Alec, I can't talk." Davey hesitated, deep in thought. "Alec, I think we may need your help."

"We?"

"Yeah, all of Grampa and Bubbe's friends and me."

"Sure."

"Where are you?"

"On my four-wheeler coming back to your place."

"Well, turn off the engine when you get within hearing distance and then walk to the edge of the clearing. Okay?"

"Sure."

"Put your cell on vibrate and don't call me. I'll call you."

Chapter Eleven

Inside the Callahan house, Agent Dennis Owen confronted Dan and Margaret in the living room, while Agents Sam Brown and Juan Cruz stalked through the house, guns leveled. From the sounds, Dan figured they were checking in closets, under beds, anywhere a person might be hiding.

Tack, at Dan's side, growled a threat Dan knew meant "Harm my humans, and you'll deal with me." The next step would be showing the teeth. Then the next, well—

Dan could tell Margaret was startled by the intensity and apparent dangerous intentions of these men. He held her hand and tried to appear nonchalant and simply curious.

"I'd appreciate if you'd keep your dog at bay," Owen said.

"He won't do anything unless told," Dan said.

Owen gulped. Dan smiled to himself. *Off-balance, just where you want to keep people who want to be in charge.*

After a moment, Owen said, "You know Bunyan Jackson."

"Sure," Dan said.

"Our … our families have been close for generations," Margaret stammered.

"You expecting him for a visit?"

Dan and Margaret hesitated.

"He's like a lot of old friends," Dan said. "We're thrilled when they drop by—expected or unexpected."

"Did he contact you about a visit within the last three days?"

"Sure," Dan said, "but he never arrived, so he may have decided to come another time."

"Is he all right?" Margaret asked.

Owen chortled. "Depends on what *all right* means to you. He's cooling his heels at our detention center in Portland."

"Detention center?" Dan asked. "Where? Why?" He took a half-step toward Owen.

"Portland HQ for the Department of Homeland Security," Owen took a half-step toward Dan.

Tack showed his teeth. Owen retreated the half-step, then another half for good measure.

Looking at Margaret, he said, "Jackson could face some hard time."

Margaret was aghast. "Bunyan? Hard time? For what?"

"You'll get no answers from me … not until I get some from you." Owen's face bore a deep scowl.

Holding Margaret's hand tightly, Dan took another half-step toward this disdainful man. Tack, his mouth closed, followed his lead.

"Exactly what are your questions, beyond 'are we expecting Jacko?'"

"Bunyan—Jacko—you two know Mr. Jackson so well you're not even sure what to call him, are you?" Owen was suspicious.

"I've known him since we were children," Margaret said, putting her hands on her hips, "and I've always called him Bunyan. That's his name."

"I met him before he was dinging homers onto Lansdowne Street," Dan said. "Even then, everyone always called him Jacko—me included. Good enough answer for you?"

"I guess."

Brown and Cruz bounded down the stairs from the second floor. "Nothing up there," Cruz said.

"We'll check the basement," Brown said. "Where is it?"

Dan pointed toward the kitchen. "Around the corner."

Owen looked down at the floor, then back at Dan and Margaret. "We have reason to believe Bunyan Jackson is helping Jews leave America and get to Israel."

"You've gotta be joking, agent. Bunyan Jackson, a conductor on an underground railroad? Ha!"

"Underground railroad?" Owen repeated.

"Yeah, as in how slaves escaped to Canada in the eighteen hundreds," Dan said.

"I know the history!" Owen spat.

Tack stirred, and Dan looked down. The hackles on Tack's back stood up straight, and the entire length of the dog's body was tense.

"Well, conditions for an underground railroad sound similar to me." He looked keenly at Owen. "Agent, Bunyan Jackson is a stalwart American who loves the country and American ideals. Central to that, of course, is freedom."

"Does freedom include leaving the country?" Owen asked.

Dan was taken aback. "Isn't travel a freedom?"

"Not for some people," Owen replied. Something flickered across Owen's face. Dan thought the agent realized the implications of what he had just said.

"Some people can leave and some can't?" Margaret asked. "How odd!"

"I'm sure you're not unaware of the resolution by the United Nations, and the vote Friday morning by the United States. Jews can no longer leave their habitation to live in Israel," Owen said.

"Yes, we are," Dan said. "Alarmed but aware."

"Alarmed?"

"Alarmed that someone's right to go where they want can be taken from them at any time by someone they don't know and to whom they can't appeal." Dan tilted his head and examined the man before him. Five-foot-nine or so, dark, handsome, well-dressed, well-spoken, well-educated, and probably upward-bound. And yet adamant about upholding an obviously un-American law. *Ah-h, young and upward-bound. Therein's the answer.*

Owen was not pleased. This was not going well. To impress Conrad and Constantine, he needed results.

Adelius Forman burst through the back door and stalked through the kitchen into the living room. The blasted dog snarled. He'd love to draw his sidearm and dispatch the beast post haste. *What a dream. Oh, well, maybe he'll present me the opportunity before we leave this place.*

“Anything?” Owen asked.

Forman shook his head.

Owen took a deep breath. His cell phone vibrated with a text message. The call was from Thompson back in Portland: “Message to Callahans read: 5 butterflies. ETA 0200.”

Owen smiled and looked at Dan. “Jackson sent an encrypted message to you.”

Dan’s eyebrows rose.

“He said: ‘Five butterflies. ETA oh-two-hundred.’ Do you know what it means?”

Dan tried to sound dumbfounded. “He was bringing butterflies with him?”

Owen cast a look at Margaret. She shrugged.

“I think we’re taking you in for questioning,” Owen said.

“On what charge? I can’t decode secret messages?” Dan asked.

Owen shook his head.

“It’s awful warm in here, Mommy,” Daisy-Rain complained. Can I stick my head outside and take a breath?

Ruth hesitated. *Could a cool breath hurt?*

“Maybe we could all stick our heads out back and take a breath,” Davey offered. He reached to open the back door a crack or two.

Moments later, they were taking turns leaning their heads out the door and breathing in fresh air. *Good Maine air. Delicious.*

Then Davey thought how the government had spoiled what could have been a beautiful day.

—∞—

Margaret was getting sick of this conversation. She cut in, "Sir, do you know my husband's service to this country?"

"No, and I don't care."

"I'll tell you anyhow." She stepped up to Owen and stood on her tiptoes to look him directly in the eyes. "My husband earned two purple hearts—two. He was awarded the Navy Medal of Honor, the Navy Heroism Medal—"

"Ma'am, I don't care. Truthfully, his service has nothing to do with the matter." Owen looked past her to Dan. "Sir, if you're aiding and abetting Jewish people in escaping this country, you can be jailed. And ma'am," he eyed Margaret, "the same goes for you. Behind bars at your age? Think about spending time in prison."

Margaret shook her head, exhibiting her disbelief. As a school teacher, she'd developed a look strong enough to shame the fibber or the guilty.

Owen frowned and returned his gaze to her. "Do you know of any Jews escaping the country?"

Margaret shook her head.

"Do you know an eight-year-old girl named Daisy-Rain Remini?"

Her eyes flickered. *Oh, my Lord! How could they know?* She steeled herself and looked keenly at Owen: "Daisy-Rain is a name I'd remember." *Not a lie.*

"Have you had any contact with Bunyan Jackson about Jews?"

"Not about Jews leaving the country." Margaret maintained a solemn face, trying her best to keep her body from shaking.

"Bunyan's vehicle contained a DS game which had the fingerprints of a Daisy-Rain Remini, age eight. She and her mother are missing, and her father's in Israel."

"I see," Margaret said. "So?"

"You have not helped any Jews pass this way?"

"No." They were not yet gone.

"No little girl named Remini, or her mother?"

She swallowed hard. "No." I'm not sure what their last name is, she thought to herself.

"Yeah, right," Owen whispered. Derision oozed from the words.

"Mommy, I'm so-o-o thirsty," Daisy-Rain whined.

Ruth sighed and put an arm around her child. "Mommy's got water right here in her backpack."

She reached and pulled out a six-ounce plastic bottle of Poland Spring water.

Daisy-Rain opened the cap, took a deep drink and mimicked, "Ah-h-h, straight from the Maine woods."

The adults couldn't help but chuckle.

"She watches too much television," Ruth said.

"A commercial, Mommy, not a TV show," Daisy corrected.

—⁂—

Agent Owen turned a hooded gaze on Dan. *He's about to crank it up.* Sure enough.

"You, sir," Owen said, pointing a finger at him. Tack quickly took a menacing step toward the agent.

Dan lowered his hand, a signal Tack knew well. The dog stopped mid-step, then sat.

"Go ahead, agent," Dan said.

"When joining the Navy, you took an oath to uphold the Constitution of the United States of America."

"This is what I affirmed, putting my hand to the Bible," Dan said. He took a breath, raised his right hand and quoted, "I do solemnly swear I will support and defend the Constitution of the United States against all enemies, foreign and domestic. I will bear true faith and allegiance to the same. I take this obligation freely, without any mental reservation or purpose of evasion. And I will well and faithfully discharge the duties of the office on which I am about to enter. So help me God."

Dan guessed what was coming. *The whole commander-in-chief thing.*

"The commander-in-chief of the military is the President of the United States," Owen said. "The president has ordered detention of Jews trying to emigrate to Israel. I know you're retired, but you swore to obey your commander."

"Actually, that's not true," Dan said. "Unlike enlisted personnel, the oaths taken by officers do not include any provision to obey orders. Enlisted personnel are bound by the uniform Code of Military Justice to obey lawful orders, *but* officers in the service of the United States are bound by this oath to *disobey* any order violating the Constitution of the United States. Whether the command comes from a sergeant or the president."

Owen began to object, but Dan stopped him with a dark glare.

"Any order," he added, "to prevent free and unfettered movement around our own country is, in my mind, against the Constitution, Agent Owen. And above all of this is my moral obligation to a higher authority than any president or king. My duty is to the King of kings and Lord of lords."

He exhaled like he was blowing a horn. "Now I don't know what you think Jacko is up to. I doubt he's harboring any Jews trying to get out of America. There certainly aren't any in our home. So I'd say your knickers are in a twist at the wrong dance floor."

Owen looked dumbfounded. Dan smiled to himself. *Knickers. Twist. Dance floor. The man's off-balance, no doubt.*

Owen fumbled for words. Somewhere in the depths of his memory bank, he seemed to recall reading something confirming what this Callahan guy said about the oath he swore.

He looked at Agent Forman, who shrugged. Sounds from the kitchen drew his attention. Brown and Cruz returned from the basement, both shaking their heads. *Nothing there.*

Off to the detention center with these two, then? Owen vacillated for a moment, then decided on a different action.

"Mr. and Mrs. Callahan," he said, "beware your actions. Medal of Honor or not, you cannot break the laws of this country. Good day, sir, madam."

He spun on his heel and walked out of the house, his team trailing behind.

On the way to the two SUVs, Cruz stepped to Owen's side. "You're not taking them in, sir?"

"We'll get no information from them. Better to simply let them take us to the Jews and others in this escape network of theirs—this new underground railroad, if such a thing exists."

He turned to Agent Brown. "Sam, be sure they can't see you, and put a GPS tracking device under their front fender."

"Yes, sir."

Seconds later, the two Homeland Security vehicles spit dirt behind them as they wheeled down the long driveway.

—∞—

Peeking through the knot holes in the spring house, Davey, Ethan, and Omri, who had replaced Ruth at the third peephole, couldn't see beyond the house, but they heard car doors slam closed. Davey leaned against the wall of the building, his eye hard against the knot hole. His cell phone vibrated on his hip.

"Yeah?"

"We've gotta talk," Alec said.

"Are those people gone?"

"Those people are feds, Davey, and, yeah, they're gone. We've gotta talk."

"Give me a minute. I'll come out and tell you all about it, okay?"

"Right."

"Hold on," Davey told his charges. "I'll be back."

He crawled to the spring house door and opened it just wide enough to squeeze through. *Could someone still be watching? Could an agent have stayed behind at the house?* Belly to the ground, he snaked his way through the high grass to the edge of the woods, then stood up under the safety of cover.

"I know who that man is, Davey. The guy who says he's an admiral." Alec sounded accusatory, but he looked disgruntled, or maybe dismayed. "The most totally cool scientist in the world."

Phew! He said, "Totally cool." A good sign.

"I've seen his photo in the MIT Student Handbook, but I didn't place him until I saw his face on TV."

Oh-oh. "TV?"

"Yeah, the Department of Homeland Security says they think he's been kidnapped."

"What? Liars!"

"So what's going on, Davey?"

Davey knew all along he could trust Alec. Heck, he'd trust him with his life. But now Grampa would have to trust him too, because the truth was all coming out. Right now.

"Dr. Zohn and the others who were with Grampa and Bubbe this morning—they're escaping the country to go to Israel."

Alec was indignant. "You shouldn't have to escape your own country—"

Davey shook his head.

"To go to your own country."

Davey shook his head.

"That's not right."

Davey shook his head.

"I want to help."

This didn't surprise Davey a bit. The only question was, how?

"I've got an idea, but the plan's gotta be between you and me."

"Grampa and Bubbe will have to know."

"If they did, they wouldn't approve."

Davey pursed his lips and considered. In the end he couldn't resist. "Tell me."

"To start with, one of those guys put something, a GPS I'll bet, under the wheel hub of Mr. C's car."

For the next several minutes Davey huddled with Alec at the edge of the woods. They bumped knuckles and did their old, secret club handshake. Then Davey hit the ground and snaked back to the spring house.

A minute later, Dan Callahan stepped out onto the back porch and walked deliberately to the spring house. He looked to the cloudless sky, wondering if a high-flying spy plane might be up to no good.

Davey must have spotted him because he pushed the spring house door open, stood up outside and waved.

Don't do that! Dan motioned for Davey to lie back down and continued walking toward him. He strode out into the tall grass, pretending to look toward the pond beyond. When he was a few feet away, he spoke just loud enough for the others to hear. "Okay, everyone. Those men were a detail from Homeland Security. They're hot to find you, Omri. They also know Ruth and Daisy-Rain are missing and Stanley's in Israel."

"How did they—" Ruth sputtered.

"I don't know. But before long they'll probably discover Ethan and Naomi are with you, too." Dan hesitated, running his fingers through his hair. "Now listen, we've got to make sure they're not waiting for us out on the highway somewhere. Then we have to get you all out of here to your next stop whether we've heard from him or not."

From inside the spring house, Omri's muffled voice said, "Perhaps we should wait right here."

"Staying's too dangerous," Dan said. "The area's only going to get more and more saturated with Homeland Security and Border Patrol looking for you."

"That's the answer, then. I'll just turn myself in," Omri said.

"No, you don't!" came Ethan's distinct voice. "Freedom's for all of us or none of us."

From the depths of the spring house, Ruth spoke up. "Right, professor. They're after us too. Plus, Stan would never forgive me if he found out I'd left Dr. Omri Zohn to the authorities of this—this repressive government."

"But you can't—" Omri said.

"Yes, I can," Ruth broke in.

"And so can Ethan and I," Naomi said. "We all give ourselves up, or we all press on—with the help of these wonderful people."

"Besides," Daisy-Rain chirped, "I don't want to *not* see you anymore, Mr. Zohn."

"You comfort me, all of you," Omri said. "Dan?"

"Yes?"

"I'd say these younger generations aren't so lost and self-centered after all."

Dan couldn't suppress a smile. "So the issue's settled," he proclaimed. "I'm sorry, I know the spring house is uncomfortable, but you all should wait in there until dark. That gives us the best chance to escape."

As Dan turned to go, Davey interrupted, "Grampa?"

"Yes."

"Alec saw a news flash on TV about Dr. Zohn being kidnapped—"

"Kidnapped?"

"Yeah, well, he called and I had to tell him everything. He's on board with keeping the secret."

Dan shook his head. He loved Alec and knew he was a brilliant kid, but he also had seen his rebelliousness through the years.

"So he and I can check out the highway to make sure the feds aren't hanging around."

"Where's Alec now?"

Davey pointed to the woods.

Dan spotted Alec's silhouette in the shadow of a tree. He exhaled deeply, concerned another person was being drawn into the intrigue. But if Alec simply helped scout the highway, maybe his involvement would be all right.

Dan nodded assent. "But wait until dusk." He turned and walked briskly back to the house. Margaret would want to somehow get food and water to the spring house. She'd be suffering vicariously with them every second of the wait.

—~~—

Back in the spring house, Davey phoned Alec to give him the okay. Alec rode home and got his father's permission to stay overnight with the Callahans, then returned to the forest edge, keeping in touch with Davey via phone.

—~~—

Inside the house, Dan's PGP cell phone rang. He answered, but a second ring never came.

He looked at Margaret, who sat in an armchair across from him. "Frank," he declared.

Her eyes went wide, and she stood up to follow him into the den. Dan strode directly to his desk, opened the bottom drawer, and pulled out his satellite phone.

"ETA?" Frank asked.

"Alan Arkin," Dan replied, hoping Frank would recall the suspense thriller *Wait Until Dark*, starring Arkin, Audrey Hepburn and Richard Crenna.

"Y?"

"Lock."

Security. Danger lurked.

Click. That meant Frank understood.

Dan consulted his navigational tables. Sunset on August fifth came at 6:12 p.m. He looked at his wristwatch. 4:47 p.m.

—~—

At Homeland Security headquarters, Shandra Constantine was seething. Drones were flying over the Canadian border from Maine and New Brunswick to Washington and Manitoba. Satellite cameras relayed images of happenings far below. Coast Guard ships roamed the shorelines. DHS experts scoured through traffic and security cameras. Agents roamed airports of all sizes. Businesses, schools, colleges, and military bases around the country were contacted to discover if any Jews—especially important scientists, financiers, and military leaders—were missing from work. Jews around the country were being rounded up at all centers of travel.

But still nothing on Dr. Omri Zohn. Or Ethan Rosenbaum and Abigail Zimmerman. Benjamin Keith, Yael Ochsenstein, and Gabriel Reichenstein had all been corralled. But compared to Zohn, everyone else—the millionaires, even billionaires trying to flee the country with their fortunes—were inconsequential.

"Petty pipsqueaks!" Constantine uttered and hit her desk with a fist. She winced in pain. Better go back to the letter opener.

She picked up a phone and punched Conrad's number.

—∞—

"Yes, ma'am." Conrad answered on the first ring, though the onset of acid reflux began its familiar rush with the knowledge he was going to upset his boss. The noise of the helicopter blades hammered in rhythm above him, driving a headache deeper into his head. He held his headphones tighter to his ears so he could better hear Constantine.

"A neighbor called to say he saw someone who looked like Dr. Zohn at Bunyan Jackson's house. You have any results?"

"I've 'coptered up to Rockland and decided to stay in the air where I can better keep track of traffic on the roads. Owen's team of six from Portland are here as well. Our main hope right now is movement from the family to whom we think Jackson was taking Zohn and some others."

"What are you waiting for? Arrest them and instill the fear of God into them!"

"I'd say they're beyond that tactic, ma'am."

"How could they be?"

Conrad recalled Owen's recount of his conversation with the Callahans. "I agree with Owen," he said. "The best plan is to spy on them and wait, then catch them making a beeline."

"Must I fly up there to do your job?"

"No, ma'am."

"Then you'd better not fail me!"

Sometimes Conrad conjured up the picture of doing dire physical harm to a criminal. But when he pictured his hands on the throat of this adversary, the face before him was—Shandra Constantine.

Just let me do my job. Nobody is better. Nobody.

Constantine hung up and poked another button on her phone.

Agent Samuel Jones picked up on the first ring.

"Sam, the media bit on our story about Zohn's being kidnapped. Go ahead and implement your idea to put our citizen-patriots on alert."

"Yes, ma'am."

"Immediately. Especially in Maine. Especially on the lookout for Zohn."

"Yes, ma'am."

"And Sam?"

"Yes."

"Include a reward. A hundred-thousand-dollar reward."

She swore she could hear Jones gulp. "Yes, ma'am."

"Make that a million."

Finally, dusk arrived. Davey was as antsy as if he were at first base (the spring house), crouching to steal second (the woods).

With his weight on the front of his feet, he sprang forward and sprinted like Mookie Betts, his favorite ballplayer.

Once he reached the trees, he pulled to a halt and straightened up. Alec was standing beside his four-wheeler.

Davey pointed at the machine and said, "Let's drive to the house as if we've been out running the trails all afternoon—just in case Homeland Security has surveillance on the place."

—ꟺ—

Seconds later, inside the house, Tack leaped to his feet, yipped and strutted to the back door of the kitchen. A "yip" from Tack meant all was okay. Taking the hint, Dan got up and followed the dog. The motor of a four-wheeler sounded out back. Dan motioned to Margaret and they met the boys at the back porch.

The boys sat back in the four-wheeler, Davey behind, holding onto Alec's waist.

"Two soldiers reporting to scout out the territory, captain," Davey said, too frivolous for Dan's taste. The boys' involvement made him uneasy. This was his and Maggie's and Jacko's calling. Not Davey's or Alec's.

And God's not in charge? The question seemed to come from the Throneroom. *Now that is a convicting thought.*

He pointed a finger. "You two are here only to scout. Your parents, Alec, would shoot me if you got in trouble."

"Yes, sir."

"This is an order, young men," he said with the same firmness he had used with his sailors on deck.

"Yes, sir," they said and simultaneously saluted.

"Do not raise any eyebrows," Dan said.

"Yes, sir."

"If you see any federal agents, do not confront them."

"Yes, sir."

"Do not act suspiciously."

"No, sir."

He pointed to Alec. "You know we love you, Alec."

"Yes, Mr. C."

"But we've never had to really, really trust you with something important."

"No, sir."

"But now we do."

"Yes, sir."

"Then don't let us down."

"I won't, sir."

"If they're out there and if they stop you, you're simply driving to the raceway to run some practice laps."

"Yes, sir."

Dan blew out a breath. "Okay."

Alec started up the machine.

"And," Dan looked pointedly at Alec, "no speeding, you hear?"

"Yes, sir. No speeding."

As Davey and Alec rode off, Margaret put a hand to Dan's shoulder. "You sure about this, dear?"

"May God watch over us all," Dan replied.

—⁓—

When darkness finally settled in, Dan and Margaret went to their knees by the living-room couch, pounding heaven's gates with their prayers. They asked God to "confuse the enemy," "blind those who would do Your people harm," "send angels to watch and protect them," "be their front and rear guard," and "change the hard hearts, dear Lord, of the leaders of this country."

—⁓—

The five fugitives lay on the hard dirt of the spring house until the field darkened around them. Even after it was safe to sit up, some continued to lie with their heads on duffel bags, lost in their thoughts. Daisy-Rain continued to cuddle up to her mother.

Omri envisioned the face of his son the last time they were together.

Benjamin's voice reflected his anguish. "Please, Dad, please consider moving back here to Israel. Otherwise, you'll miss your grandson growing up."

"I'd love to, son, but my life, my work is in America."

Then Benjamin had asked the question now causing Omri's consternation. "What's more important, Abba, work or family?"

Benjamin had landed the sharp blow, using the intimate "abba." Daddy. A child's call to his father.

Omri squinted, trying to more clearly recall Benjamin's face when he'd uttered that question. *Was the look one of condemnation? Censure? Criticism?*

No, none aligned with his son's character. The look was more a challenge. Even concern, mixed with love and sincerely missing his dad. All this mingled with worry about how his father was coping with living without his wife and daughter.

He smiled a melancholy smile,then with renewed determination, he began to anticipate being home again.

Years before, the Spirit of God had moved Frank Reid to build a boat for the express purpose of transporting Jews to Israel. At that time, taking on the challenging task had made no sense, but, like Noah, he'd acquiesced and obeyed God's will. "A boat you want, God; a boat you'll get," he'd said. Three- and-a-half years later, the boat was completed—and a beauty to boot.

Today, standing in his back yard, Frank spoke again to God, praying for wisdom, discernment, and the prophetic ability to see things transpire before they did.

He looked to the narrow tidal river where his boat was moored and prayed that Dan Callahan and his *butterflies* would arrive on time. If the ebb tide went out too far, they'd be dry-docked for eight hours, waiting for the next high tide. He checked his watch. That time was drawing dangerously near.

—∞—

Dan and Margaret rose from their time of prayer. She had prepared a large picnic basket full of food. Dan carried the hamper, placing it in the back seat of the extended cab.

Omri and the others would hide in the cap-covered bed. Tack would stay behind with Margaret for protection.

Margaret looked heavenward. The sky was turning dark. Tonight, it would be pitch black with no stars and a puny little fingernail moon. *Was this good or bad?*

—∞—

High above them, a passing satellite, armed with infrared night-vision and thermal-analysis cameras, spit out images of the Callahan property.

Constantine watched from the DHS communications room, the nerve center of her operation. "What's Callahan carrying?" she asked, pointing.

The woman manning the computer monitor shrugged. "Let me zoom in."

As she did so, Constantine stepped up and bent over her shoulder.

"Go in tighter, Muriel!"

"Yes, ma'am." The grainy image was inconclusive.

"Is this the best this camera can do?!" Constantine fumed, then swore.

"Maybe he's holding a batch of baseballs. Callahan coaches Little League." Agent Jones had joined her from his office.

"Right, and he's holding a practice at night. Good thinking, Sam." She shook her head in disbelief. "You're the Rhodes scholar, right?"

He nodded.

"Amazing education system," she spat out. "Well, besides this brilliant deduction, do you have anything?"

He shook his head.

The satellite passed by. Another wouldn't come into range for three minutes.

Using a throwaway phone, Dan called Davey.

"Anything?" he asked.

"We've been up and down the highway and seen nothing," Davey replied.

"Then we're a 'go.' Give us ten minutes, then come back here and keep your Bubbe company."

Dan laid loving eyes on his Maggie. "Keep to the plan, darlin'. Man the house. If any federal agents come knocking, stall and obfuscate." As a captain he'd had charge of five thousand men aboard an aircraft carrier. She didn't argue.

"Wish me luck?" he said.

"God's hand trumps chance every time."

"Spoken like a good pastor's wife."

"Captain's wife too."

Dan cupped her chin in his hand. "We'll pick up this conversation later, young lady."

He pointed at Tack, who suddenly stood as if at attention, his ears up. "Stay here with Mom and protect her, boy."

Tack barked twice. That was a "Yes, Dad."

After a lingering kiss, Dan clicked his tongue with a half-smile and a wink. "My princess," he said.

"My knight." She smiled.

Dan sensed her strain. Danger indeed lurked out there in the darkness. He and the others would, indeed, need God's hand.

Seconds later, Omri and the others scurried out of the spring house, duffle bags on their backs, following Dan to his truck in the yard.

Dan picked up Daisy-Rain, kissed her cheek, and set her in the back. The others tossed duffel bags into the bed and pulled themselves up. When they were settled, Dan closed and locked the gate.

"God go with you, Dan," Omri said.

"With us all," he replied.

"Amen."

From the front door, Margaret extended a hand toward them, praying silently. Dan wasted no time putting his foot to the accelerator, the tires spitting up dirt as he drove down the driveway.

The night's as dark as the heart of our government, as dark as the heart of the United Nations, as dark as the hearts of the people who hate Jews simply because they're Jews. Simply because—

—∞—

In the DHS operations room, Shandra Constantine leaned forward and peered at the satellite image. "Where's the truck?" she asked.

"Truck?" Jones echoed.

"Callahan's truck's gone!"

"Can you find that vehicle, Muriel?" Constantine's question was more of a demand.

Muriel furiously maneuvered a joystick and started scanning the area.

"Three minutes and we lost them?" Constantine slammed her fist into the back of Muriel's chair. "Did they leave in that specific window of time?"

Constantine pointed to the phone. Jones speed-dialed Conrad.

CHAPTER TWELVE

As the call came in to the DHS vehicle, Agent Juan Cruz, hidden in the Maine woods, gazed at the display on a GPS tracking device and announced from the back seat, "They're moving!"

Hearing the conversation via radio, Owen said to Conrad, "We're on 'em. Their cargo, no doubt, is with them."

Owen rubbed his hands in anticipation of catching his quarry. This would propel him to fame within the department. He smirked as he punched a button on the communications module.

—ᴧᴧᴧ—

Conrad's voice was strained, anxiety tightening the tendons along his throat.

He was in a helicopter, flying along the coast just north of Rockland. At this point, he'd rather be on the ground in the chase, but there was something to be said for the speed of a helicopter versus an SUV confined by roads.

The night was so dark he could gather no sense of distance. Lights from cars and houses below helped little.

He wondered what they'd do with Zohn when they caught him. *Place a twenty-four/seven guard around him at his home and his lab until he finished the nuclear fusion project, then let him go free? Or put him in a cell where he belonged?*

The scuttlebutt about Senator Frank was he faced impeachment at the very least. The President was having the solicitor general investigate what powers Smith could impose on the Jewish lawmaker.

It'll serve him right. Put the two in the same jail cell. Maximum security. Ha!

—∞—

Dan turned north out of the driveway. In forty seconds, he was headed east onto Route 105 toward the coast. He tried not to make the ride in the back uncomfortable for his charges, to not go so fast he would draw attention, and to see into the darkened woods on both sides of the road for hidden Homeland Security or Border Patrol vehicles.

The tension of the battlefield, the fear of hand-to-hand combat, the adrenaline rush of setting a plastics charge and blowing a bridge—all these resided in his memory banks. But this emotion was something different. The feeling possessed a sort of thickness, sucking the air out of the cab. He opened the driver-side window an inch. The night air was cool but didn't cut into the density. He practiced the deep-breathing tricks so effective in battle and on the control deck of his ship, while recalling the Navy SEAL motto: "The only easy day was yesterday."

He chuckled wryly at the incongruity of this moment. Here he was, a man who started his career "diving the world over so others may live," putting his life in peril for his America, living by *"non sibi sed patriael!"*—not for self but country.

Now, here he was, a man defying that same country and the whole new set of values for which its government now stood. He had committed his entire existence to America. Now he was committing his life to God and the hope of delivering his people out of bondage.

Finally, he prayed. *Honor, courage, and commitment, Lord. Those form the bedrock of my life, and I apologize for my pride in that life. I realize my honor, courage, and commitment should always be to you first. Forgive me for it ever being otherwise. But now I recommit them to your service. Help and guide me, Father. Direct and protect all of us in this vehicle. Amen.*

In the back of the truck, wanting to ease the tension, Omri spoke softly to the little girl sitting across from him in her mother's arms. "Daisy-Rain, you must be excited to be going to see your Daddy."

"Oh, yes!" she said with a lilt. "I miss him awful."

"I know you do, child," Ruth said. "Won't be long."

"It may be longer than you think," Ethan said.

Naomi elbowed her husband, hushing him.

"Think, child," Omri said in wondrous tones, "you're going to the country where Abraham saw the burning bush, where Isaiah and Jeremiah heard the voice of God, where David wrote the Psalms, where the rich heritage of the Hebrew people blossomed."

"Daddy and I have spoken of this, haven't we?" Ruth said.

"Yes," Daisy-Rain answered, "and guess what, Momma?"

"What, dear?"

"We have a Ruth and Naomi right here in this truck, don't we?" Delight sprinkled her words. Omri could not help but smile.

"We've actually shared that thought together, sweetie," Ruth spoke into the darkness. "And Ruth said, 'Ameikh ami, ve'Elohaiikh Elohai.'"

Omri translated, "'Your people shall be my people and your God my God.'"

"'Wherever you go, I will go,'" Ruth continued. "'Wherever you lodge, I will lodge. Where you die, I will die.'"

"A sentiment," Omri said, "that came from a Moabite woman, a gentile."

"Kinda like Bubbe?" Daisy-Rain asked.

"Kinda like," Ruth answered.

Omri grinned and wondered if, after this evening, he would ever see Dan or Margaret Callahan again and if his escape had endangered their lives.

Free choice. My free choice to leave. Theirs to help. God will honor them for facing such danger. Right?

—~—

A set of headlights appearing in his side-view mirror broke Dan out of his prayers. Those headlights were quickly gaining on him. They were high off the ground—like those of an Escalade. They were wide apart—like an Escalade. And Escalades were what the federal agents drove. Oh-oh. There was no escape, no old tote road to pull into and hide.

He stepped down further on the accelerator and picked up speed from forty-five to fifty-five miles per hour. He went over a rise and down a hill. In his side-view mirror, the SUV's headlights shone toward the tops of the trees as it crested the hill, then it bore down on him on its descent.

He accelerated further. Fifty-seven, Fifty-eight, fifty-nine miles per hour. But the SUV steadily gained ground.

An S-shaped curve lay ahead, a dangerous turn Dan knew well. He let up on the pedal but only to slow as much as he must to stay safely on the asphalt. Coming out of the curve, he accelerated again.

The headlamps of the SUV tilted as the vehicle struggled to stay on the road. Dan took advantage to pull further ahead.

In the Callahan house, the telephone rang. Margaret picked up the headset.

"Mom!"

Annie, their daughter.

"Yes, dear."

"I woke up in the middle of the night. It's two a.m. here, you know, and I felt like somebody nudged me awake, like something's terribly wrong. Is everything all right?"

"Pray, Annie. Pray!"

"What the matter, Mom?"

"The hunters," Margaret said. "The hunters have come!"

"How far away are we?" Conrad hollered into the headset to the helicopter pilot.

"About five minutes, sir."

The helicopter had been reconnoitering the coast and just got the call from Owen that the action was inland. Conrad slapped his knee and swore. Every second counted. He wanted to be on the scene the moment Zohn and this Callahan guy were caught.

Conrad had plugged into the internal communications, so he was wired to Agent Owen's team. He could hear them. They could hear him.

Thompson's voice sought out Owen.

"Yes!" Owen answered.

"Sir, this Daniel Callahan is an ex-Navy SEAL and has been awarded the highest medals you can think of. Besides that, he captained an amphibious assault ship and then an aircraft carrier before he retired. Congress is considering naming one of the new cruisers after him."

Conrad cursed again, then crossed himself. Might as well be on the right side of God, he thought.

Agent Hank Bye, seated beside Conrad, asked, "What's the matter, sir?"

"Just what we need. We're going to arrest a war hero." He uttered several words usually constrained to a football locker room, then crossed himself again. *Sorry, Big Guy.*

Owen cut in. "We're hot on their tail. We'll have them in a minute."

"Give me your coordinates."

In the back of Dan's pickup truck, Omri got flashes of the faces around him. Fear blanketed each one. But he himself felt calm, like being in the eye of a hurricane.

They were in a chase, for sure. The cap's opaque rear window allowed a view of the oversized vehicle catching up to them.

"This is playing out just like the last time … with Jackson," Ethan declared. "Only this time we're going to get caught."

"Oh, my!" Ruth put a hand to her mouth and pulled Daisy-Rain close.

"Mommy, we can't get shot. We've got to get to Daddy." The child wept.

"Ethan said *caught*, not *shot*, darling," Ruth soothed. "And we never know, do we. God knows."

Omri repeated in a murmur, "God knows."

Behind the wheel, Dan tried to stay on the asphalt along the winding stretch of road. Then he came to a familiar straight-away at least a half-mile long. A car approached from the other direction. When the vehicle passed, Dan peered into his side-view mirror to see if the headlights illuminated the car chasing him. It did, and indeed, behind him was a big, black Escalade.

He inhaled a gallon or so of air, knowing he could no longer outrun his nemesis. He let up on the accelerator and raised his eyes in a plea toward heaven.

The SUV wheeled into the passing lane and slid up beside him. His heart went to his throat. No flashing lights … yet. As Dan's chest deflated, the lights flashed from low beam to high to low again, then the vehicle accelerated and flew past him—and kept going. Its angry driver laid on his horn and hastened off in a race to somewhere.

The stale air of defeat was suddenly saturated with oxygen. *What just happened?* Again Dan raised his eyes to the heavens, this time with thanksgiving.

On another stretch of Maine back roads, Alec and Davey hurtled along in Alec's Pontiac GTO. Davey wouldn't tell his friend, but fear played heavy fingers along his spine and he guessed Alec's too. Their plan was working, but how would everything play out? Federal agents had detected them and were in serious pursuit.

Alec turned and shot a look at Davey. Davey couldn't tell if it was a Funtown- or Splashtown-type smile or a look of anguish. Maybe some weird mixture of the two.

This had been Alec's idea, and Davey had been thrilled to go along with the scheme. While Davey and the Jews were hiding out in the spring house, Alec had been standing watch under cover of the forest when the Homeland Security agent had deftly placed the tracking device under the Callahan truck. Alec had just as adroitly snuck to the driveway and removed the device.

And now Davey held the GPS in his hand as they led two SUVs, probably filled with federal agents, on a chase in the direction opposite his Grampy's route.

Alec was driving his race car. No way they could be caught, right? Well, maybe?

For a brief moment Alec entertained the thought of what would happen to his education, his life, if they were indeed apprehended. Forget MIT. Forget racing. Forget freedom! Then the memory of the finish line at Monday night's race flashed before him. The checkered flag.

An announcer's voice in his head said, "The young man had a checkered past."

A guttural laugh escaped him as he made the connection between "checkered flag" and "checkered past"—and Davey looked askew at him.

"No way an Escalade can catch us, Davey," he declared and straightened his shoulders. "No way, man!"

"Nope." Did Davey feel as confident as Alec was? Probably not, so he decided to encourage his best friend.

"We could drive this road in our sleep, right?" Alec declared; there was no doubt.

"Yep."

"All we gotta do is stick to the plan."

"Right."

Alec grinned and shifted gears, accelerating around a curve.

—∞—

In his truck Dan's body felt the relief, but his mind searched for answers. Had Homeland Security *not* been watching? Did God do something spectacular? He pressed down the accelerator. Frank's house was only six or seven miles away.

Dan could hear voices in the back of the truck. Shouts of "Hallelujah!" It sounded like even Ethan was joining in.

—∞—

In the Callahan home, Margaret prayed fiercely.

Eyes closed and one hand on Tack's fine head, she listened as in London, Annie read Psalm 91: *"The Lord will give His angels charge over you to watch you in all of your ways. They will lift you up in their hands—"*

—⁂—

Davey had just finished tightening his seatbelt when Alec said, "Let's show 'em what we're made of, girl." Patting the leather-covered steering wheel, he yelled, "Yahoo!"

A second later, the skin on Davey's face was forced back. *Is this like the G-force an astronaut experiences on takeoff?*

—⁂—

Driving the lead Homeland Security vehicle, Agent Adelius Forman watched as the taillights of the vehicle they were following disappeared around a curve, obviously speeding up, not slowing down.

"They're on the run!" he said. Forman was proud of his driving grades at the Federal Law Enforcement Training Center in Brunswick, Georgia. He'd been at the top of his class and would never forget that he would have "won the gold" if not for a blown tire in the final test.

"Well, catch them!" Owen said, sounding exasperated.

Didn't need to even say that! He smirked at the easy catch ahead. Gripping the wheel tight, he downshifted to fourth gear as he approached the curve, then accelerated out of the bend. Behind them, the second DHS vehicle lost ground. Forman smiled.

—ꙮ—

Flying over a rise in the road, the GTO's front tires slammed onto the pavement. Thank God we're strapped in, Davey thought, or my head would've hit the ceiling. And thank God Alec is driving, not me!

Davey turned to look behind them. The vehicle in pursuit was just coming over the knoll.

"Do an O'Reilly," Davey ordered.

"No spin?"

"Yeah."

Alec sped around a curve to the left, downshifted, then downshifted again. He hit the brakes, sliding the car sideways and turned down an even narrower dirt road.

—ꙮ—

In the back seat of the Escalade, Cruz's eyes were keen on the tracking device. He pointed ahead, "There must be a road up ahead on the left that's not on the GPS map."

Forman slowed down.

Cruz peered ahead and cursed. There weren't any street signs out here in the woods—not a one—and the moon was nonexistent. Black as a pirate's heart.

"There!" he declared, pointing to a narrow opening in the forest.

Forman hit on the brakes, slamming Cruz into the back of the bucket seat. He barked another curse, bolder than the last.

Davey looked in the side-view mirror. The headlights from the SUV called "the hound from hell" were faint in the distance.

Shortly, he and Alec came to an abandoned gravel pit.

"Do a reverse O'Reilly," Davey suggested.

"Right, plenty of spin!" Alec agreed. "Yeah!"

Alec twirled the wheel, sending the car into a series of tight circles, kicking up dirt and dust into a plume, so much that dark powder seeped into the car, causing Davey to cough.

But they both shouted in delight at the heavy cloud of sand, then Alec yanked the car out of the spin and floored the accelerator.

Davey's head flew back; he screamed a "Yahay!"

Thirty seconds later, Forman approached the gravel pit and slammed his palm into the steering wheel in frustration. A dust storm confronted him, worsened by the blackness of the night.

"I can't drive into that!" he roared.

Behind him, Owen ordered, "Wait for the dust to settle!"

Of course, boss. Geez.

As Forman waited, drumming the steering wheel with his fingers, Owen asked Cruz, "Where in the name of God would they be going out here in the forest? What's up ahead?"

"Looks like woods and more woods."

"An airstrip? Like a personal strip?"

"If so, none appears here."

Exasperated, Forman decided to edge his way through the dust storm.

—∾—

Up ahead, Alec raced through a series of slow curves and rises and falls in the road. He knew this stretch well. This place was home. It was … his special place, where he practiced to improve his reflexes.

"Almost there," he announced. "Get ready!"

Abruptly, he spun the car to the right onto an old tote road used for logging a few years earlier. About twenty yards down the narrow passage, he slammed on the brakes.

Davey hopped out before the car stopped and heaved the tracking device, wiped clean of his fingerprints, as far as he could down the tote road.

He slipped back into the car and shouted, "Touchdown!"

Before Davey's could close the door, Alec had the GTO spinning backwards the way they'd come. Kicking gravel into the air, the car came back to the dirt road. Alec turned off the lights and sped up over a ridge.

In his rearview mirror, he spotted the dim lights of the DHS vehicle flicking one direction then the other. The car had entered the series of curves.

Alec drove cautiously ahead, then spotted the vague silhouette of a barn in a field, about fifty yards to the right. If a person didn't know the structure was there, they'd never spot it and keep on driving down the old dirt road to nowhere. He sped up again, racing to the structure.

Davey jumped out of the car and opened wide the barn door. Twenty seconds later, Alec and Davey stood atop a loft, hayforks in hand, furiously throwing hay and straw down on top of the GTO.

"That enough, you think?" Davey asked.

Alec sneezed once, twice, three times. "Better be. Let's go!"

He slid down a ladder, his feet on its sides as if he were fireman slipping down a firehouse pole.

Davey came down so fast, he almost bopped Alec on the head.

"Whoa!" Alec hollered.

They hustled to the back of the barn and opened a door to an old horse stallwhere two well-used dirt bikes were waiting.

"We'll meet up at the old treehouse," Alec said.

"It's still there?" Davey asked.

Alec shrugged. "Well, the tree's gotta be there."

With that, he and Davey kick started their bikes and left the stall by a back door, heading into the pasture beyond.

—ɱ—

"What in the world?"

Owen stepped out of the Escalade and stood, hands on hips. The vehicle's headlights lit up the sorriest piece of road he'd ever seen.

Tree branches hung low over a track that narrowed into the distance. A couple of four-wheelers might, just might, be able to ride side-by-side down this path. But if they'd taken four-wheelers, where was the vehicle?

Cruz got out of the car and joined Owen. "According to my tracker, they should be straight ahead," he said, "about forty yards."

He squeezed his hands into fists. He could roast a potato in his palms right now.

He turned to look inside at Forman who was obviously seething.

"Go slow, and we'll walk along beside you," Owen instructed.

Finally they reached the tracking device, lying on the ground.

Owen picked up the GPS. *Incredible.* "So, did it fall off Callahan's truck?" he asked. "Was he really bringing them into these woods?"

Cruz shrugged. "Doesn't look like anyone's been down this road in a long time."

Owen ground his teeth. "They threw the thing down here." He hesitated, thinking it through, then tapped his throat mike. "They've been leading us on a rabbit chase!"

Conrad, his helicopter hovering somewhere nearby, bellowed something unintelligible and hung up.

Owen hung his head. He saw Jacko's face, slapped at the SUV, and shook his head, cursing Jackson and his friends.

Conrad picked up his secure radio and contacted Boston headquarters.

"Satellite images," he demanded when Denise Richards answered. "Get the satellite images for the Callahan house. We've been chasing the wrong vehicle!"

"Lost them? You said you lost them!?" Shandra Constantine stood in the middle of the operations room.

Her fury was beyond description. She spun around, glared at the half-dozen agents in the room and swore, thinking if her mouth were a machine gun, she'd mow them all down.

You could have all the scientists, every last billionaire, the cream of the IT world, and it didn't matter. Not to the president. Not to her.

Zohn! He was the icing, the crown jewel.

But he wasn't in hand. Indeed, they didn't know where he was at all. A world-class intelligence agency, and they couldn't track one truck in one state in a one-horse town with no traffic? Imbeciles!

Nickles? She could have spit JFK dollars! A sizzling-hot steam pipe held no quarter to her.

"Destination?" she asked. "What could be their destination? The border? An airstrip?"

"The coast!"

The voice was Conrad's, heard above the whirring blades of the helicopter.

"Call the Coast Guard," Constantine ordered. "Make sure they have a photograph of Zohn and have them stop and search any boat—*every* boat."

Five minutes earlier, the doorbell rang at Frank Reid's home. Frank had just returned to his back yard after walking to the river to see how close the tide was to "D Day," his term for the last moment he could get his boat down the narrow tidal river to the ocean. He ran to the door, expecting Dan Callahan. Instead, Bob Masters, his pastor, stood before him.

Oh, this is not good.

"Frank," Masters said, "I felt I had to speak to you tonight."

This is very bad.

"I sensed the bad feelings. Then you weren't in church today."

Frank glanced over Master's shoulder, anticipating Dan's truck to come into view any second.

"Bob, there are no bad feelings. Maybe hurt feelings. Or hurting because I know in my heart you're not only wrong theologically but erring on the side of a belief system that points people toward hatred of those whom God calls the apple of his eye."

"Your beliefs are up to debate, Frank."

"Not with me. And not with God."

"It's in his Word."

"What? Hate the Jews is in his Word?"

"Well," he shrugged, "not exactly."

"Not at all." Frank looked at his watch, then over Masters's shoulder. Nothing.

"Frank," Masters said, "can we make time tomorrow or the day after to discuss this in a more quiet fashion? When we've both wound down a bit? Perhaps in my office?"

Frank hesitated.

"Listen, I know your feelings about the Jews, my friend. But you know the government just announced on the radio citizens are being asked to report any Jews trying to leave the country for Israel. So now—subliminally at least—even our government doesn't trust them. This is a matter of law, and Romans eight verse one admonishes believers to follow the laws of our country."

Frank stiffened, anger growing within him.

Dan maneuvered down into a little fishing village, then turned right along a street hugging a shoreline much more forgiving than most of the state's coast. To his left, he spotted Frank's Cape Cod home.

A white sedan was parked in the driveway and a man was standing in the door entering a breezeway between the house and a two-car garage.

Who could he be? Was there danger? The feds?

Dan flicked his headlights on and off and cruised past.

Frank spotted the headlights approaching.

Turning his attention back to Masters, he said, "Pastor, I'll check my schedule and get back to you soon for a meeting." He moved to close the door.

Masters must have noticed Frank's attention was diverted toward the road because he turned and watched Dan's truck pass by. Frank could see Masters' eyes narrow, and his thoughts turning.

At last, Masters turned back to Frank. "Please do so, my friend."

Frank shook Masters's hand good-bye—not the usual Christian hug but a distant sort of "nice-to-see-you."

Moments later—and not too soon for Frank who was counting the seconds before the tide would be out too far for departure—Masters drove away in the direction Dan had gone. Odd, he lived the other way. Maybe he was visiting Amy Rand to see how her broken ankle was mending.

Chapter Thirteen

A hundred yards up the street, Dan turned into a driveway and started to back out, only to wait a moment as a white sedan passed by at a leisurely pace. The car appeared to be the one parked in Frank's driveway. By the luminance of a streetlight, Dan could see the man inside was peering at him.

What manner of person is this? Dan wondered.

When the sedan had disappeared around a bend in the street, he turned the truck around and hurried to Frank's home. Two flashes of his headlights and the garage double-door opened. Dan drove into an open bay, and the door closed behind him. Frank hurried around a corner, wearing an Army-green jacket, hat, and high-top boots.

Dan stepped out of the cab. "Frank, we've got no time to waste."

He hurried to the back of the truck and let down the tailgate.

"Time to waste?" Frank said. "We'll miss the tide if we don't jump aboard the boat *this very minute!*"

Frank waved to Omri and the others to climb out. Omri handed Daisy-Rain, dressed in pink Tinkerbell pajamas, to Dan, while he and Ethan hopped down and began to help the others. Everyone scrambled to get out, dragging their duffel bags with them.

"Okay, folks," Dan said, "this is where we part." He kissed Daisy-Rain on the top of her head. "This is Frank, a brother of mine since we served together with the SEALs a hundred years ago. He'll take good care of you."

"But we've gotta hurry," Frank said. "Miss the tide and who knows what will happen."

Omri stepped forward and shook Dan's hand. "God bless you for all you've done for us."

Dan put an arm around Omri and handed him the picnic basket. "I know He'll go with you. And I know you couldn't have a better ship captain than Frank."

"Would you somehow let me know what's happened to Bunyan?" Omri asked.

"He'll be in touch, I'm sure."

Dan placed a paper in Omri's hand. "Please hold onto this and read over these Scriptures when you get the time, my friend. I believe you'll find them eye-opening."

Omri slipped the paper into his pants pocket.

Dan stepped back. "Let's grab all the gear and get going."

In a moment, Dan and Omri and the four other "butterflies" were racing behind Frank out the back door from the garage and along a yard that led to a long dock where the waters of the narrow tidal river sped toward the ocean.

—⁓—

"Hurry, hurry!" Frank grabbed duffel bags and tossed them into the back of the boat. Frank had built this boat, right down to the spinnakers—with a little help from Dan and other friends. He knew the boat, and he knew how low the water would get before the hull touched the riverbed. Another two or three inches lower and they wouldn't be able leave on this tide. The boat had to stay bouyant the half mile to a small bay and then into the open ocean beyond.

Frank's job was to take his cargo all the way to Israel, non-stop.

He'd just seen the Homeland Security spot about Dr. Zohn on television and realized how desperate they were to capture him.

Within seconds, Dan had loosened the ropes tethering the boat to the dock, Frank started the engines and pulled the vessel slowly into the river flow.

Little Daisy-Rain's voice called out of the darkness, "I love you, Mr. Dan."

Dan waved at the boat's receding profile. "I love you too, little princess."

Frank had no fear his boat could get his passengers all the way to Israel. She was a forty-four-foot sail and power boat with very heavy displacement and a full keel. She could make a hundred nautical miles a day, and he'd stored a month's worth of food and water for a half-dozen people. But the trip would be wearisome and fraught with the dangers of a deep ocean and storms that often challenged the best of sailors.

Pastor Bob Masters turned onto a side street and parked on a bluff high above Frank's house. Turning off his car lights, he gazed through the darkness, trying to figure out what was unfolding below.

Frank had acted so strangely at his home, never mind his obstinacy at the Bible study the other day—so adamant that the Jews were still God's people, despite the Scriptures Masters threw at him. *Where had he been since then, and who were these people? Why did they driven past Frank's house and wait until he left?*

Frank wouldn't have anything to do with Jews escaping the country, would he? Homeland Security is pulling out all the stops to prevent such a thing. Any help would be breaking the law and Romans 13:1 says: "Everyone must submit himself to the governing authorities."

Leaning out his window, Masters tried to get a closer look. Were people boarding Frank's boat?

Meanwhile, Dan turned and clambered back to the house. He locked the doors, stepped from the mud room into the garage, closed the tailgate of the truck, opened the garage door, and backed out of the driveway. *Home to Maggie, and to a life perhaps never the same as before.*

He drove out of the village. The country road was quiet. Darkness enveloped the few houses he could see. He had gone from hectic and fearful just an hour ago to serene and peaceful.

Dan let his shoulders relax. His mind wandered to Maggie and the boys and the tale he'd tell about the scare with the black SUV. Phew! He chuckled and admonished himself for having been so frightened.

He passed the last curve he'd slowed for without touching the brakes. Suddenly, all hell seemed to descend on him. Bright flashing lights flashed in his face. A high-intensity beam lit up the highway like high noon from above.

Blinded, Dan slammed on the brakes. He held his hands in front of his face and spread his fingers, trying to see what was happening. In front of him, two Escalades squeeled to a stop in the middle of the road. Behind him, a helicopter, rotoblades whirling, dropped down, kicking up dirt, and planted itself across both lanes.

Bodies rushed at him, guns raised. The metallic sound of the tailgate being lowered was followed by cusswords he hadn't heard since the Navy. Both truck doors flew open. Arms reached in and dragged him from his seat.

Still fighting the lights, Dan kept his eyes on the ground.

Two shiny black shoes came into his vision.

"Captain Callahan!" The voice was familiar. Agent Owen.

"So this is Callahan?" This voice he didn't recognize. "Doesn't look like a war hero."

"No, he doesn't, Mr. Conrad. He doesn't, indeed," Owen said.

—∞—

An hour later, Dan was being grilled by an irate Agent Joseph Conrad. Dan marveled at how Conrad's face turned various shades of red as Dan refused to answer his questions. The more belligerent the questions, the more peaceful Dan's visage. The higher the voice rose, the more tranquility reigned in Dan's heart.

Since the day he'd given his heart to the Lord, Dan had become familiar with this calm. He was a sojourner here on earth. Life, a fleeting time, but a promise of eternal tranquility awaited on the other side.

Conrad's questions all led to dead ends. As they did, Dan observed the federal agent and thought of a lush, plump plum drying up into a hard prune. The man was becoming a prune before Dan's eyes. Amazing!

Standing silently behind Conrad was Agent Owen, looking dejected. Probably wanted to be in charge, probably hoped to bust the whole underground railroad and get promoted to DC. Poor man. Lost in more ways than one.

Conrad's questions had dissipated into threats, each delivered with a raised eyebrow, or a snarl, or a poisonous cussword about Dan's lack of patriotism and how Conrad would have his name removed from the Navy ship being built.

At one point, Dan looked with sorrow at the man. He was just like Owen, only more so—bound to his job, chained to ambition, needing to prove to Shandra Constantine that he was the best.

Finally, Dan asked, "Intimidation tactics normally work for you, do they, agent?"

"Tell you what, bud. Jailtime. That's the tactic that works for me. Every time … 'cause every minute you're languishing behind bars will be a minute I'll be enjoying the thought of you there.

Scrubbing dirty bedsheets in the laundry. Hoping you're the flavor of the month. Yeah, that's my favorite tactic, Seaman."

"I'm afraid you don't have the authority to bust me down in rank, agent. Besides, my commanding officer isn't the same as yours."

—∞—

While Margaret and Annie were praying on two continents, Davey and Alec sat ten feet off the ground in the remains of their old clubhouse, munching on stale Cheetos and sharing a bottle of warm Moxie they'd found in one of their dirt-bike saddlebags, and Shandra Constantine stalked the halls of the Homeland Security offices on the St. Elizabeth's Hospital campus, looking for someone, a janitor even, to scream at. She didn't dare speak to President Smith. This might very well be a career-breaker.

—∞—

As Frank Reid steered his boat from the bay into the Atlantic Ocean, blinding floodlights blasted his eyes. Moments later, a Coast Guard cutter sliced in front of him, leaving an eight-foot wall of water in its wake. Thankfully, Frank's passengers were in the cabin below deck.

He hollered down to them, "Hide behind the false wall!" His warning referred to an inner wall that was built for the sole purpose of concealing people.

He heard chair legs scrape the floor, feet scrambling for cover, and a man's voice say, "Hide the luggage back there too!"

The cutter was the smallest of its class, a sixty-five-footer, but its waves were big enough to rock Frank's vessel. *I hope no one gets sick below deck.*

A voice on a loudspeaker bellowed, "This is the United States Coast Guard. Stop your boat and prepare to be boarded."

Even before Frank's boat stopped rolling, adrift in the wake of the cutter, a motor surf boat pulled alongside. A lieutenant, seaman, and chief warrant officer all stepped aboard. Frank put on his best look of bewilderment.

"Jimmy," Frank said, using the naval term for lieutenant. He directed his statement to the broad-shouldered, six-foot-tall, thirtyish man. "I'm Frank Reid, Senior Chief Petty Officer, US Navy retired. To what do I owe the pleasure of your boarding?"

"We're stopping all vessels, looking for a Dr. Omri Zohn."

"Oh?"

"His capture is vital to our nation's defense."

"I've heard of him. He's the nuclear-fusion guru, right?"

The lieutenant nodded. "What're you doing out in the middle of the night, Senior Chief Petty Officer?"

"Just tripping out to Job Island. I want to get an early start tomorrow. The blues are running out there. I hate to lose time, lieutenant. Like to get there by four bells."

"Job Island … and by midnight, huh?"

Frank nodded.

"Awfully big boat you have here for fishing," the lieutenant observed.

"I normally use my Boston Whaler, but she suffered some damage to her hull, starboard aft, so I'm putting this baby into service for the time being."

"Whaler, huh? What model?" Frank could tell the lieutenant doubted him and was putting him to the test. No problem.

"Twenty-three Conquest with a Suzuki four-stroke."

"Hmm." The officer hesitated, eyes hooded, looking deep in thought. "Mind if we check out your rig, sir?"

"No. Have at it." Frank swallowed hard. "Light switch is on the right."

The lieutenant nodded to the chief warrant officer and the seaman. The warrant officer, who could have passed for the generic grizzled veteran in an old John Wayne movie, had a handgun holstered at his side. The seaman, a kid who probably shaved every other day, carried a Mini-50 rifle.

Frank looked the lieutenant in the eye and silently prayed. *Little to read there. No cutting slack for a comrade in arms.*

The chief warrant officer, whose name patch identified him as CWO Hubbard, scrambled down the steps ahead of the seaman and flicked on the small circular lights inset in the ceiling. Before him was a small galley with a door opening to a tiny head. Nothing unusual here—except the overhead lighting was faint, making the cabinets look a little fuzzy.

The room was very neat. The galley countertop contained nothing but three aerosol spray cans.

Beyond the galley and through a narrow doorway was another cabin, this one larger. Hubbard stepped through, followed by the seaman. The boat was rigged to sleep six. *Talk about overkill for a one-man fishing excursion.*

Hubbard signaled for the seaman to start searching. First he opened a tiny closet. No signs of anyone. Then another. Nothing. Then a foot locker. Nothing. Then another. Nothing.

Hubbard spotted a couple of fold-up beds that were attached to both the port and starboard sides of the boat. He pulled them down. Empty. How many boats were they going to board, anyhow? A waste of time, and the lieutenant darn well knew it. But orders were orders.

"Let's go, Brown," Hubbard said. But as he turned to leave, something drew his attention. *What's this?* A piece of cloth stuck out of the corner of the rear wall portside, about three feet off the floor.

He bent down for a closer look. The material appeared to be part of a child's pajamas, colored pink with the likeness of a fairy.

"Tinkerbell."

"What's that, chief?" Brown asked.

"Tinkerbell," he repeated.

He tugged on the material, but it didn't budge.

"You suppose the wall was put up with a piece of pajamas sticking out?" Brown asked.

"Don't be stupid." *Why are kids nowadays as dumb as a hammerhead?*

Hubbard knocked on the wall. Sounded hollow. "Go get the lieutenant and the owner," he commanded. *Well, even dumb kids are good for something.*

—⁂—

Seconds later, Frank stepped into the cabin, with the lieutenant and seaman behind him.

When he spotted what had roused curiosity, Frank nearly choked. *The jig's up, and we're not even in international waters.*

CWO Hubbard pointed to the patch of pajama fabric and asked gruffly, "What's behind this wall, sir?"

The lieutenant slipped past Frank and leaned in for a closer look at the cloth.

"Tinkerbell," he said. "Not something I'd expect a retired Navy man to be wearing, Chief."

"My, ah, my granddaughter," Frank murmured. "Must be my granddaughter's."

"A-huh." The lieutenant yanked. The material didn't dislodge.

"Funny how the cloth's wedged into the edge of the wall, isn't it?"

Frank nodded.

The lieutenant knocked on the wall. Solid wood, but it sounded hollow. He turned to Frank. "What's behind the wall, Chief?"

"Nothing."

"Unless you want my seaman here to take an ax to your wall, I want you to show me."

"Then you'll have to do that, lieutenant."

"Brown," Hubbard said, "There's an ax above deck. Retrieve it and put it to use."

"Yessir."

The seaman left the cabin and returned shortly, hefting a hatchet in one hand and his Mini-50 in the other. He set down the rifle and stepped up to the wall.

Frank eyed the rifle and had a fleeting thought of taking charge of the situation. Then he remembered the sixty-five-foot cutter had a full crew of armed Coast Guardsmen, and he came back to reality. *Oh, Lord!* he prayed.

The low ceiling prevented the seaman from lifting the ax above his head, but shoulder height was high enough. When he slammed the wall, it splintered. Frank then realized his passengers could be injured in the assault. And they'd certainly be captured, whether harmed or not.

"Stop!" he hollered, motioning with his hand.

He walked to a bookcase and pushed a hidden button. A hydraulic arm, centered on the wall, pushed it toward the men, stopping after moving three feet, then turned enough so that a person could step behind the wall from the left side.

"Aha!" The lieutenant pulled his sidearm from its holster and stepped to the opening. Frank looked to the floor, blew out a breath, and waited for the inevitable. Five of God's people had been so close to freedom. But now …

The lieutenant stared inside, looking for his quarry. Then, astonished, he stepped back. "Nobody! Nothing!"

Frank looked up quickly, his eyes wide. Trying to hide his own surprise, he choked out, "What'd you expect?"

"Something more than this," the lieutenant said, picking up a little girl's pajama shorts. He handed them to Frank. "You can give this back to your granddaughter. What's her name?"

Frank hesitated, trying to conjure a name, any name. Then he smiled and answered: "Deborah. A brave little tyke."

"Why'd you let us damage your boat when there was no need?" the lieutenant asked.

Frank narrowed his eyes at the man. "I risked my life for my country. I just wanted to see if she remembered and respected my service. Guess not."

The lieutenant hung his head. "I'm sorry, Chief. Send an invoice to HQ, and I'll authorize a repair." He saluted Dan and added, "We'll leave you to it. Good fishing to you."

With that, the other two Coast Guardsmen headed up the steps to above deck, but the lieutenant spotted the spray cans. His eyebrows knit together as he picked up an aerosol can and looked closer. The can was white all around, with no lettering, no logos.

He turned to Frank. "What's this, anyhow?"

"Shellac."

"No brand name?"

Frank shrugged. "I'm field-testing for Dow Chemical. I've done some work for them in the past."

"Hm-m-m." The lieutenant hefted the can. "Empty."

"Yeah, I used all three cans on the cabinets just yesterday." The tiny hairs on his neck bristled.

The lieutenant stood in place for several seconds, pondering. Frank followed his eyes to the cabinets. They possessed an odd opaqueness. *Oh-oh. Something's up.*

"I don't think the stuff works too well," the lieutenant declared, setting the can back down on the countertop. He turned back to the steps and began to climb. *Contrary to your opinion.* Frank hurried up the stairs and watched as the Coast Guardsmen reboarded their surf boat and headed back to the cutter.

—m—

Standing at the helm of his boat, Frank watched the cutter sprint away in search of another vessel. *You're getting colder. Colder!*

He let a minute or two pass. *Now, you're cold as ice!* He stepped down into the cabin, wondering where on earth his five guests could be.

Subconsciously, he was thinking perhaps his eyesight was worsening, or possibly just the effects of a very long day turned into night, because, indeed, the cabinet seemed fuzzy to the eye. Then he picked up and turned one of the aerosol cans in his hands. "Hmmm." Looking around, he called, "All clear!"

He heard movement immediately to his left and, clear as day, Omri and Ethan appeared in front of the stove and refrigerator. Omri appeared dumbfounded; Ethan sported a self-satisfied grin.

Frank allowed his jaw to fall. In front of Omri and Ethan, as in a vague faraway dream, Naomi, Ruth and Daisy-Rain began, ever so slowly, to appear.

At first, it seemed as if he were looking through ten feet of water. Their forms were wavy and opaque. They seemed to be there in the cabin, but he could see through them. Frank closed his eyes, rubbed them, shook his head, then looked again.

The women and girl, moment by moment, became less transparent. First, their silhouettes were clearer, then their clothing, then their faces. Miraculous!

Flustered, he stepped back in surprise. He could only muster a weak, "What?"

"The spray-can version of my invisibility cloak," Ethan said, his grin at Guinness Book proportions.

"Invisi—" Frank stepped closer and touched Ethan's shoulder.

"Has to do with light refraction and other strange and exotic things," Omri said.

"Strange, exotic … and life-saving." Ruth's face beamed.

"Yeah, you couldn't see any of us, could ya'?" Daisy-Rain giggled.

"No, I couldn't, young lady. Not even you!" Frank again shook his head in disbelief. "I'm—I'm going to go back above-deck. Wh-why don't you all get some sleep? We have a long trip ahead of us."

"Frank," Omri said, "I know I speak for all of us when I say thank you. Thank you for all you've done and all you're doing. Thank you for putting yourself in jeopardy for a group of people you don't even know."

Frank smiled. "The Messiah said, 'What you do for even the least of these my brethren, you do unto me.' I know the Jews always have been and always will be God's people. And his land has long been Israel. I can do nothing else than to love you and love taking you home. I embrace the task ... actually, my calling."

Omri stepped forward and hugged him.

Chapter Fourteen

Seventy-five hours after the Senate approved the UN ban, seven of the top ten on Shandra Constantine's A List were accounted for, but one of the three missing was *the* number one. Constantine was fuming. She stalked from her desk to the windows. The sun was rising in brilliant oranges and yellows, but the beauty didn't come close to soothing the unfettered wrath spilling out of her. Nor did the sunrise affect her heavy feeling of dread. She had just ended a phone call from Conrad, after filling his ear with the foulest words she could mine from the dark pit inside her. She'd already started another list, this one of the people who'd pay for their ineptitude.

The dread? The call she now had to make to the president. Despite the manpower, the technology, and the commitment, Dr. Omri Zohn had somehow slipped through the net, and Rosenbaum with him. They had vanished with no trace. And DHS didn't even have evidence against this Jacko Weird-Name-and-All Jackson or the Callahans. How could she explain people in Podunk, Maine, outwitting what she'd always claimed was the world's finest law-enforcement agency!

As she stepped back to her desk to call President Smith, her intercom came alive. "Madam Secretary," her secretary said, "Mr. Pinto is on the line."

"Put him through." Constantine snapped up her phone. "Speak."

"We caught Abigail Zimmerman and her husband boarding a small private plane out of a little town in northern Minnesota," Pinto said with some enthusiasm.

"Zimmerman." Constantine repeated the name like it was fourth prize in a small-town speaking contest, then hung up. It was time to make the call she so dreaded.

Since President Harold Smith had risen at five o'clock, he had fought the temptation to call Constantine for an update. He sat atop his desk, reading a national newspaper—*my newspaper*—with each day's talking points set in play by the White House Communications Department and its pals in the mainstream media.

When the first two words came out of Constantine's mouth, he knew she'd never be part of his United Nations leadership team.

When the first sentence was out of her mouth, he'd resigned himself that not *all* of the Top 100 List would be prevented from leaving America.

When the conversation was finished, Smith simply shrugged. *Was this a defeat? Naw! Hey, overall, the vote on the UN resolution and carrying out Operation Cork were, combined, an immense success. For the country. And, more succinctly, for one Harold Reynold Alfonso Smith. That is, Secretary-General-to-be Harold Reynold Alfonso Smith.*

The door of the private entrance to the Oval Office opened, and a lady's hand appeared. His wife, Theresa, the future First Lady of the United Nations. Smith's grin spread from ear to ear.

The rising sun shimmered over the Atlantic Ocean. Frank Reid's hand-built boat, now under full sail, rode a sea as calm as a bathtub. He recalled the old saw, "A smooth sea never made a skilled mariner," reminding himself not to be overconfident.

He looked around him. Almost all of his charges had spent some time leaning over the side, but all seemed to be gaining their sea legs now.

Omri stood at the bow with Dan Callahan's tiny Bible in one hand and a slip of paper in the other. The paper, in Dan's handwriting, listed the following Scriptures:

- Isaiah 52:13 to 53:12
- Psalm 22 (Matthew 27:34-50)
- Psalm 16: 10-11 (Acts 1:3 and 2:32; Matt. 28:5-9);
- Psalm 22 (Luke 23:33; John 19:18 and 20:19-27)
- Genesis 3:15 (Galatians 4:4)
- Genesis 12:3 (Acts 3:25-26)
- Deuteronomy 18:15-19 (Acts 3:22-23)
- Psalm 22:7 (Luke 23:11, 35-39)
- Psalm 41:9 (John 13:18, 21)
- Psalm 69:21 (Matt. 27:34; Mark 15:23)
- Psalm 72:10-11 (Matt. 2:1-11)
- Isaiah 7:14 (Matt. 1:18-25; Luke 1:26-35)
- Isaiah 50:6 (Matt. 26:676; 27:26-31)
- Jeremiah 31:31-34 (Hebrews 8:6-13)
- Micah 5:2 (Matt. 2:1; Luke 2:4-7
- Zechariah 9:9 (Matthew 21:1-11)
- Zechariah 13:7 (Matthew 26:31, 56).

Omri had read only the first Scripture from Isaiah, the one chapter forbidden to be read in the world's synagogues. The richness of its fulfillment left him stunned and deep in thought.

He was shaken as he contemplated Frank's announcement: "Nothing but sea ahead of us!"

"Sea and a new chapter in all our lives," Omri had replied.

"Mommy, Mommy!" Daisy-Rain pointed at the sky. "Look at the pretty colors."

"Notice how a sunrise is much more beautiful when there are clouds in the sky," Ruth said, putting a hand on her daughter's shoulder.

"Yes." Omri nodded. "Just think—If there were no clouds, there'd be no billowing pillows of pinks and reds and yellows, no swirls of flourishing colors sweeping across the sky. The same when God comes into our lives, shines light on a dark situation, and appears in the midst of a personal storm."

"If there were no hard times, no clouds, his appearing wouldn't seem quite so marvelous," Frank agreed.

"We've certainly been through some hard times the last three days," Ethan acknowledged.

"Well," said Naomi, "if this sunrise is a promise, I see it as marvelous and glorious to behold—the most beautiful sunrise I've ever witnessed."

"Out here on the ocean, the most beautiful parts of the day are sunrise and sunset," Frank said. "Sunrises like this always remind me of God's presence, his incredible creation and constancy. Always rises, always sets. You can count on it."

"Like you can count on God," Omri added.

"And my invisibility cloak," Ethan said.

"Ha! Yes, and your cloak, Ethan," Omri agreed. "God can even use a nonbeliever to accomplish His purposes. Do you still not believe, my friend?"

All eyes were on Ethan; his eyes were on the sunrise. It was apparent he was keeping his thoughts between him and God.

Omri recalled part of a quote from *The Pilgrim's Progress* that Margaret Callahan's ancestor, Caleb, had asked Bunyan's ancestor, Tice, to read: "There (in Jerusalem) your eyes shall be delighted with seeing and your ears with hearing the pleasant voice of the Mighty One."

Omri thanked God for Dan and Margaret Callahan, their grandson, Davey, and his friend, Alec. He prayed Bunyan would be released and safe, and they would see each other again—though a reunion would have to be in Israel, or perhaps Canada. He exulted at the thought of being reunited with Benjamin and Sharon and his grandson in the Holy Land. A broad smile filled his face as he shook his head at the magnitude of the adventure. His group's exodus. Its aliyah.

Bunyan stood on the deck and looked out over the edge of his lawn to the Atlantic Ocean. The tide was coming in, and waves were building in size, but beyond them, the sea looked languid, like one could take a leisurely swim north to Portland Headlight. Of course, such a thing wasn't possible except for one in a million swimmers. *We do what we can, what we're equipped for, physically and mentally—and spiritually.*

Since retiring from baseball, he'd tried to do this with his life. Since his CeCe had passed away, he'd filled his days with the Boys and Girls Club, YMCA, Special Olympics, free clinics for Babe Ruth and Little League kids, visiting cancer patients at Children's Hospital in Boston, talking to the residents at elder-care homes ...

Looking at the ocean, Bunyan shivered, remembering the time he even did the Polar Bear Swim at Higgins Beach in January to raise money for cancer research.

The next moment he offered up a prayer for the little group of Jews out there somewhere, on board a boat to Israel. He determined to fly to Israel to visit with Omri and perhaps see the Rosenbaums and Reminis. Maybe Omri would give him a personal tour of the country. *Imagine—a tour of God's land by one of His people!*

In his right hand, Bunyan clutched Grampa Tice's copy of *The Pilgrim's Progress*. Its leather was dried, and the edges of its pages had yellowed over the last one-hundred-and-fifty-odd years. But the insight on those pages remained indelible in his memory.

He recalled the Shining Ones who'd given Pilgrim peace, saying, "Your sins are forgiven." And he recalled the passage in the ninth chapter of the Book of Amos: "'I will bring back My exiled people Israel; they will rebuild the ruined cities and live in them. They will plant vineyards and drink their wine; they will make gardens and eat their fruit. I will plant Israel in their own land, never again to be uprooted from the land I have given them,' says the Lord your God."

A smile spread across Bunyan's face, for he knew some of God's people were finding their way back to Israel on this very day—exactly like Pilgrim … and like his own ancestor, Tice. *Yes, Lord, You're doin' it. One at a time, two at a time, five at a time.*

The doorbell rang back in the house. Moments later, Lana stepped out onto the deck. "Someone's here to see you, Bunyan. Says he's from Homeland Security."

Oh-oh! Bunyan's shoulders drooped. He nodded. "Bring him out, Lana. And if I'm taken away, call Steve Whiting for me, will you? He's in my Rolodex under 'lawyer.'"

Lana's eyes flew to the ground, and her shoulders sagged.

"What if I'm taken away too?"

"Then I'll call him for both of us." Bunyan released a crooked smile.

Lana nodded and looked beyond him to the ocean. With a sureness that comforted Bunyan, she said, "They're safe."

Just then, Agent Owen strode past Lana and up to him.

"They want me to arrest you, Jacko."

"The charge?"

"Like I said before, aiding and abetting a fugitive."

"So this is on your shoulders."

"And I do so willingly."

"You don't get it, do you, agent?"

"Get it?"

"A hundred and fifty years or so ago, my great-great-great-great granddaddy was a slave. He was held in a plantation against his will. But he escaped from Kentucky over the Ohio River to Ripley, Ohio, and all the way up here through Portland and into New Brunswick. A couple of the people who helped him along the way in the Underground Railroad were Jews.

"Helping Grampa Tice was against the law, but the righteous thing to do. They decided *right* was more important than *law*."

By his expression, Owen had an idea what was coming. He pushed his hands into his suitcoat pockets in obvious resignation, waiting for Bunyan to continue.

"Today, Jews are on their own plantation, agent. It's called America. By law, they're not allowed to escape. So what's the righteous thing to do?"

Owen shrugged.

"As a black man, I'm repaying a debt," Bunyan paused, "and I'm putting myself in right standing with the Lord. I remember someone saying once, 'Climb out on a limb. That's where the fruit is.' I ask you, son, will you stand up for what's right?"

As he waited for the answer, Bunyan clutched his book and turned to gaze out over the ocean. He couldn't see Omri Zohn, nor Ethan and Naomi Rosenbaum, nor Ruth and Daisy-Rain

Remini, but a broad grin filled his handsome face. And he bet the satisfaction matched that on the face of his very good friend, Nobel Laureate Omri Zohn.

Lunchtime at the Callahan home. Dan couldn't remember the last time he'd slept until mid-morning, but he had today. Finally, Tack was done with waiting and dashed upstairs, hopped on the bed, and licked him awake. Dan laughed and wrestled with his dog. He dressed in jeans and a T-shirt and went downstairs. About the same time, Davey and Alec trekked in after spending the night in their old tree house of all places.

Margaret had prepared a luncheon spread, and they all sat on the rear porch, munching sandwiches, chips, and homemade pickles.

"So, Davey and Alec …" Dan began, "unbeknownst to your Bubbe and me, you removed a tracking device from my truck and took it with you, leading the agents on a wild goose chase, speeding through dangerous roads. Then you escaped on your dirt bikes in the pitch-dark of night. Do I have that right?"

Davey and Alec simply smiled back at him.

Dan narrowed his eyes on Alec. "Your dad's going to kill me when he finds out."

"Nah! He's cool."

"Yeah?"

"Yeah—ah, yes, sir."

"And, Maggie." Dan turned to his wife. "Our Annie calls you from England, knowing something's happening and requires, even compels, prayer."

Margaret shot her "ain't God great?" grin back at him.

"And, if my message from Frank is correct, he and our friends have escaped into international waters and are on their way with keen winds at their back." Dan drank deeply from a glass of iced coffee. "I think the Lord's writing that 'great epic poem.'"

"Poem?" Davey asked.

"Ephesians two, verse ten, Davey. 'For we are God's workmanship, created in Christ Jesus to do good works, which God prepared in advance for us to do.'"

He looked to Margaret, who beamed at the telling for she knew what he was going to say.

"Workmanship here is the Greek word *poéma,*" Dan explained, "which translates 'great epic poem.' Just imagine, each of us is a great … epic … poem God is taking the time to write. And He's writing us into something truly wonderful, a poem beautiful enough to inspire and encourage those who read us."

"Like when the apostle Paul said we're living epistles?" Davey asked.

"Exactly! We're to reflect God and his character and integrity. God wants us to be poems of honor and great accomplishment for his kingdom."

"So, did we just write a chapter in our poems?" Alec asked.

"No, Alec. God wrote the poem and you allowed him to do so," Margaret replied.

"Yeah, sometimes when we're working on your GTO, we get pretty inky," Davey quipped, punching Alec on the arm.

"Ha! Funny!"

Dan's encrypted phone rang. The Spirit of God had impressed on him to bring it out to the porch with him. A text message read: "SOP x 3 @ 9."

Dan grinned at Margaret and winked. "For such a time as this. Better make up those beds, Maggie."

—THE END—

(Dear reader, please take a few minutes and write a brief review of The Last Aliyah at www.Amazon.com.)

Endnotes

While conceiving the plot for the The Last Aliyah, it was not difficult to visualize the anti-Semitic, anti-Zionist United Nations proposing a ban on Jewish emigration to the state of Israel. Indeed, though it was created as a world body dedicated to peace, justice, and morality, the UN has largely devolved into a front for Arabic and Muslim interests and has become the largest organization promoting Palestinian interests against Israel.

All the while, Palestinians are given full voting rights and representation in the Knesset, Israel's legislative body. Most notable is Joint List, which in 2015 boasted thirteen members of the one-hundred-twenty-seat body.

At the same time, the UN's Arabic-Soviet-Third World bloc has turned a blind eye as totalitarian and theocratic Islamic countries have driven nearly all Christians and Jews out of their countries and made life unbearable for those who remain. For instance, Iraq, which once had 190,000 Jews, now counts 100. Following mass violence in 1945, Libya's Jewish population dropped from 60,000 to 20 by 1974. Morocco's 60,000 Jews were reduced to fewer than 2,500 following the 1948 massacres. Synagogues were destroyed, land confiscated, lives threatened. And the Christian population in all Middle East countries, except Israel, has plummeted just as drastically.

In spite of this, as of 2013, the UN's Human Rights Council, created in 2006, had condemned Israel in forty-five resolutions—nearly as much as the rest of the world.

From 2012 through 2015, the United Nations General Assembly adopted 97 resolutions criticizing countries, 83 of which were against Israel.

Each year, the United Nations Educational, Scientific and Cultural Organization (UNESCO) adopts around ten resolutions criticizing only Israel.

An exception occurred in 2013, when, under pressure from UN Watch, UNESCO adopted one resolution on Syria.

In the mid-1950s, the UN criticized Israel for retaliatory strikes it launched against Palestinian Fedayeen bases in neighboring Arab countries while it was silent on the terrorist attacks that provoked the reprisals. And when Nasser closed the Straits of Tiran to Israeli shipping and encouraged terrorist attacks on Israel, it was the Jewish state that drew resolutions of condemnation for its "aggression" against Egypt.

The infamous 1975 resolution equating Zionism (the return of Jews to their homeland) with racism is illustrative. Not just sheer prejudice, but stupid.

Meanwhile, as seen in France, England, the Mid-East, and elsewhere around the world, anti-Semitism is being taken to heights not seen since Nazi Germany. Not the least of these countries is America, whose relations with Israel deteriorated enormously under President Obama.

Also, in the wake of more than eighty congressmen's overnight turnabout in their vote opposing the TransPacific Partnership in June 2015, I find it highly believable this legislative body could also be cajoled and arm-twisted into backing a worldwide ban on Jewish emigration to Israel.

The question is: Who will be there to help Jews escape America if and when this scenario plays out for real? And if there is a certain Jew whom the US government is adamant about keeping in America, what then?

Who can argue that the Jews are God's chosen people? History tells the story in both Old and New Testaments and in modern times:

It was a miracle that for the first time in human history a nation, long ago dismantled, was recreated in 1948.

In 1919 in World War I, after defeating the Ottoman Empire along with Germany, England took control of Palestine—which the Romans had named after the Philistines as an insult to the Jews—until 1948. In 1947, the United Nations voted to create two states in "Palestine," one for the Jews on a narrow strip of land that by all accounts was indefensible because it was divided in the middle. The state for the Arabs was a large territory to be called Jordan.

When Israel declared her statehood in May 1948, the entire Arab world, armed and thirsting after Jewish blood, attacked the little-armed Jews from all sides. Certain of victory because of overwhelming odds, and because Great Britain had made it illegal for a Jew to own a firearm, the Arab armies warned Palestinians to leave their homes until the war was won.

Indeed, although Palestinians today were claiming that a million fled, the actual number was around six hundred thousand, including some driven out by Jewish forces in the ensuing battles.

At the same time, more than eight hundred thousand Jews were banished from their homes in Arab countries.

An astonished world looked on as miracle after miracle delivered victory to—the Jews.

In 1967, Egypt, Jordan and Syria conspired to attack and overwhelm Israel but a forewarned Israel struck first, taking control of Jerusalem; the Golan Heights, from which Syria had bombed Israeli communities in the Galilee; and the entire Sinai Peninsula.

Israel later returned the Sinai and, in 2005, forcefully removed nearly ten thousand Jewish citizens from their homes in the Gaza Strip, even though those lands were legitimately hers, having been won in a defensive war.

Although the United Nations continued to pass resolutions demanding Israel return the territories she had gained, the Jewish nation was not obligated to oblige the UN.

Jordan was created as the homeland for the Palestinians, but the controlling Hashemite king never had allowed such a habitation.

While Arab-controlled countries didn't allow the few remaining Jews living there to vote, Israel not only permitted Arabs to vote but allowed them seats in her governing body, the Knesset.

Read *True North: Tice's Story*, the prequel to *The Last Aliyah*. Here is the first chapter:

CHAPTER ONE

The Year of Our Lord 1860

Tice stood at the banks of the swiftly flowing Ohio River, contemplating his future, or the end of it—the man with the gun chasing him close behind. Try to swim the river, he'd drown. Stay here, he'd get whipped half to death or maybe all the way to death. That's what happened to runaway slaves.

He struggled to catch his breath. *Lord, how'd your boy get here? What on earth I done?*

Like flipping the pages through a fast-moving picture book, the last hour or so of his life spun before his eyes. The day had begun so quietly, so drearily, like always.

There he was, maybe nineteen, twenty years old, standing with hoe in hand in his Massah's field, reflecting on his short life. This day like all the others. Still hackin' away in the dirt, still pickin' cotton, still sleepin' on a board.

He swung the hoe and joined in singing with the other slaves:

"Swing low, sweet chariot—"

Tice stood working in the cotton field, hoe in hand, singing with his fellow slaves, the words of the spiritual distracting him from the monotony of the chore that would consume his day. Singing helped. Sometimes the less you had on your mind, the better. Sometimes when you're not thinking of your Momma, God bless her soul—or your Pappy—*I hope you're still alive!*—the quicker the day goes. But today was different.

"Comin' for to carry me home—"

Tice's arms were swinging the hoe, his mouth was forming the words. But lately, his mind was on his Pappy and the freedom his father had whispered about to him a few summers ago, before being sold by Massah. Pappy had remembered that freedom with happiness.

"I looked o'er Jordan 'n what did I see—"

Tice continued working and singing, making his way across the field with the others under Massah's watchful eye. He had to keep up, do his share, or Massah would whip him, sure.

Just then, Massah gave a random crack of his whip, a frightening reminder of what he did to those who displeased him.

Tice struggled not to look toward the edge of the field, to the road where he'd met a stranger not two weeks prior.

The man had seemed to appear from nowhere, leaned down from his horse toward Tice, and said quietly, "Young man, if you can ever escape, do so by crossing the Ohio River just south of the ferry and ask for the Randolph house. That's my place. Do that and we'll get you free. Remember that? Randolph?"

"A band o' angels comin' after me—"

Tice had nodded. *Randoaf.* He thought of another slave, a skinny old man the women called a "randy oaf."

He didn't know what that meant, but, as the man hurried off, Tice repeated, "Randoaf."

Since then, Tice had worked as usual. But the thought of escape stayed in the forefront of his mind, the taste of Pappy's freedom inhabiting his dreams at night.

"Comin' for to carry me home."

Tice blinked hard twice, shook his head and nearly lost his grip on the hoe as he scolded himself. *Freedom 'n such is fool thinkin'.*

Suddenly, the whip smacked the ground by his feet, and an icy hand laid firmly on Tice's bare shoulder. It sent a chill down his spine and cut the hymn short in his throat. His friends all around him in the cotton field took notice and stopped singing as well.

Clutching the neck of the hoe in his hands, as if to drain the life out of the wood, Tice turned an eye toward the firm grip and knew from the white, square-fingered hand whose it was.

"Yes-sir, boss," Tice said, turning toward the man who owned him and another hundred slaves who toiled the fields as well as the plantation that spread for a mile in any direction. Tice dare not look his boss in the eye, so he focused on the man's chin.

"You're one of my strongest workers, Tice," Julius Lykins said, "so I need you to go down to the village, to the railroad station."

"Yes-sir, Massah Lykins."

"A shipment's arriving on the train. Morgan'll be down there, along with Gilly, waiting with a wagon. You get down there and help them unload."

Tice nodded.

"The shipment should arrive about the time you get there if you head out now. If you don't get there in time, you'll get the sting of this whip, boy." Lykins pushed his horse whip in front of Tice's eyes.

Tice cringed. He'd felt that sting before and had the welts across his back to prove it.

"Well, get on down there, boy. I expect you, Morgan, and Gilly back here in an hour or so."

Tice handed his hoe to Elijah, his friend standing nearby, and started to quick-step out of the field toward the road to town.

"Clock's ticking, boy," his master said.

Tice started jogging.

"Tick tock!"

Tice set out in a full run, his hardened bare feet unaffected by the hard-packed dirt as he reached the road to the quiet Kentucky town of Maysville.

"Gotta get there or feel the whip. Gotta get there or feel the whip," Tice repeated to himself. As he ran, his brief life flashed across his mind. He was born on this plantation and knew nothing else. His Momma died of fever when he was a boy. A few years later his Pappy was sold to another plantation who knows where. He had no brothers or sisters, except brothers and sisters in the Lord.

An' here I is, still livin' for nothin'—'cept my relationship with my Lord. Here I is, runnin' into town for my Massah, goin' to load my Massah's stuff for my Massah's plantation, for my Massah's farm animals maybe, or my Misses's parlah.

The hymn lingered in his mind.

"If you get there before I do—"

Someday he'd have a manshun, he thought, a big old house in the sky. But until then, he was hoein' 'n pickin' 'n runnin' 'n loadin' here on earth for a man who beat him 'n his friends for fool reasons, or no fool reason t'all.

Tice was a speedy runner when need be and soon he looked up to see the rail station ahead. Sure enough, he could see the steam from the engine floating skyward, drifting side to side—same as he'd like to do. He began to sprint, not wanting Morgan, his Massah's foreman, to get upset with him. Morgan packed a more powerful whip than his Massah when his Massah wasn't watching.

"Comin' for to carry me home—"

Shortly, Tice reached the train and saw Morgan talking to a man wearing a funny-looking hat. Gilly, another slave, stood behind Morgan. The man motioned to another fellow, who reached up and tugged at a rope on a door on the train, then slid the door open. Tice ran to Morgan's side and lowered his eyes to Morgan's chin.

"Let's get to it, boy," Morgan said. A burly man, Morgan twisted his handlebar mustache with a forefinger and thumb. "Hop up there and hand down the boxes to Gilly. He'll pass 'em to me and I'll load 'em up on the wagon."

"Yessir."

Tice sprang onto the train. Box upon box filled the rail car. What was in the boxes, he didn't know at first. Soon he discovered, though, from the sheer weight of them, that the cargo was dishes, plates, pots and pans and such items for the mansion. *This'll mean the manshun's old pots and pans for us-uns, maybe.*

In short order, Tice passed the last box to Gilly, a big fellow slave Tice hardly knew—indeed, nobody hardly knew 'cause he hardly spoke. A grunt here and a grunt there defined Gilly.

After loading the boxes onto the wagon and then strapping them down with rope, Morgan turned to Tice. "Gilly'll ride with me. No room for three. You'll hafta walk, boy. But don't ya' be dallyin'."

Tice liked that idea. He'd step along the side of the road where it was grassy and cooler under the shadow of the trees. He began the walk back and watched the wagon disappear ahead of him. As he stepped one foot in front of the other, a thought began to ferment in his mind. An exciting idea. An educated person might call it an epiphany.

He looked up. Morgan and Gilly had disappeared over a rise in the road. Tice stopped in his tracks and repeated to himself, "Randoaf."

He glanced around him. Was anybody watching? Maybe the workers at the train station? No. Anyone ridin' or walkin' down the road? No.

"Tell all my friends I'm comin' too—"

Quickly, he set his feet to motion toward the plantation. Then, a hundred yards up the road, looking again to make sure no one was watching, Tice veered into the woods, eastward toward the Ohio River.

Pushing branches out of his face, Tice plowed through a woodland. "South of the ferry. Randoaf." His destination was etched in his mind. He knew the river. He knew where the ferry left Maysville and floated over to Ripley, Ohio, north of the Mason-Dixon Line, separating slave states from free states.

"Comin' for to carry me home."

As he hustled towards the land of freedom, doubts about that very liberty filled his mind. Sure, he'd be free. But where would he sleep? What would he eat? What work would he do—*could* he do? Who would be responsible for all this—all of him? First his Momma, then his Pappy and always—yes, always—Lykins saw to it that his hunger, thirst and shelter were taken care of. Now Momma was gone, Pappy was gone and he was leavin' Lykins.

Oh, Massah. Tice thought of more than one whipping at the hands of Lykins. At that memory, he hastened his steps, remembering Lykins saying he expected Tice back to the plantation soon. *When I doesn't arrive, Massah'll be furious 'n he'll come lookin' for me, and he'll have that whip in his hand. Oh, that whip!*

Several minutes later, he pushed another branch out of his face and came to a meadow. Nothing planted here. No cotton. No tobacco. Tice hesitated and looked around slowly, wanting to make sure no one would spot him if he made a mad dash across the field.

"South of the ferry. Randoaf," he muttered aloud as he sprang into the meadow at a speed that even surprised him. "South of the ferry. Randoaf."

Hay in the field tickled his ankles, but his focus remained on the river. Just then he heard a loud voice hollering, "Hey, you!"

It was a white man's voice. "You there!"

He pretended not to hear the man and continued to run.

"Stop your runnin', boy!"

Stop? Could he stop now? Doubts flooded in again.

He hesitated. Yes, he could stop. Maybe that would keep him out of trouble. Maybe the man wouldn't tell his Massah. Then he wouldn't have to worry about food on the table, a roof over his head, chores to do. No. No worries. He slowed down but didn't look in the direction of the voice.

What should he do? What would Pappy do? he asked himself. Then again he remembered his Pappy talking to him about being free until neighboring tribesmen raided his village, tied them up, then sold the whole village to a white man on a boat. Tice remembered the smile on his Pappy's face when he talked about being a free man, and he speeded up his pace again.

"Comin' for to carry me—"

"Stop or I'll shoot!"

Chills went down Tice's back. His knees almost buckled. Shoot? The man had a rifle? *Well, maybe dyin' wouldn't be bad, neither, Lord—compared to hoein' someone else's fields for the rest of my life.* He hurried on as fast as he could and finally reached the end of the pasture. No lead bullet was fired, only a missile of fear.

Tice dove into the forest, landing on the ground and rolling into a bramble bush. "Ouch!" he screamed, looking down in pain as blood began to leak out of his right arm. He gingerly pulled his arm away from the bush and touched his forearm. "Ow!"

He heard the man call to someone else, "Hurry up and tell Mister Lykins that I think one of his slaves is runnin' away toward the river! I'm chasin' after him!"

"Chasin' after him," Tice repeated. Oh, no. Hurry, he told himself. South of the ferry. Randoaf.

He pushed himself off the ground to his feet, got his bearings and ran off. How long could he go? How long had it been? Was Lykins missing him already? If not, that man was going to tell him. Fear rippled through him like tendrils of ice as Tice thought of the consequences of being caught.

"Dear Momma," he called out. "Dear Pappy. Save me."

"Dear Lord!" he said louder as he came to a hillock, "Where's my band o' angels?" He looked up and the top of the hillock appeared a mile away even though it was only probably fifty yards. "Oh, Lord, help me!"

Tice clambered up the mound. Was this the Blue Ridge Mountains? he wondered. He'd heard stories and thought they were far beyond the river. Was his mind workin' okay?

Just when his legs gave out, he reached the top of the hill. Falling to the ground, he looked up and saw the river in the distance. He took a few seconds to rest and draw his breath, knowing he couldn't wait long; the man was chasing after him. The man! Tice turned to look behind him. The man was nearing the base of the hillock!

"Stop right there!" The man scowled and pointed a finger at Tice. "Stop there and it may spare you a beatin'!"

Tice shook his head. He knew that weren't true. *Not true t'all. I's long past bein' spared no beatin'. A beatin's a comin'. A bad beatin'—if'n I gets caught. If'n.*

The thought of the whip spurred him on, giving him a second wind, and he hustled down the hill, ducking away from alder branches along the way. He reached the bottom and skirted around another bramble bush. *Gotta get distance. Gotta get distance 'tween me 'n him. A long way.* He didn't see that the man had a rifle, but maybe he did.

Suddenly he splashed through a brook, his toes hit a rock and he fell to the bank of the brook, screaming in pain. He grabbed for his big toe. Had he broken it? He sat up and held his foot. Blood seeped out of his big and second toes. He put his foot back in the water, hoping the coolness would help numb it.

But he couldn't wait, couldn't linger a second longer. The man must be nearing the top of the hill by now and might spot him. His Pappy's face flashed before him. *"Git ov'r it, son. Buck up! Git up and run!"*

"Yes, Pappy," Tice said aloud. He lifted himself out of the water, stepped up to dry ground and set out running again as fast as he could while trying not to touch ground with those two injured toes.

And here he was, several minutes later, wheezing for breath, a sharp pain in his ribs, standing at the riverbank, fixated on the spring runoff streaking past in a maniacal race downstream. Yep. The choice: certain death or certain torture. Here was his future, or the end of it

Struggling to catch his breath, Tice said aloud, "Dear Pappy, save me!"

Editor's note: The story of Bunyan "Jacko" Jackson's great-great-great-great grandfather Tice, entitled *True North: Tice's Story*, is available from all bookstores as a softcover and can be read as an e-book available for Nooks and Kindles at www.barnesandnoble.com and www.amazon.com.

Please take a minute and write a brief review of *The Last Aliyah* at www.amazon.com/books.

About the Author

Having received wide acclaim for his first historical novel, *Midnight Rider for the Morning Star*, and for another historical novel, the *Publishers Weekly* Featured Book *True North: Tice's Story*, Mark Alan Leslie jumped into the realm of modern action/thrillers with his Thrill of the Chase Series beginning with *Chasing the Music*, released in 2016, and *The Three Sixes*, released in December 2017.

A longtime journalist and editor, Leslie has won six national magazine writing awards. A golf writer for twenty-five years, Leslie has compiled two golf-industry e-books—*Putting a Little Spin on It: The Design's the Thing!* and *Putting a Little Spin on It: The Grooming's the Thing!*—based on his hundreds of interviews with luminaries like Arnold Palmer, Jack Nicklaus, Sam Snead, Gene Sarazen, Ben Crenshaw, Gary Player, Kathy Whitworth, and Patti Berg as well as scores of people famous within the world of golf like Pete and Alice Dye, Robert Trent Jones Sr. and Jr., Tom Doak,

Joe Jemsek, Brent Wadsworth, Tom Fazio, Ted Horton and Tim Hiers.

Leslie lives in Maine, with his wife, Loy. The couple has two grown sons and four granddaughters.

www.ingramcontent.com/pod-product-compliance
Lightning Source LLC
Chambersburg PA
CBHW070405260626
47161CB00001B/283
9781946638892